PIRATE ACADEMY

VAMPIRES AND GODS, BOOK TWO

Eva Pohler

Copyright © 2021 by Eva Pohler.

Eva Pohler Books
20011 Park Ranch
San Antonio, Texas 78259
www.evapohler.com

Publisher's Note: This is a work of fiction. Names, characters, places, and incidents are a product of the author's imagination. Locales and public names are sometimes used for atmospheric purposes. Any resemblance to actual people, living or dead, or to businesses, companies, events, institutions, or locales is completely coincidental.

Book Layout ©2017 BookDesignTemplates.com

Book Cover Design by B Rose Designz

Pirate Academy/ Eva Pohler. -- 1st ed.
Paperback ISBN 978-1-958390-49-8

There is no room for both love and war, and there's a war going on.

—DELPHINE

Contents

For the sailors of the Mediterranean Sea.

The Code

As much as Hestie wanted to help save the world, she'd been hoping for a longer reprieve.

She sat beside Poros in the salon of the *Marcella II* marveling over how good everyone looked. They'd just finished shopping in Malta, and all of them—even the vampires—were sporting new digs. The stores had carried the newest back-to-school styles. Hestie had found a gray romper and wore it with a matching wide-brimmed hat. Beside her, Poros looked sharp in a white t-shirt with an unbuttoned blue plaid shirt and jeans, which brought out the gray in his remarkable eyes.

She wasn't sure she trusted Gertrude Morgan. To Hestie, the girl was an attention whore, who, for all Hestie knew, may have invented the prophetic dream just so she could return to the center of drama.

Alastair lifted his brows at her. *Morpheus confirmed her vision.*

Stay out of my head, she said to him telepathically.

You are broadcasting your thoughts to every vampire here.

Hestie glanced at the other vampires. Their eyes avoided hers. She nervously twirled a strand of her long, red hair with a finger and wished she knew how to keep her thoughts to herself.

We do, too, Raimo said without speaking.

Morpheus stretched his silver wings. "I'm headed to Mount Olympus now to inform the others."

"Thank you, Morpheus," Hermes said before the winged god of dreams disappeared.

Prometheus, their captain, turned to Hermes. "When do you want to begin?"

"Immediately," Hermes said.

"No offense, Uncle Hermes," Hestie said. "But my brother and I have been training since we were kids, and so has Poros. Maybe you should focus on the *mortal.*"

Alastair shot her another look, and Taavi, who'd become extra friendly with Gertie, frowned.

Hestie hadn't meant to sound snobby, especially since Jinsoo, the newest god in the pantheon, was also inexperienced. Yet, it wouldn't hurt Gertie to be taken down a notch. Hestie hadn't imagined there could be a bigger and more annoying know-it-all than her brother, but she'd been wrong.

You are angry at her for saying that you are shallow and materialistic, Taavi said to Hestie telepathically. *But she did not know you then.*

She doesn't know me now, Hestie shot back.

Gertie's face had reddened. "I fought in the vampire wars. I may not be as skilled as you, but I'm no rookie."

Prometheus patted Gertie's shoulder. "I don't think Hestie meant to imply otherwise."

Hestie had been about to insist that she *had* meant to imply otherwise when Poros squeezed her hand and said to her telepathically, *Is something bothering you?*

Before she could answer, Hermes moved to the center of the salon and, pacing, said, "I think you misunderstood me, Hestie. When I said you need to train, I wasn't talking about sailing, and I wasn't talking about fighting. In fact, my V-Team avoids fighting as much as possible."

Hestie's brother put his finger in the air, as if to speak, but before he could, Gertie said, "Thievery is the art of invisibility."

"Which *you* don't have," Hestie muttered.

Gertie scoffed. "I didn't mean *literal* invisibility."

"Can you two let our lord do the talking?" Del suggested, as she combed her long black hair from her beautiful bronze face.

"Thank you, Del," Hermes said. "That's a great idea! Why didn't I think of it?" Then, sarcasm rant over, he added, "First things first. You need to learn the code."

"I'm relieved to hear you have one," Prometheus said. "Because there are some things I won't abide on my ship."

Hermes scratched his dark curly beard. It looked almost identical to Prometheus's.

"Why don't you hear us out, Captain?" Hermes suggested. "Then, if you want to add anything, we'll hear *you* out."

Prometheus nodded.

"So that you don't have to listen to the drone of my voice," Hermes said, "I'd like each of my pirates to call out one of the rules in our code, one at a time. Who's first?"

The others turned to Del and Alastair since they were their leaders—after Hermes.

Del, who looked extra-stylish in her short dress with thin straps, spoke first: "Rule One: Only steal from greedy thieves."

"That's right," Hermes said. "Those who steal to survive are off limits."

Hestie bit her lip. The pirates' definition of "thieves" was a little vague. The vampire pirates took her ancient Persian coins, coins that *she found* at the bottom of the sea, because they believed the coins weren't rightfully hers—that they belonged to Persians. But *she* found them. What about finders, keepers?

Then Alastair, looking spiffy in his Marvel t-shirt and light gray vest with skinny black jeans, licked his pouty lips and said, "Rule Two: Land first, sea last."

"Exactly," Hermes said with a nod. "Transactions at sea are much more dangerous than those at port. Whenever possible, we follow the greedy thieves to land and, after they've left ship, we take the stolen goods."

"Hey," Jinsoo said. "That's what you did to us, when you took Chidori and the coins."

Chidori, perched on Jinsoo's shoulder, hid her beak in his hair.

The vampires turned a shade paler.

Even Mahdi, whose skin was as dark as the night sky, seemed to pale with mortification at the mention of the pirates' attack on the *Marcella II*. He cleared his throat and said, "Rule Three: Avoid confrontations."

Hermes nodded again. "Better to slink and hide than to fight."

Hermie cocked his head to the side. "A rule often broken?"

"Only when threatened," Del said coldly.

Hestie glanced at her brother. The sting of Mina's death had hurt him most, after Jinsoo. She wondered if he'd ever be able to forgive Del, even though everyone there but Jinsoo understood why she had done it.

Raimo's voice brought her from her reverie. "Rule Four: Scout and plan."

"Absolutely," Hermes said. "Avoid spontaneity and rash behavior. Always be smart and a step ahead of your victims."

Hestie blanched at the word *victims*. She hated the idea of becoming a *victimizer*. Not for the first time, she wondered if joining the pirates was the right move, even if they avoided people whom they considered innocents. Didn't stealing from thieves put you on their level? As much as she wanted to stop Sailfish Trading and Shipping from delivering the warheads to their buyer in Syria, the rest of it still seemed fishy.

Pun intended? Alastair asked telepathically.

What pun?

Sailfish, fishy?

Hestie grinned. Leave it to Alastair to lighten the mood.

You are welcome, he said. *And I will grant that* target *is a better word than* victim.

"Rule Five: No modern weapons," Bach said. "Only blades."

Poros turned to Prometheus. "That's a relief."

"Keep in mind that our targets usually have them," Raimo pointed out.

"Then why do you have this rule?" Gertie asked.

"As a precaution," Del explained.

"That's exactly right," Hermes said. "My vampire pirates are gifted, as are you and Prometheus's crew of young gods. But our targets are generally mortal, and it wouldn't be prudent to carry such weapons around those so vulnerable."

"*Generally* mortal? Hermie asked.

"Occasionally the gods get involved," Penny said. "You saw how it was when the *Tarantula* was destroyed."

"And Penny and I were taken prisoner," Bach added.

Penny and Bach exchanged glances in a way that made Hestie wonder if something had happened while they'd been detained on Mount Olympus. Was there more to their story?

As if in response to her thoughts, the faces of both vampires turned a light shade of pink—a vampire's blush, Hestie supposed.

"Sometimes you gods forget that we lost people, too," Penny said.

Hestie thought about Kagan, Farouch, Chloe, Edric, and Cade. The vampires had known one another—had been a family—for centuries. She could only imagine how hard it had been to lose almost half of their family members in one day.

Alastair glanced at her with moist eyes.

"The loss of loved ones should be all the more reason for working together," Prometheus said. "Right now, we need to focus on finding those warheads, before they end up in the wrong hands."

"If they're being sold to a buyer in Syria," Hermes said, "I would guess my brother Ares knows about it."

"He may even be the one orchestrating the sale," Prometheus pointed out.

"So, as always, we proceed with caution," Del said.

Despite her reservations, Hestie was glad she was there to help fight against corruption. When she'd first been transformed from a demigod to a god, she'd been shocked to learn that not all the Olympians were fair and just. It had been heartbreaking to watch the entire pantheon at odds with one another. She had been equally dismayed at the Olympians' destruction of the *Tarantula*. Even Athena, whom Hestie had admired most, had been a disappointment. Hestie wanted nothing more than to liberate people around the world, to fight against oppression. Bringing medicine and technology to those in need had been one step. Finding the warheads would be another.

"Rule Six: If forced to fight, fight to wound, not to kill," Penny said. "And before you mention our attack on this vessel *again*, we didn't kill Prometheus until we realized he was a god and would come back. We thought the same was true of Mina."

"Right," Hermes said. "We are *not* in the business of killing."

Hestie glanced at Jinsoo, who frowned.

"Rule Seven: Avoid taking prisoners," Sophia said. "Unless they are gods trying to kill you."

"We weren't trying to *kill* you," Poros said.

"Well, *I* was," Hermie said sheepishly.

"But that was *after* they took me and Poros," Hestie said.

Penny climbed to her feet. "Dude, you were trespassing on our ship."

"After you stole Chidori!" Jinsoo cried.

Hermes lifted his arms. "Enough. You all need to get over the past and focus on the present. There's a lot at stake."

"Sorry, Hermes," Poros said. "We're ready to listen."

Gertie stood up. "Rule One: Only steal from greedy thieves. Rule Two: Land first, sea last. Rule Three: Avoid confrontations. Rule Four: Scout and plan. Rule Five: No modern weapons—only blades. Rule Six: If forced to fight, fight to wound, not to kill. Rule Seven: Avoid taking prisoners. Is that everything?"

"Show off," Hestie murmured.

Gertie's face reddened as she sat back down.

"No," Taavi said with a grin, apparently impressed with his new girl-friend. "There's one more: Rule Eight: Be an expert at basic trickery."

"And that's where we'll begin," Hermes said. "I suggest you go to port and allow my team to demonstrate some basic schemes. Then try your hand at a few. Don't return to the ship until each one of you has stolen something without being detected. But do give whatever is taken back to its rightful owner. Tonight is for practice and nothing else."

"Aren't you joining us?" Hermie asked.

"I've got things to do and places to go," the god of thievery replied. "But call if you need me."

Hermes vanished.

"Is this really necessary?" Hermie asked Del as he followed her and the others from the salon. "I don't see how lessons in trickery will help us to steal the warheads."

"You might be surprised," Alastair said as he walked past.

Hermie flew in front of Del, forcing her to stop and to face him. When her dark eyes finally met his, he felt unnerved.

Before she could break away, he said, "I'm sorry I asked if the rule to avoid confrontations was often broken. It was insensitive of me."

Del shrugged and moved past him. "No worries."

Although she sounded sincere, there was something about her de-meanor that made him feel as though she were angry with him. Why was she acting so coldly toward him? And why did it pain him so deeply?

Let it go, she said in his mind.

He followed her from the ship to the dock. *Let what go?*

She didn't answer. Instead, she picked up speed, making her way to the front of the group, where Prometheus, Poros, and Hestie were lead-ing the way.

Hermie quickened his pace, nearly knocking Taavi into the sea.

"Sorry, man," Hermie said to the vampire.

Taavi shrugged. "It is nothing."

Hermie had never felt this way about anyone before, and he needed to pursue it, to find out where it would lead.

As Hermie was about to catch up to Del, Alastair grabbed him by the arm. "Leave it for now, my friend."

Hermie studied the vampire. "Do you know what's eating her?"

"We all do," Alastair said. "And she will tell you, when she is ready."

Hermie followed the others from the docks, nearly suffocated by his misery.

Jinsoo walked beside him with Chidori perched on a finger. "Where are we going, Captain?"

"There's a café I know a few blocks ahead," Prometheus called from the front of their group. "It's a popular area, especially at night."

Instead of heading inland, they walked along the marina toward the island point, where there was a plaza with a fountain surrounded by bars and cafés. When they reached The Black Pearl, they sat at round metal tables on the patio, splitting into three groups, but close enough to one another that even the mortal would hear what any one of them might say. Hermie and Jinsoo sat with Penny and Sophia. Hermie had tried to sit with Del, but the chairs around her table had been filled before he had reached them.

"I have questions," Hermie said.

Penny, who was round and busty with her curly brown hair tied high on her head, leaned forward, exposing her cleavage. "Shoot."

They were interrupted by a waiter, who took their drink order.

Once he'd gone, Hermie asked, "How do you define a thief?"

"Oh, I want to hear this," his sister called from the table next to his, where she sat with Poros, Del, Alastair, and Bach.

Hermie's back was to Del. He was glad that, if they weren't going to be at the same table, at least they were close to one another. It gave him pleasure and pain in equal measure.

"We could all stand some clarification," Prometheus said from the table on the opposite side of Hermie, where he sat with Gertie, Taavi, Raimo, and Mahdi.

The other vampires looked at Del and Alastair.

"I will take a stab at this," Alastair said.

Then, instead of speaking aloud, he said to them telepathically: *A thief exploits a weakness in others for his or her own gain. Rather than earn, the thief takes.*

Del's voice soon followed Alastair's: *And while smugglers are not always thieves, if what they are smuggling is a person, or a dangerous weapon, or cultural artifacts stolen or previously stolen by someone else, we consider them thieves, too.*

Then Bach added: *Greedy capitalists are also thieves.*

"Hold on," Gertie said. "The line is getting blurry."

Hermie had been about to say the same thing. Although he admired the vampires' concern for the disenfranchised, he worried they crossed an important ethical line.

"Well, Bach is a bit of a communist," Alastair explained.

Bach put a fist in the air. "Marx was a genius."

Hermie lifted a finger. "Smart, hard-working capitalists who build wealth are not thieves."

Del's voice startled him from behind. "But those who build wealth on the backs of the oppressed are."

Her words seethed through her teeth. Hermie liked what she had to say—in fact, he was impressed by it—but the way she had said it hurt him. He felt as if she were driving a knife into his heart.

"And how can we know the difference?" Hestie asked.

"Research," Gertie answered. She turned to the vampires. "Am I right?"

The waiter returned with their drinks, delivered them, and left.

"This is a very interesting conversation," Prometheus said with a grin. To Poros, he added, "I wonder what your sister would say about building wealth."

Poros shrugged. "Who knows?"

"Athena would support the builders," Hestie said. "And sometimes capitalists are the builders."

"And sometimes the builders are in a sweat shop," Del said curtly.

"Amen," Bach said, lifting his fist into the air again.

Hermie couldn't resist a glance back at Del, for a chance to read her face. Why was she so angry? Was her anger directed at him? If so, what had he done to deserve it?

Alastair's voice came into Hermie's head again as the lessons continued. *Let us begin with a simple scheme. The best way to rob someone is with two parties. One party creates the distraction while the other steals the goods.*

Del added: *The two best distractions are violence and sex.*

Hermie's mouth fell open.

Penny laughed. "The expression on your face, dude."

"Hermie never had sex," Jinsoo said, matter-of-factly.

"Shut up. Neither have you, bro'," Hermie said, fighting the blush crossing his cheeks.

I did not mean actual sex, Del said.

She meant a flirtation, Taavi said, *usually with the target.*

Del, we should demonstrate on the man sitting by himself across the plaza, Mahdi said. *See him?*

Yes.

"I have another question," Gertie said. "You're vampires. Why not use your power of invisibility?"

"Shh," Penny warned. "No need to tell the entire island of Malta."

Gertie lowered her voice. "Sorry."

"We *do* use it," Taavi said.

"Even so," Raimo said, "a distraction makes the target less likely to notice us. Invisibility is not foolproof. We can still be heard and felt."

"And smelled," Bach said with a laugh. "Some of us smell worse than others."

Hermie relished the soft chuckle from Del behind him. It was the first hint of laughter from her all day.

"Do not speak ill of the dead," Sophia chastised.

"Kagan liked to be teased," Bach insisted.

"As you may already know, Gertie," Taavi said, "vampires cannot make their clothes invisible."

Gertie nodded. "The vampires I used to know never wore them. They created an illusion of clothing for mortal eyes. Why don't you do that? Wouldn't it be easier to use your power of invisibility without clothing?"

"Indeed, it would," Alastair said. "But the wind on the sea can be beastly to our skin."

"The cold does not bother us," Taavi said. "But the wind constantly tickles, like flies."

"If there are no more questions," Mahdi said as he climbed to his feet, "Del and I will demonstrate."

Del stood up and walked around the plaza. Along the way, she plucked a few flowers from the raised borders of the cobblestone path. Hermie's breath caught at the graceful yet strong silhouette Del made in the dark night. Her long curly hair begged him to touch it. Her stunning figure made him forget why they were there. But most of all, it was her deep black eyes that haunted him.

Then Mahdi sauntered to the other side of the fountain and sat at a table not far from the target. Like Taavi, Mahdi was charismatic and a bit of a clown. As he sat down, he gave a grin and a thumbs up toward Hermie and their group, causing Penny to roll her eyes. Hermie watched as Del approached the table, where the man was sitting beneath the dim lights of the patio cover.

Del tripped and fell to her knees, dropping the flowers on the ground. Hermie resisted the instinct to help her.

"Oh, no!" she cried, rushing to collect the flowers before the wind could sweep them away.

The target jumped to his feet and scooped as many of the flowers as he could from the ground.

"Thank you, sir!" Del said in a pleasant voice and with a charming smile. "Am I silly to want them so much? They are for my mother's grave. They remind me of her, you see. Do you speak English?"

"No, I mean, yes, I speak English. And no, I don't think you're silly. I think you're sweet."

"Thank you, sir, but it is you who are sweet, for helping me."

Mahdi moved in from behind and bumped against the distracted target.

"Excuse me, sir," Mahdi said before he continued across the plaza.

Once he'd passed the fountain and was returning to their group, Mahdi stuck his front teeth out, grinned, and did a little dance.

Penny rolled her eyes again.

Alastair said telepathically: *Notice how Mahdi made physical contact with the target? If the object to be stolen is* on *the target, firm pressure must be applied to the body so the object can be lifted without being felt by the target.*

Del put one of her lovely hands on the stranger's shoulder. "Thank you again for helping me."

"Would you like to join me for a drink?"

Hermie did not like the way the stranger was looking at Del. Seeing the man's attraction, his earnest desire for Del, made Hermie check himself. He had to control his feelings. He was acting insane.

Then Hermie noticed that Mahdi had left the stranger's wallet behind on the pavement near Del's feet.

"Oh, sir. Is this your wallet?" Del asked.

"Huh? Um, yes! It must have fallen when I stooped to pick up the flowers."

"I think we are even, are we not?"

The target frowned. "I believe I am in your debt, miss. How about a drink?"

"I must go, sir. Thank you, anyway."

When Del returned to her seat, she said to Hermie, "Your turn."

CHAPTER TWO

Fails

When it was Gertie's turn to participate in a practice scheme in the plaza on the island of Malta, she felt at a distinct disadvantage, being a mortal among vampires and gods. She'd been feeling especially self-conscious, ever since Hestie had called her out for being the only one in need of training.

Plus, she was cold, having forgotten her jacket, though she wasn't about to complain. She hadn't eaten dinner, either, but she'd rather starve than appear weak before the others.

If only Taavi could be persuaded to drink from her. The thought of the extreme euphoria that swept through someone who'd been fed upon made Gertie's mouth water—as if she could taste the vampire virus on her tongue. After the euphoria, the strength would follow, along with speed, x-ray vision, and mind powers. Best of all, with the vampire virus, you could fly and make yourself invisible to mortal eyes. Gertie longed for that.

"You and Taavi create the distraction," Alastair said to her. "Fight or kiss—your choice. And Hestie, you be the thief this time."

Gertie clenched her fists. If she screwed this up, it wouldn't help Hestie's opinion of her. No pressure.

She glanced at the captain, who seemed amused by the pirate training as he enjoyed his beer.

He lifted his mug and said, "Good luck."

"When will it be the captain's turn?" Gertie asked Taavi.

"Never," Prometheus said. "Never, ever, ever will I go by the name of pirate, no matter the cause. But cheers to you." He lifted his mug again.

Their group had moved down the plaza from The Black Pearl to The Galley Bar and Restaurant, so they could work on new targets without arousing suspicion. Their newest target was a middle-aged woman sitting alone at a table across the street, where she sipped from a glass of wine and gazed at the dark, shimmering sea.

Follow my lead, Taavi said to Gertie with a wink as he took her by the hand.

For a split second, he reminded her of Jeno.

As they crossed the street together, Gertie said, "I like your new clothes."

"Thanks."

He was wearing a gray t-shirt with a black leather vest and black jeans.

Taavi stopped near the deck, not far from where the target was sitting, and stood close to Gertie. His body was long and lean, and he took Gertie into his arms and gazed down at her with his golden eyes from beneath dark, thick brows. His dark, wavy hair blew in the wind. She had her hair tied in a ponytail at the nape of her neck. When Taavi smiled, a single dimple appeared in his left cheek.

I am going to kiss you, okay? Then you slap me and call me a terrible name. Pretend you do not appreciate my advances. He winked again. *Of course, you and I know otherwise.*

Gertie chuckled. *This should be fun.*

Gingerly, Taavi caressed her bottom lip with his. Then he pressed his mouth firmly against hers as he pulled her into a tighter embrace. Gertie lost herself. She hadn't been kissed like this, with so much longing and so much hunger, in such a long time. Part of her knew that Taavi was acting, but another part of her hoped that he wasn't.

Still dazed moments after the kissing had stopped, Gertie looked up at Taavi, bewildered. Where she had previously been drawn to him by the prospect of his bite, she was finding herself longing for more.

He grinned. *Any moment now, you can slap me.*

"Oh," she whispered, snapping out of it.

Remember to be dramatic, he added.

"Um, okay."

He lunged for her again, his mouth covering hers. Her body shivered with pleasure. She didn't want it to end.

He pulled away, laughing. "Gertie! Concentrate!"

She slapped his cheek so hard that it stung her hand. "Leave me alone!"

Taavi took a step back, looking shocked by the blow.

"How dare you!" Gertie added. "You, you…" she couldn't think of a bad name to call him.

He pulled her toward him, and she tried to fight him off, but when he pressed his lips against hers again and circled his arms around her waist, she kissed back. Before she knew it, she had grabbed fistfuls of his hair.

The others are watching, he said.

Again, she snapped out of it and slapped his cheek. She glanced at the target and noticed the woman was walking away from her table, her purse in hand, and leaving the bar altogether.

"Did Hestie have a chance to…"

"No," Taavi said.

Hestie flung her head back in frustration. It had finally been her turn to be the thief, and Gertie and Taavi had blown it for her.

Earlier in the evening, she had enjoyed playing the distraction with Poros, as Hermie had made the steal. Poros had pretended to propose, and everyone in the plaza had applauded when she'd pretended to accept. Hermie had had no problem slipping the purse from the back of the chair of his target.

It had been fun to pretend that she and Poros were getting married. It had made her wonder if that could be their future.

She'd also laughed with delight when it was Jinsoo and Chidori's chance to distract as Poros stole. The yellow canary had fluttered above Jinsoo and had pegged him with peanuts. Jinsoo had pretended to be annoyed, crying "Stop that, you crazy bird!" The people in the plaza had been in stitches while Poros had lifted the wallet from his laughing target.

Then they'd moved down to another outdoor café, where Hermie and Mahdi had staged a brawl while Jinsoo stole bags from three targets sharing the same table.

After each success, the crew had toasted to the victors, who were high on adrenaline, before the spoils were inconspicuously returned to the targets. Hestie had been itching to play the thief.

Now, she returned to her table, where Poros rubbed her back and said, "There will be other chances."

"I know. I thought I had it. I was so close."

When Gertie and Taavi caught up to them, Hestie asked, "What happened, guys?"

Gertie's face turned as red as a beet. "Sorry."

Taavi, in his usual happy-go-lucky way, said, "That target was ready to leave. We will get the next one."

Hestie nodded and lifted her glass of iced cola. "Cheers to that."

"I say we shake it out," Taavi said with a gleam in his eyes.

"What do you mean?" Hestie asked.

"It is something we do," Alastair said.

"We shake it out," Penny repeated.

"We should not waste time," Del objected.

"Oh, come on," Taavi insisted. "We need to regain our focus."

"I agree," Mahdi said. "This is an important part of our process. They should learn it."

"I want to learn it," Gertie said eagerly. "Please?"

Hestie found herself wanting to learn it, too, out of curiosity, if for no other reason.

Del shrugged.

Taavi's grin widened. "Good. So, this is what we do. All together, we clap twice," he clapped his hands together twice, "snap twice," he snapped his fingers twice, "and then one person in the group sings a word or phrase. Then we clap twice, snap twice, and the next person adds a word or phrase to the song."

"Huh?" Hermie asked.

"We make up a song," Alastair explained. "And if you cannot think of a word or phrase to go with the song when it is your turn, you are eliminated from the game."

"We should keep practicing our techniques," Del said.

"I want to play the game!" Jinsoo cried. "Please?"

"Please?" Gertie said, too.

Del shrugged. "Okay."

Taavi and Mahdi high-fived one another, and then Taavi led the group with two claps, two snaps, after which he sang, "My love."

Penny moaned. "It is always love with you."

Despite her objection, Penny and the group continued with the game. They clapped twice, snapped twice, and then Mahdi sang, "is like."

Hestie laughed as she watched each player struggle to come up with the next word or phrase in their made-up song. They had begun to attract the attention of others. A few people had gathered in the street to watch and to listen.

Hestie laughed gleefully when Jinsoo added a phrase about kimchi to the song. By the time it was her turn, the song had become a little convoluted, but she had known what her part would be from the very be-ginning. She sang, "Oooh, baby."

That makes no sense, her brother said to her telepathically, but the rest of the group was in near hysterics—even Del, who'd been moody all day.

Once they'd made it all the way around the group, ending with Ger-tie, they all sang the made-up song, claps and snaps included, in its en-tirety:

My love
Is like
The ocean
At night
Shimmering
Brightly
Like stars.
But kimchi
Is sour
Oooh, baby
Unlike
Our love
Will forever be.

Then they laughed so hard that Hestie thought she would pee in her pants.

Once they'd recovered, Del said it was time to move on.

Prometheus settled the bill, and then they strolled through the cool, windy night down a cobblestone path.

"That's a good spot," Penny said, pointing to a string of benches in front of Beans Café. "There are a handful of people dining across the street—not too few and not too many."

Poros took Hestie's hand and led her to one of the benches.

"Hestie, try again," Alastair said as he raked a hand through his sandy-colored hair. Then he turned to Gertie and Taavi. "And you two distract. But this time, try fighting."

Hestie didn't think the mortal's cheeks could grow any redder, but they did.

Laughing, Taavi said, "No worries."

"Don't blow it for me this time," Hestie said to Gertie before she crossed the street.

Hestie lingered near a potted palm, inspecting its leaves, a few yards away from the target. She was startled when Gertie's voice rang out, loud and clear, over the patio.

"Who *was* she? Tell me her name, you cheating douchebag!"

Taavi backed away with his hands in the air. "Please. There is no one else but you."

"Liar!" Gertie cried. "I trusted you! I gave you my heart! And after a year of being together, you kiss the first pretty face that likes you in my absence! How dare you do this to me!"

As the target gawked at the spectacle Gertie was making in the street with Taavi, Hestie strolled through the tables where others were eating and drinking. The adrenaline coursed through her, exhilarating her as she snatched the purse from the chair beside her target and continued toward the street, in the opposite direction of Gertie and Taavi.

She wanted to shout with joy at her victory, but she hadn't gone far when someone approached her.

"Excuse me, miss?"

Hestie turned to see a man in uniform—a security guard.

"Yes, sir?" Hestie asked as her throat tightened.

"Does that bag belong to you?" he asked.

In less than a second, Alastair was at her side.

"May I help you, sir?" Alastair asked the guard.

"No. This is not your concern. I saw this woman take this bag…"

Hestie made the purse disappear. "What bag?"

The security guard gaped.

"Look here, sir." Alastair stared into the eyes of the guard, mesmerizing him. "You are mistaken."

The guard's face slackened. "Pardon me. Good night."

The security guard walked away, but the woman whose purse had been stolen was now approaching them from the restaurant.

Alastair mesmerized her before she could complain. Then Hestie used her powers to place the stolen purse on the chair where the target had been sitting.

The woman returned to her chair and, seeing the bag, glanced around, baffled.

Gertie and Taavi continued to argue, distracting the others seated on the patio. Hestie was grateful that at least their side of things had been a success, or she might have found herself in worse trouble.

A thief must never draw attention to herself, Alastair scolded as they returned to the others. *You should have removed your big hat before going in. Who wears a hat at night, anyway? You could have carried it and used it to conceal the purse.*

"Got it," she said. "I'll do better next time."

The trick is over, Taavi said to Gertie telepathically. *Stomp off angrily, toward the others, and I will meet up with you shortly.*

She was still reeling with anger. Nikita would have been proud of how well Gertie had played her part.

"I never want to see you again!" Gertie shouted before she turned away from Taavi and crossed the street to join the others on the benches in front of Beans Café.

Despite her Academy-award-worthy performance, Gertie was feeling dizzy, cold, and weak. When Taavi rejoined her a few moments later, she asked him, telepathically, *Please, take a drink from me. I hate being the weakest one here.*

I do not think that wise, he replied. *Perhaps you should ask another.*

She was about to ask Taavi what he meant but supposed she already knew: Their relationship was on the verge of becoming toxic. Her body had responded to him against her will, and it had angered her, because she wanted to be faithful to Hector. To make matters worse, she longed for Taavi's bite. Without a doubt, he longed for her blood.

Once they had rejoined the group, Raimo, whose dark stringy hair hung over his dark eyes, said, "We need to feed. We know a place across the sea in Sicily—a bar where the regulars know what we are and what we have to offer."

"Drink from *me*," Gertie said.

"There are eight of us," Del pointed out. "And we need more than a pint between us."

"We'll meet you back at the ship," Prometheus said to the vampires.

Gertie turned to Del. "Take me with you. Just drink enough from me to give me your powers."

"Come on, Gertie," Prometheus said. "You need food and sleep."

Hermie followed the captain and the others back to the ship, wondering where he'd gone wrong. He thought he'd had a connection with Del, but now she wasn't giving him the time of day. Maybe that's how vampires were. Maybe they were incapable of having deep feelings.

The *Marcella II* seemed empty without the vampires there. Jinsoo asked Hermie if he wanted to play *Urban Fighter*, but Hermie wasn't in the mood.

"I think I'll go to bed," Hermie said.

On the way to his cabin, he passed the vampire crates in the laundry room. Still troubled by Del's aloofness, he sat on her crate and decided to wait for her. Only a few minutes had passed, however, when he thought of a better idea: He would look for her in Sicily.

Not wanting to risk the scrutiny of the others, he told no one before god-traveling from the ship to the night sky. He stopped near the peak of Mount Etna, which towered from the east coast of Sicily, near where the Mediterranean reached the Ionian Sea. He scoured the land below, searching for his vampire friends. Compared to Malta, Sicily was an enormous island, its landscape teeming with people, even at night. Where should he begin?

As he hovered there beneath the stars, wondering what to do next, he sensed Selene not far above him, making her rounds in her silver, iridescent chariot. Her long, silver hair blew in the wind, as did her long, luminous robe. Her chariot was pulled by two silver horses with manes as long and iridescent as hers.

"Hello, Hermie!" she called from above.

"Hi, Selene!" He flew toward her and stroked the manes of her horses.

"What are you doing out here, all alone?" she asked him.

"Looking for my friends. They're, er, vampire pirates who work for Hermes."

The moon goddess smiled. "Hecate's friends. Yes, I know them."

"I don't suppose you noticed where they went tonight?" he asked, highly doubting that she had.

He was surprised when she said, "Of course, I did. What else have I to do alone in my chariot but to study the creatures of the night?"

Hermie's mouth dropped open "Really? Wow! Could you point me in their direction?"

"La Luna Rossa," she said. "The Red Moon. It's a pub in Syracuse, on the coast between The Musciara Resort and Hotel Sbarcadero. It's very old. That's why they like it. It's nearly as ancient as they."

"Thanks!" Hermie cried. "Have a nice night!"

"You, too, little god. Be careful."

Hermie flew through the windy night toward the coast of Syracuse, where the streetlights lit up the city, and music could be heard pouring from the bars and cafés and into the streets. The streets were filled with the sounds of people talking and laughing. He spotted La Luna Rossa not far from a marina filled with ships. Two men stepped from the pub and stumbled across a parking lot toward the docks. One of them was singing while the other laughed. They were passed by another man leaving the docks for the pub. La Luna Rossa appeared to be a popular place for sailors.

Hermie followed the sailor into the pub, where it was loud, smoky, and crowded, and scanned the dark room for the vampires. They weren't difficult to spot, because they were the most beautiful people there. Mahdi and Bach played pool with sailors, who, by the appearance of blood on their wrists, seemed to have been fed upon already. Penny and Sophia sat at a table with two men who had blood stains on their necks. Taavi stood near the jukebox with a blonde in his arms swaying to the slow music. His lips pressed against the woman's neck. Alastair sat alone at the bar, staring at Hermie with a quizzical brow. He'd probably noticed Hermie the moment he'd entered the establishment.

Hermie sat on the empty barstool beside Alastair. "Where's Del?"

"How did you find us?" Alastair asked.

"Does it matter?"

Alastair shrugged and pushed his sandy-colored hair from his eyes.

"Where's Del?" Hermie asked again.

"She went to the ladies' room."

"I didn't think vampires…"

"She went for a drink."

"Oh."

Hermie glanced around for the bathrooms and, after seeing a sign, followed it down a long, narrow corridor, where a man was standing against the wall outside of the ladies' room. Del emerged seconds later and immediately noticed Hermie. Instead of greeting him, she went into the arms of the stranger. He kissed her on the mouth. Hermie shuddered as Del kissed the stranger back.

Hermie didn't know what to do. He resisted the urge to pulverize the mortal. Should he return to the ship with his tail between his legs? No. He refused, no matter how awkward he felt.

Approaching them, he said, "Hello, Del."

"Who's this kid?" the man, probably in his mid-thirties, asked. He spoke Italian.

"No one, really," Del said with a laugh before she resumed kissing the stranger.

Hermie fumed. "Can't I have just a moment of your time? I came a long way to talk to you."

"You are interfering with my dinner," she said. "I promised Lorenzo that I would take him flying. Siete pronti, Lorenzo?"

"I'm always ready for you, Del," he said.

So, he wasn't a stranger, Hermie thought.

Go away, Hermie, Del said to him telepathically.

But, I don't understand. I thought we were…friends.

Friends? With, what did you call it? An animal magnetism? A chemistry?

Yes.

To Lorenzo, she said, "Un momento per favore."

She took a few steps toward Hermie, until they were so close that he could reach out and touch her long, curly hair, if he dared.

"You need to understand something," she said. "The sooner you get it, the better."

"I'm listening," Hermie said, feeling lost in her deep, dark eyes. Was she mesmerizing him? No. She had once told him that her powers only affected mortals, not gods.

"We are on a team with an important mission. There is no room for romantic entanglements."

"But, Del…"

"Besides, we both know it could never work. What happened to Mina—what I did to Mina—will always be between us."

Before Hermie could object, Del flew to Lorenzo with lightning speed and vanished from the corridor.

Hermie thought of following her, but, in the end, he returned to the *Marcella II.*

CHAPTER THREE

How to Clean a Ship

After a week of practicing the vampires' schemes with the group in different areas of the island each night, Gertie felt like a pro. She didn't need the powers of speed, invisibility, or mind control to be successful—though she wouldn't have minded having them.

Then, one evening, as they were about to set out from the docks, Hermes appeared.

"Hello, Hermes," Prometheus said, tipping his white captain's hat.

"Hello," the god of thievery replied. "You have a talented crew, it seems."

"Indeed," the captain said.

Gertie beamed and glanced at the young gods. Hestie rolled her eyes at Gertie.

"Do you bring us news from Mount Olympus?" Poros asked. "Are the others on the lookout for the warheads from Gertie's dream?"

Hermes frowned. "I'm afraid they are distracted by other concerns."

Gertie's jaw dropped open. "What? I would think this would be a top priority."

Hermes scratched his beard. "That's because you are unaware of just how often this sort of thing happens. Weapons are smuggled around the world on a regular basis."

"Weapons of mass destruction?" Poros asked, looking as incredulous as Gertie felt.

"That's the thing," Hermes said, now scratching his head. "Mortals rarely *use* warheads. Machine guns and milder explosives tend to be more deadly, more dangerous, statistically speaking. The other gods believe the warheads are for show, for maintaining leverage. Once used, the leverage is gone."

"I can't believe they're willing to chance it," Hermie said. "Better safe than sorry."

Hermes looked uncomfortable as he said, "The thing is, even if we succeed in capturing and destroying these warheads, the mortals will make more. This is an ongoing effort that the other gods feel is futile. If we want to stop STS, we'll have to do it ourselves."

Gertie hung her head, her faith in the Olympians shattered.

"You may as well face that truth sooner or later," Alastair said to Gertie and the young gods. "Except for Lord Hermes and our fearless captain, we're on our own."

"Right then. It's time to move on," Hermes said. "It's time to teach our rookies how to clean a ship."

"Oh, I'm an expert at that," Jinsoo said. "Captain makes us keep the ship spic and span."

The vampires laughed.

"Not that kind of cleaning, you cute boy," Alastair said.

Jinsoo grinned with embarrassment. "Oh."

Chidori comforted him with a kiss.

Hermes turned to Del and Alastair. "I'll leave you to it. Call me if you need me."

Then, just like the last time, Hermes disappeared as quickly as he'd arrived.

"Where do we start?" Gertie asked Del.

"Scout and plan," Del said. "Case the docks and find the target. We want a ship full of goods but empty of people. Got it?"

Gertie nodded.

"We should split up," Raimo said. "Less conspicuous."

"Good idea," Alastair agreed. "Let's scout and plan tonight and thieve tomorrow."

Gertie raised her hand and then felt embarrassed when Hestie seemed to scoff at her. What was Hestie's problem, anyway?

"Gertie, do you have a question?" Prometheus asked.

"What if the ship we choose as our target leaves in the morning?" she asked.

"That would be unlikely," Taavi said.

Penny nodded. "If we collect our intel correctly."

"But what if it does?" Gertie persisted.

Del shrugged. "Then we begin again."

"Wouldn't it be smarter to scout, plan, and thieve in the same night?" Gertie asked.

"No," Alastair said abruptly.

Gertie sensed he and the others were annoyed with her, so she said nothing more.

As Del divided them up into groups, Hermie came up to Gertie. Unlike his sister, he gave her smile. He was beautiful with hair as dark as the night sea and eyes as blue as the morning sky. His skin glowed, like the other gods, as though it had been kissed by Helios.

"I was thinking the same thing as you," he said. "There ought to be a better way. In fact, we should be able to search up the float plan of any commercial vessel at port. That would tell us everything we need to know: How many crew members, what type of cargo, how long the ship will be in port, where it came from, and where it goes from here."

"That's awesome, Hermie," she said. "You should tell the others."

"I don't think it would do any good."

Taavi came up beside her and said, "It looks like you are with me."

Hermie gave her a shrug and walked the other way, toward his group. Gertie continued along the dock with Taavi, followed by Raimo and Mahdi.

"You have been avoiding me," Taavi said to her.

Gertie blushed. "You know why."

"If you are still with Hector, why are you here?' he asked. "Or why is he not here with you?"

"It's hard to explain."

"If you were mine, I would be with you."

Gertie swallowed hard, not sure what to say. Hector had *wanted* to return to the ship with her, but she had told him not to. Now, she wondered why. At the time, she'd been thinking only of Hector, of his need to figure things out with his music. But now she worried that she'd done it for herself. She glanced up at Taavi's dark eyes sparkling down at her from beneath dark brows. He grinned, and a dimple appeared. As she recalled the way he had held her and kissed her during that first night of training, she was drawn to his mouth.

Then her phone vibrated. Taking it from her pocket, she saw it was Hector calling.

Hermie, along with Jinsoo and Chidori, followed Penny, Sophia, and Bach from the marina, where the *Marcella II* was docked, toward the point, where the larger vessels were housed. They passed a Royal cruise ship before approaching a string of barges, including one with a logo that Hermie recognized as belonging to Sailfish Trading and Shipping.

Hermie pulled out his phone, saying, "Hey, guys. Hold up."

Sophia glared at him impatiently. Penny put her hands on her hips. Bach crossed his arms. Jinsoo fed Chidori a sesame seed from his pocket.

"I'm searching the internet for the float plan for this STS barge," Hermie said. "If I can find it, it'll save us a lot of time."

"That is not how we do things," Bach complained as the wind blew his blond hair into his face.

Hermie clicked on the top of his search results, struggling to keep his own hair out of his face. "That doesn't mean you shouldn't."

"He has a point," Penny said to Bach. "We should hear him out."

"I smell something bad," Jinsoo said.

Chidori chirped her agreement.

Sophia sighed. "We smell it too."

"You probably smell your kimchi back on the *Marcella II*," Hermie teased.

"Something died," Penny said, her ponytail whipping in the wind. "Probably rats."

"Gross." Jinsoo shuddered.

Hermie raised his hand. "I found it. The float plan for vessel 122947. That's this one." He scrolled through the pdf document. "Let's see. She transported slabs of granite from Syria to St. Petersburg, Russia and is on her way back to Syria. She sets sail first thing in the morning."

"Unfortunate," Bach said. "It would have been good to do a practice run on an STS ship."

"We could snoop around," Penny said. "I do not sense anyone aboard." She turned to Hermie. "Do you?"

"It's hard to tell." He used his god vision to look through the shipping containers, but his perspective was hindered. He would see better from above. "I think there might be two or three people, possibly."

"I do not smell blood or hear any beating hearts," Bach said.

"Just dead blood," Jinsoo said with another shudder.

"What happened to the rule about scouting and planning?" Hermie asked Penny. "We can't go snooping around. It's against the code."

"*Thieving* without a plan is against the code," Penny said as she stripped from her clothes, shocking Hermie and, from the look on his face, Jinsoo. "*Snooping* is encouraged. Make yourselves invisible and follow me."

Hestie stood between Poros and the captain as Del and Alastair studied a shipping barge docked in the marina among dozens of other ships.

She supposed x-ray vision came in handy for the pirates. She used her god vision to see what was in the shipping containers. They were filled with cigarettes, cigars, and cans of chewing tobacco.

"Black market goods," Del said.

"How do you know they aren't legitimate?" Prometheus asked.

"Legitimate goods are packaged differently," Alastair explained. "The same brand per case. These crates contain units of mixed brands. See?"

"Ah, yes," the captain said. "I see what you mean."

"I sense one or two sailors aboard," Poros said.

Prometheus nodded. "Probably guards."

"This would be the perfect vessel for our purposes," Del said.

Alastair dropped his clothes onto the pier and lifted into the night air. "Let us board and scout it out."

Even though gods could see through clothes, Hestie was still taken aback. She looked away when Del stripped from hers, too.

"I'll wait for you here," Prometheus said.

"Make yourselves invisible and follow us," Del said to Hestie and Poros.

Hestie glanced at Poros.

He shrugged. "Let's follow their lead."

Hermie followed Penny, Sophia, and Bach into the air above the barge, where they could get a better look into the shipping containers. Jinsoo and Chidori were right behind him.

"I see people," Jinsoo said, pointing to one of the containers.

"Dead people," Bach said.

Hermie's stomach turned. Three bodies—two male and one fe-male—were heaped in a corner.

Why were there dead people inside a shipping container on an STS vessel?

Gertie ended her call with Hector and turned to the three vampires, who were now staring at her suspiciously.

"I had no idea," she said to them. "You heard how shocked I was. Besides, Hector could be mistaken."

"He sounded *certain*," Mahdi said.

"Even if my stepfather does own the majority of STS, that doesn't mean he's aware of all the smuggling going on," Gertie insisted.

"Highly doubtful," Raimo said as he pushed his dark, stringy hair out of his eyes.

"We need to report this to our lord," Taavi said.

As the group headed back to the *Marcella II*, Gertie felt sick to her stomach. The gods and vampires would never trust or accept her if what Hector had learned about her stepfather's involvement in STS were true. She needed to go home and face James Morgan. She needed to know the truth.

Hestie was relieved when, back on the *Marcella II*, Hermes finally appeared in answer to their prayers about the dead bodies on the STS ship.

It was nearly dawn, so, to avoid the vampires getting fried by the sun, they met in the ship's hull in the laundry room, where the vamps sat on top of their crates and the other gods stood in the connecting corridor. Gertie, fighting sleep, sat on the floor with her back against the wall. Hestie almost felt sorry for her, especially because the vampires had been treating her differently, ever since they had learned about the connection between STS and her stepfather.

"You need to stay focused on your training and the warheads," Hermes said to them. "Let me worry about the dead bodies."

"What will you do?" Poros asked. "Something *will* be done about them, won't it?"

"I've already alerted the port authorities," Hermes assured him. "As soon as I can, I'll go to the Underworld to interview the dead."

Gertie lifted her sleepy lids and asked, "How? Don't they lose their memories?"

"The Furies have ways of helping them to remember," Hermes said.

Hestie shuddered. Hermes meant torture. It didn't seem fair that those poor souls, who had likely suffered before death, would be made to endure more pain. But one dip in the Lethe—the river of forgetfulness—and they'd forget again. She supposed that if their temporary pain would help Hermes to find out what had happened, then it was worth it.

"And what do we do about James Morgan?" Raimo asked Hermes.

"Should Gertie even be here?" Penny asked.

"She could be a spy," Bach suggested.

Gertie climbed to her feet. "I'm not a spy."

Hestie noticed tears in Gertie's eyes. She wished the vampires would back off.

"Don't you vamps remember how Gertie risked her life to save as many of you as she could when the *Tarantula* was attacked?" Hestie asked. "And this is how you repay her? By accusing her of being a spy?"

Wow. You go, girl, her brother said to her telepathically.

Gertie turned to Hestie with wide eyes. "Thank you. I didn't think you liked me."

Blood rushed to Hestie's cheeks. She *hadn't* liked Gertie, but only because the mortal always tried too hard to show off. "I'm just saying you deserve better."

Poros squeezed Hestie's hand and gave her an approving smile, but instead of making Hestie feel good, it made her feel defensive. Hestie stuck to her guns in believing that the know-it-all had needed to be taken down a notch; even so, Gertie had proven her loyalty more than once.

"I should go home," Gertie said, surprising Hestie. "To learn what I can from my stepfather."

"Agreed," Hermes said. "But first, complete your training on how to clean a ship. Participate in tonight's practice run, and then one of us will take you home afterward."

"Let me take her," Jinsoo said. "I haven't gotten to fly enough."

"You don't know where she lives," Hermie pointed out.

"So?" Jinsoo said.

"Let's not worry about that now," Prometheus suggested.

"No," Hermes agreed. "You need to continue your training, to prepare for tonight."

The pirates gave their lord a nod.

"I'll leave you to it," Hermes said before he vanished.

"I'll take my leave as well," Prometheus said. "I'll be at the helm smoking my pipe, if anyone needs me."

Gertie could barely keep her eyes open as the vampires talked about the hazards of cleaning a thieving ship. She slid down the wall to the floor and sat on her bottom as she listened.

Del, who sat on her crate with her legs stretched out, one crossed over the other, moved her dark hair to one shoulder and said, "The most important thing is to know where your enemies are before you strike, so you can plan properly."

Alastair lay on his crate on his side, with his head propped on an elbow. "We aim to thieve when the crew is off ship, but, if the job must be done at sea, things can be more complicated."

"Even at port," Raimo, who hovered above his crate, crosse-legged, reminding Gertie of the Genie from *Aladdin*, said, "most pirates station guards to protect their booty while the rest eat and drink at the taverns."

"And when that happens," Penny said, "we use the distraction techniques you have already learned to trick the guards."

Sophia lay down on Penny's crate and rested her head in Penny's lap. "Wake me up when this is over. I am sleepy."

Mahdi, ignoring Sophia, held up three fingers. "There are always three teams: The lookout, the distractors, and the burglars—Team One, Two, and Three."

"We usually put our best fighters on lookout," Del said. "Raimo, Penny, and Mahdi. But tonight, we want you trainees to perform the mission without us."

"Awesome!" Jinsoo cried.

"Seriously?" Hestie asked.

Hermie lifted a finger. "Are you sure we're ready for that?"

"Shouldn't we pull something off with you there, first?" Poros asked.

Gertie was relieved that she wasn't the only trainee with reservations.

"We will be with the lookout," Alastair assured them.

"And will intervene, if necessary," Mahdi added.

"First, we will show you some of our previous jobs by sharing our memories with you," Del explained. "But before we do that, we want to outline the important components of a successful mission."

"The members of the lookout are stationed around the perimeter of the ship," Alastair said. "If guards are posted near the booty, the distractors move in."

"And if no guards are posted?" Gertie asked.

"Then the distractors join the lookout," Taavi said. "That way, if the crew members return before the mission is completed, the distractors can get to work, to avoid conflict."

That made sense to Gertie. She hadn't realized pirating was so meticulously orchestrated.

Along with the other trainees, Hermie watched Del's memory of one of the pirates' prior jobs. The memory played inside his head. It was fascinating, how vampires could share information. What made it even more fascinating was his ability to experience the memory from Del's point of view. It made him feel close to her, even though she continued to give him the cold shoulder.

In the memory, Penny, Raimo, Mahdi, and Farouk were the lookout team and were stationed along the perimeter of a Turkish-built frigate designed for Russia but hijacked by Syrian rebels. Del, Alastair, Taavi, and Edric were the distraction team. They maneuvered the *Tarantula* in the frigate's path, pretending to need aid. The rest of the vampires functioned as the burglars. In this case, since the ship itself was the stolen good, the job of the burglars was to capture the Syrian pirates and save the Turkish crew without killing anyone.

Hermie was astonished when, in the memory, he saw Del jump aboard the frigate in time to put herself between a Syrian bullet and a Turkish crew member. The bullet wouldn't kill a vampire, but Hermie could feel, through Del's memory, how painful it had been. Taking the bullet had allowed her to save a human life.

Hermie had found it difficult to concentrate, though, because he kept pulling himself out of the memory to gaze at Del sitting on her crate. Why was he so drawn to her? It couldn't be her beauty, even though she was, without a doubt, the most beautiful girl he'd ever seen. Hermie knew himself to be made of better stuff than that. It couldn't be her skills, because the other vampires were just as skilled as she. And, as much as he admired her attitude about the disenfranchised and her mission to help liberate them, it was the same for her team. So why was he drawn to her, specifically?

It suddenly occurred to him that he was drawn to her because of the pain and sorrow she felt over having taken Mina's life. She had shown him her mind and had shared her overwhelming regret and grief. Maybe the other things—her beauty, her amazing skills, her awesome attitude, her admirable mission—only added to this other thing: He wanted to alleviate her suffering because he felt responsible for it.

When the vampires had finished with their instructions for the day, they climbed into their crates to rest. Hermie didn't like the feeling of being away from Del, of not having her in his sight, but he couldn't very well crawl into her crate with her, could he?

"Let's go the bridge with Captain," Poros said to Hestie.

"I'm going to bed," Gertie said. "I can't keep my eyes open."

"Sweet dreams," Hermie said to her, knowing she could use some moral support.

"Thanks," she said as she opened the door to her cabin. "I'll be sure to pray to your cousin for help with that."

Hermie followed Jinsoo, Poros, and Hestie onto the bridge.

Prometheus waved when they appeared. "All done for now?"

"It appears so," Poros said.

"I'm going shopping for more supplies," he said. "You should rest up before tonight."

"Can we come with you, Captain?" Poros asked.

"*We* want to go shopping," Hestie added.

"Oh, Chidori and I want to shop!" Jinsoo agreed.

The Captain lifted his chin. "Aren't you tired? You've been training nonstop for days."

That was true, Hermie thought. Even during the day, while Gertie had slept and the vampires had hung out in their crates, Hestie, Poros, Jinsoo, and Hermie had continued to practice their trickery.

Jinsoo frowned. "We're gods, too. Don't forget."

The captain mussed Jinsoo's hair. "Even gods need their rest. But I suppose you can come along, if you want."

"Thanks!" Hestie said with a smile.

She and Jinsoo bumped fists.

"Chidori may need her rest," Hermie pointed out. "Why not leave her with me?"

"You don't want to come?" Jinsoo asked Hermie.

Hermie shook his head.

"What about you, Chidori?" Jinsoo asked the bird.

In reply, she flew from Jinsoo's finger to perch on Hermie's shoulder.

"Fine. Be that way," Jinsoo teased.

Hermie was glad to be left alone in his room with his bird. He hadn't minded the bond she'd made with Jinsoo, but, sometimes, if he was being honest, he was a little jealous.

He supposed he was feeling sorry for himself. And why shouldn't he? The girl he'd been dating had been tragically killed just as they'd been getting close, and the girl that he felt drawn to more than any other, in ways he had never thought possible, wanted nothing to do with him.

"At least *you're* here with me," Hermie said to Chidori as he plopped onto his bed and stretched out onto his back.

Chidori fluttered in the air and then landed on his chest.

"Sweet dreams," she chirped.

He doubted he would sleep. His mind was spinning with images of Del and with questions about her attitude toward him. If her feelings for him had been anything like his feelings for her, she wouldn't have said those things to him in Syracuse.

You do not know the whole story, Del said in his head.

Then tell it to me, he replied.

I will. But now I must sleep.

A pang of disappointment gripped his chest.

Sweet dreams, he said to her.

You, too, Hermie.

He hadn't closed his eyes for very long when he heard something. Was it music? The most beautiful sound flowed softly from the corridor outside his room. It took him only a moment to realize that it was the vampires singing themselves to sleep.

CHAPTER FOUR:

A Practice Run

At dusk, Gertie accompanied the vampires and gods—all save Prometheus, who'd remained on the ship with Chidori—down the docks toward the adjacent marina, where the shipping barges and other large vessels were docked. The dark water was restless, crashing against the ships as if it wanted to suck them out to sea. The wind, too, was wild, and dark clouds blotted out the stars. Even Selene was not visible to Gertie as she folded her arms across her chest, trying to keep warm.

She was the only among them not in invisibility mode, which made it appear to any mortal who might be watching that she was walking alone. Being mortal, she couldn't see the others, either. She may as well have been alone.

She'd tried to convince the vampires that she should be bitten, so that she could make herself invisible, too; but none of them wanted to risk encouraging what they saw as a tendency toward addiction.

She hated that her flaws had been so obvious. Despite her ability to shield her thoughts from being overheard, she felt transparent. Transparent and weak.

And nobody trusted her, especially after learning what Hector had discovered in his research.

She almost wished Hector had stayed out of it, because she was sure that there was no way her stepfather could be aware of the smuggling that took place on STS ships.

Gertie was surprised by how many sailors were leaving their ships for port, probably to have their dinner, and maybe their drink, before returning for sleep. Some of them eyed her up and down as they passed her, probably wondering why a teenage girl was walking alone at night on the docks. Maybe they thought she was somebody's booty call.

Are you still there? Gertie asked the others.

Yes. It was Hermie who answered her.

Taavi briefly showed himself flying alongside her, naked. He winked and vanished.

Gertie blushed, forgetting how immodest vampires were with their bodies. But she was glad Taavi had winked at her. He'd been standoffish toward her ever since Hector's phone call.

Hearing Hector's voice on the phone had reminded Gertie of how much she missed him, but now that the decision had been made for her to return to Athens, she had mixed feelings. She hadn't seen Hector since the day of the memorial on the *Marcella II*—though they had spoken on the phone a few times. On her last night in Athens, when Morpheus had come for her, Hector had told her on the phone that he loved her. She'd wanted to believe him. Her love for him remained unchanged. But he had left her. He had left her to figure things out. It had broken something inside her. It had broken her faith in his love for her. She was scared to death that he was going to break her heart.

She was jealous of how devoted Nikita and Lajos were to one another. Hestie and Poros were the same. It made Gertie fear that she and Hector were lacking. Why had he gone? He'd said he wanted to come back, but why had he gone in the first place?

Gertie's grandmother had been the only person who had stuck with Gertie throughout most of Gertie's life, but even she had eventually left. As much as she loved Gaia, Gertie still felt used by the goddess. She felt used—and abandoned—by her father, Dionysus, too. Even her mother, Diane, had used her and had been willing to give Gertie up. Gertie's eyes moistened. Had Jeno used her? Whether he had ever loved her or not, in the end, he had left her, too. Why had it always been so hard for her to find love, to make friends, to get people to like her?

This was exactly why Gertie preferred fiction, and fictional friends, to reality. Before meeting Nikita and the Angelis family, Gertie's friends had been exclusively fictional. Gertie wiped a tear from her cheek. She missed Nikita.

After she'd walked over half a mile in the wailing wind, she turned and continued down the dock where their target was anchored. By now, most of the sailors had cleared out. She saw one coiling a rope on the deck of one of the barges, but he hadn't seemed to notice her.

Gertie quickly climbed the ladder toward the deck of the target. The wind hurled against her, as if warning her to abort the mission. Then Jinsoo appeared on the ladder above her, just as they had planned, and she was relieved.

The two guards were sitting on the deck on barrels in front of the first shipping container. They were large men in their twenties and appeared to be twins, with red hair, almost as shocking as Hestie's. Two rifles leaned against the barrels.

"Excuse me," Jinsoo said. "We're your new interns."

As Gertie stepped onto the deck after Jinsoo, she noticed the two guards look at each other, puzzled, before turning to her with the same look of confusion.

"From the university," Gertie added. "Our counselor said to report here tonight."

"You look too young to be a university student," one guard said to Jinsoo.

"Are you racist?" Jinsoo asked him.

"What? No! I just meant…" his voice dropped off.

Gertie was glad they could speak English. Otherwise, Jinsoo would have had to do the talking.

"The captain didn't tell us there would be interns," the other one said. "I think you got the wrong ship."

Gertie resisted the urge to smile. It was almost as if the guards knew the script.

Jinsoo flung his hands in the air and turned to Gertie. "I knew it. That counselor is crazy. I knew she didn't know what she was doing!"

Gertie shook her head. "You're wrong, Jinsoo! This is the right ship! My transcript said the *Legacy*, and that's this ship!" She turned the guards. "This is the *Legacy*, isn't it?"

The two guards nodded.

"But, like he said," the first one said. "Our captain didn't say anything about interns boarding."

"Maybe he forgot," Jinsoo said. "My counselor said this was arranged a while back."

"Could be," the second guard said. "But I doubt it. I don't think our captain would be interested in training university students."

"We're already trained," Gertie said. "We're basically free labor. In fact, aren't *we* the dumb ones, because we are actually paying our university to allow us to work for you?" She forced a laugh.

The two guards chuckled.

"That does sound backwards," the first one said. "What's in it for you?"

"College credit," Jinsoo said. "And an easy A."

"And a reference for our resumes," Gertie added.

Gertie hoped Hermie was nearly finished stealing the cartons of cigarettes, cigars, and tobacco from the shipping container behind the guards. She and Jinsoo were running out of script.

Jinsoo sat on a nearby barrel. "I guess we should wait here for your captain."

"He'll be able to clear things up," Gertie said.

The two men shrugged.

"Suit yourself," the first one said.

Gertie leaned on the ship's railing and asked the guards, "So, what made you choose this profession?"

The second one laughed. "I didn't have much of a choice. You, Fred?"

"I love the sea," Fred said. "And the money isn't bad either."

Status update? Gertie prayed to Hermie.

When he didn't reply, she became anxious.

Poros? Hestie? Any word yet from Hermie? she prayed to the gods on lookout.

Again, nothing.

Jinsoo? Have you heard anything from the others? she prayed.

Nobody answers, he replied.

Just then, another sailor emerged from behind the shipping container. Gertie hadn't realized that another crew member was still aboard.

"Hi," she said sweetly. "We're…"

"Lies," the sailor said. "I found your friend. You better come with me, or I'll slice off his head."

Gertie's heart skipped a beat as she turned, dumbfounded, toward Jinsoo. *How could this human have captured a god?*

Jinsoo shrugged. *I don't think he's human.*

"What's going on?" the second guard asked.

"These kids are crooks, that's what," the third one said. Then to Gertie and Jinsoo, he repeated, "Come with me or your friend dies."

He's bluffing, Gertie prayed to Jinsoo. *He has to be.*

Do you want to risk it? Jinsoo asked her telepathically.

No.

Immediately, Gertie reached out in prayer to Poros, Hestie, and Prometheus.

She was dismayed when even Prometheus failed to reply.

The guards took up their rifles, and the third one led Gertie and Jinsoo toward the back of the barge, to the last shipping container. He opened the door and told them to enter, where they found Hermie in a cage.

"Hermie?" Jinsoo cried. "Can't you get out of there?"

"It's adamantine," Hermie said. "He tricked me into it."

The sailor laughed. "Believe me when I say I'll chop his body into pieces and feed them to the sharks if you two don't get into the cage with him."

Gertie and Jinsoo did as they were told. Tears stung Gertie's eyes and her entire body trembled as she continued to pray to the gods for help. Why would this ship have an adamantine cage? she wondered.

Just then, the vampires appeared with Poros and Hestie.

Hermie grabbed the bars of their prison. "Where have you been?"

When their captors didn't react to the presence of the supernatural beings who appeared on the ship, Gertie lifted a brow. "What's going on?"

"This was part of your training," Del explained.

"A test," Alastair added.

Taavi folded his arms over his chest and winked at Gertie. "Mainly for you and Jinsoo."

Gertie and Jinsoo gawked at one another.

Penny put her hands on her hips. "And you failed."

"What?" Jinsoo narrowed his eyes. He looked at Poros and Hestie with reproach.

"We had no idea," Poros insisted, raising his hands in the air. "I promise."

"Never agree to be captured, no matter the stakes," Raimo said.

"Hold on," Gertie interrupted. "They threatened to chop Hermie into pieces and…"

"We know," Del said.

"Even so, you made things worse by surrendering," Raimo said.

"An enemy only takes you prisoner as leverage," Del explained. "Otherwise, he would not bother to keep you alive."

"As leverage or for information," Raimo corrected.

"Right," Alastair said. "If that had been a real situation, and the sailor had threatened to kill Hermie if you did not enter the cage, he would have been bluffing, because the moment Hermie is dead, the leverage for the sailor is gone. You understand?"

Gertie gnawed on the inside of her lower lip.

"You should have made a run for it and returned with reinforcements," Mahdi said.

"Never agree to go with the enemy," Penny said. "It is better to risk death and run for it than to allow yourself to be captured."

"Because once you are captured, you are pretty much screwed," Bach said.

"But the gods took *you* prisoner," Gertie pointed out to Bach.

"We were taken by force," Bach said. "We did not surrender."

"Oh." Jinsoo smiled a sheepish grin.

Blood rushed to Gertie's cheeks. Could she do nothing right? She wanted to go home. She missed Nikita and Nikita's parents— Mamá and Babá—who were more like parents to Gertie than her own.

"Who are these sailors?" Gertie asked.

The sailors revealed themselves. Gertie recognized them as Ares, Phobos, and Deimos—the gods of war, fear, and panic. Jinsoo, being a god, should have been able to see through their disguise. Maybe he hadn't met them before. But Hermie had.

"It was a rotten trick." Hermie frowned with disgust.

Ares shrugged. "We owed Hermes a favor."

"But now we have to run," Deimos said.

"Later," Phobos said just before the three gods vanished.

Alastair brushed his hair from his eyes as he turned to Gertie and Jinsoo. "We hope you learned a valuable lesson."

Gertie felt even more blood rush to her cheeks as she clenched her fists and fought tears. She wanted to go home.

Once they were back in the salon on the *Marcella II*, where the vampires began to go over more details about how to clean a ship, Hestie took a moment to pull Gertie aside.

Hestie said, "I would have done the same thing."

Gertie seemed unmoved. Maybe she didn't believe Hestie.

"Thanks," Gertie said. "But I guess I'm not cut out for this. My powers are limited, compared to everyone else. I'm glad I'm going home."

"Don't sell yourself short," Hestie said. "You're very brave."

Tears filled Gertie's eyes. Hestie looked away, embarrassed.

"Thanks," Gertie said.

"I mean it," Hestie said. "And I'm sorry for giving you a hard time, it's just that…"

Gertie met her eyes. "What?"

"You come across as a show-off," Hestie said, reluctantly. "Don't you realize how off-putting that is to everyone around you?"

To Hestie's horror, Gertie ran from the salon and went below deck.

The others glanced at Hestie with looks of disapproval. They'd overheard everything she'd said, even though Del had also been talking.

Way to go, Hermie said to her telepathically.

After the night's lessons were over, and it had been decided that Taavi would fly Gertie home, Hermie hoped for an opportunity to speak alone with Del. But Mahdi had convinced everyone to play their "shake it off" game. The vampires sat in a circle on the floor of the main deck. Prometheus, Poros, and Hestie were above them on the flybridge, watching. Jinsoo had decided to join the vampires. Taavi and Gertie had already gone.

Hermie stood on the main deck not far from the merry circle. He enjoyed watching Del smile and laugh as they played their game—two claps, two snaps, and a new element to the song. He was jealous of how easily Jinsoo sat between Del and Alastair, without an ounce of self-consciousness or worry or fear. Chidori perched on Jinsoo's shoulder. She tweeted a hello to Hermie. He waved back.

Jinsoo noticed Hermie lurking in the shadows behind him. "Hermie, come play! It's so fun!"

Hermie hesitated, but when Jinsoo scooted over, making room between him and Del, Hermie couldn't resist the opportunity to sit beside her.

"Okay," he said as he squeezed in on the floor between Jinsoo and Del.

Del glanced at him, and he was surprised that she wore a smile on her beautiful face. It filled him with overwhelming joy. He was alarmed by his excessive feelings for her, by the overreaction of his body and emotions to what should be a small thing.

You look happier tonight, he said to her telepathically.

I am ready to tell you my story, she replied. *After our game.*

CHAPTER FIVE

Discoveries

Gertie trembled in Taavi's arms as she flew with him through the dark sky from the port in Malta toward Athens. She trembled—partly because the night was cold and windy, and partly because the feel of Taavi so close to her made her body react in ways she couldn't control.

She'd had mixed feelings when he'd volunteered to take her. On the one hand, she'd wanted a vampire, because a god would have *god-traveled* her home, and what would have been the fun in that? It would have been over in a split second. She'd wanted to enjoy one last superhuman experience before returning to her regular, old life.

On the other hand, she worried that being so close to Taavi for the two-hour flight would further confuse her about her feelings for Hector. Now that she found herself practically spooned by Taavi, his chin tucked against her shoulder, his cheek close to hers, and his arms tight around her waist, her head was spinning.

"You need to learn to love yourself, Gertie," he said, seemingly out of the blue. "You try too hard to be liked. It should not matter to you what others think."

Gertie gnawed on her lower lip. He was right.

"This was a lesson I had to learn at a young age," he continued. "My father was a bully. For the longest time, I thought he was strong and formidable because his angry tirades were so frightening. By the time I was twelve, I realized that he was merely an overgrown baby who could not control his anger. I learned not to associate my worth with his treatment of me."

"You are the opposite of your father," Gertie said. "I've never seen you angry."

"I feel anger often," Taavi said. "Especially when I see people treated poorly. But I know how to control myself."

"You always seem so happy-go-lucky," Gertie said.

"I *am* happy, most of the time. I have never felt so fortunate as I do now."

Gertie wondered if his feelings had anything to do with her. She was too afraid to ask for clarification because she wasn't sure how she felt about the possibility.

"I was thirteen," he continued, "when the very first vampires killed the rest of my family, and I was forced to move into the orphanage. I went from being the son of a successful merchant to someone who had nothing. Before that, I was well-liked. But after my parents and brothers were gone and I had nothing, people scorned me."

"Why would anyone scorn an orphan?" Gertie asked.

"They *pitied* me," he said. "But they also *mistrusted* me. Back then, the orphans attended the same school as the other children from the village. They were cruel to us—the children, the parents, and the teachers. People hate the poor. They say otherwise, but their actions tell a different story. People despise the poor as much as they do poverty."

"That's hard to believe."

Taavi laughed. "For someone like you, I imagine it is."

Blood rushed to Gertie's cheeks. "I know I have no right to complain. I've lived a life of privilege. But it hasn't been easy, either. My house was not a place of love or affection or support. I've been alone for most of my life."

"That explains a lot," Taavi said.

After a few minutes of silence, Gertie asked, "How did you do it? How did you learn to love yourself?"

"It happened while we were a choir," he said. "Del and Alastair received most of the praise and attention. Del is the only one of us who can reach high C, and Alastair the only one who can hit low C. They sang most of the solos. Except for being chosen to be in the choir in the first place, my talents went largely unnoticed. But I knew I was good. I decided that it was enough for me to believe in myself. I did not need praise or approval from others."

"I don't know if that's something I can just decide to do," Gertie said.

"It takes constant work," Taavi explained. "You must remind yourself constantly that you are good enough, that you have gifts, that you have worth and deserve to occupy the space you live in."

A flood of tears filled Gertie's eyes.

"Promise me you will try," Taavi said.

Gertie's voice cracked when she said, "I promise."

They flew in silence for a long while after that. During that time, Gertie began thinking of Jeno, recalling their time together, when she was a vampire. She missed him. And, although it hadn't been perfect, she missed living the life of a vampire.

After at least twenty minutes had passed, Gertie asked, "By any chance, did you know Jeno Mimikopoulou? He was from the same area as you."

"Yes. He and his sister were older, but I knew them. Calandra had a beautiful voice."

Fresh tears stung Gertie's eyes at the mention of Calandra. "I was there when she died."

"How did it happen?"

"It was the beginning of the vampire wars. Athena set fire to the caves beneath the acropolis, to smoke out the vampires. She did it during the day. The caves collapsed. The Parthenon crumbled. Athena literally destroyed her own temple in her attempt to destroy the vampires. I was there. I saw it all. I was a vampire then, too. And in our escape, Calandra, she hadn't fed in a long while and was more vulnerable to the sun, and she was…" Gertie's voice trailed off.

Taavi gave her a squeeze. "You are such a kind and loving soul."

"I was just thinking the same of you."

While Poros helped Prometheus to mend a sail, Hestie joined the vampires on the main deck to listen to their stories. They had finished their singing game and were reminiscing about their lost friends. Jinsoo and Hermie were with them. They shared stories of Mina, too.

Hestie didn't join their circle. She leaned against the ship's railing and watched from afar.

At one point, Jinsoo became emotional and said, "I hate Poseidon. This is all his fault. My sister and your friends would be alive if…"

Hermie nudged him. "Be careful what you say. Don't forget how powerful he is."

"Oh, you cute boy," Alastair said with a roll of his eyes. "Never speak ill of the god of the sea as long as you remain a sailor."

Jinsoo's cheeks reddened.

Hestie realized that the hatred Jinsoo had felt for the vampires in the wake of his sister's death had been transferred to Poseidon. She hoped Jinsoo was smart enough not to do or say something that would bring on the god's wrath.

Penny and Bach exchanged glances.

Then Penny said, "We saw firsthand what can happen, while we were prisoners of the gods."

"What do you mean?" Del asked.

Sophia gave Penny a warning look.

Bach's mouth was set in a line of anger and reproach.

"I think we should tell them," Penny said to him.

Just then, Athena appeared as a great owl and landed on the top of the center mast, above where Prometheus and Poros were working. She didn't go unnoticed by the vampires.

Penny glared up at Athena and said softly, "Athena and Poseidon gave us a glimpse of our future, if we ever cross them again."

"What future?" Hermie asked.

"Not death," Bach said. "Something far worse."

Mahdi leaned forward. "Stop being so cryptic and tell us what they showed you."

"The Titan Pit," Penny said. "They took us there."

"That's not allowed," Hermie said. "Not without at least three of the most powerful gods, or two of the most powerful gods and all three Furies. And Hades has to sanction it."

"Hades was there," Bach said.

Hestie's back stiffened.

"Seriously?" her brother asked. "What happened?"

Penny took a deep breath. "Athena and Hades guarded the door while Poseidon took us in and showed us the miserable lives led by the Titan prisoners."

"Pain and boredom for all eternity," Bach said. "Can you imagine?"

"But I gave them technology," Hermie said. "It was one of the first things I did when I became a god. Mortal prisoners have access to movies, video games, and the internet, so I figured they should, too."

"I guess Netflix can't keep up with their needs," Jinsoo said with a laugh.

But no one laughed at his joke.

"What kind of pain?" Raimo asked. "What, like torture? I thought that only happened in Tartarus."

"They were not tortured by the Furies," Penny said. "They were tortured by each other."

"What?" Jinsoo's face turned white.

"They turn on one another and take pleasure in tormenting," Bach explained. "It seems to be their favorite way of fighting the boredom."

"How grotesque," Hermie said.

Hestie had been thinking the same thing.

"We have to be careful," Bach said. "Our mission is important, but we cannot afford to cross the gods again."

Athena lifted her enormous wings and flew away.

Hestie felt sick to her stomach.

When the city of Athens came into view below, its bright lights sparkling in the dark night, Taavi said, "Do you mind if we stop at the acropolis before I take you home? I have not visited in quite some time."

"I'd love to," Gertie said. "I could fly with you all night."

Taavi gave her another squeeze. "I *would* fly with you all night, if I did not need to get back to my crate before daybreak."

They landed near the Parthenon, which was still under construction. It had been over a year since Athena had collapsed the caves and killed Calandra and others like her. Gertie shrugged away those dark memories to focus on the present. Tonight, it was quiet and still, save for the breeze. Gertie immediately thought of Jeno and the many nights they spent together gazing at the lights of Athens below. So much for remaining in the present, she thought.

Taavi broke their silence. "You and Hector…"

Gertie shook her head. "I honestly don't know."

He tilted his head to one side. "What has changed your mind?"

"Fear, I think."

Taavi studied her and waited patiently for her to explain.

"He left me, Taavi. He said he needed time to figure things out. Now he wants to get back together, but what if he leaves me again?"

"Do you love him?"

"Yes. But I also loved Jeno. And, if I'm being honest," Gertie took a deep breath, "I think I have feelings for you, too."

Taavi closed the distance between them in less time it took for Gertie to draw her next breath.

"It pleases me to hear that," Taavi said with a smile. "Does that mean you are free to kiss me, for real this time?"

Gertie gazed into his eyes. His lips parted, and she lifted her face toward him. When their mouths finally touched, she closed her eyes and relished the feeling. His hands circled her waist. She moved her arms around his neck and pressed her body against his.

"Oh, Taavi," she moaned.

You are a pleasant surprise, he said in her mind.

"So are you," she said.

Despite her words, Gertie felt less pleasure than guilt as thoughts of Hector plagued her. She loved Hector, so what was she doing in Taavi's arms? Was this her pathetic way of protecting her heart? Had she made Taavi her backup plan?

Not wanting to think, not wanting to feel the guilt and anxiety, wanting only to enjoy and relish the moment, she said, telepathically, *Will you feed from me? Please?*

Taavi gasped and closed his eyes.

She combed his dark hair from his face. "I'm sorry. Never mind. I didn't mean to upset you."

She had barely spoken the words when his mouth opened, and, fangs protruding, he punctured the side of her neck.

As dawn approached, the vampires made their way below deck to their crates. Hermie felt a mixture of sadness and delight—sadness over the stories they'd shared about those they had lost and delight over having had the opportunity to sit so close to Del. Now, he followed her with anticipation.

"You're still going to tell me your story, aren't you?" he asked at the bottom of the steps leading to the hull.

"Yes," she said.

"Would you like to come to my room? It stays dark in there, even with the portal to the sea. There's no direct sunlight."

"I do not think that wise," she said. "I will tell you my story from my crate. It will be easier that way."

Hermie lifted a brow. "Easier for whom?"

"For us both."

She continued down the corridor. He watched as she climbed inside her box and closed the lid. Not ready to have her out of his sight, he used his god vision to gaze at her through the wood. He was astonished to see her break down in tears. Her thin frame shook as she covered her face. He wondered what was making her cry. Was it the memories of her lost beloved friends? Was it the guilt over Mina? Or was it the story she had promised to share with him?

Hermie went to his room and climbed into bed, preparing to listen. His heartbeat was faster than usual as he anxiously waited for Del's voice to enter his head.

When it did, he was relieved. He had worried she'd changed her mind.

A long time ago, I fell in love.

Hermie rested his arm across his forehead and stared at the ceiling. *How long ago?*

A very long time ago. Like I told you before, time is less relevant to immortals. You will soon discover that for yourself.

I guess so.

I was seventeen when I was turned, she continued. *Do you remember my story?*

Of course, Hermie said. *How could I forget it? You were orphaned by the first vampires when you were twelve. At the orphanage, you were put into a traveling children's choir for five years, until all of you, including the priests, were attacked and turned. The villagers killed the priests but weren't able to kill you and the other teens, so you went into hiding.*

Yes.

Not long after, you and your choir moved to Piraeus, where new people arrived daily, right?

Right.

The locals eventually drove you away.

Yes. We lived there for three years, I think, before they could no longer stand us.

That's when you joined a merchant ship.

You were listening.

Hermie sighed with frustration. *Of course, I was listening. Haven't I made it clear that I'm interested in you, Del?*

Yes, you have.

You and the others worked on that ship for a decade, you said. Right?

For over a decade. That is when I fell in love with Lucas.

Hermie took a deep breath and released it slowly, steeling himself for what must be a heartbreaking story.

Lucas was a sailor who worked for the merchant. We fell in love, and he convinced me to turn him, so I did. I cannot remember a happier time than when I loved him—before the pirates came.

Hermie chewed on his bottom lip, hoping she wouldn't go into detail about her love for this other guy. It pained him to imagine her in the arms of another.

When the pirates came and killed the captain and his human crew, Lucas stayed with me and my friends to live in that depraved symbiotic relationship I told you about.

The low time in your life.

The lowest, she said. *We vampires told ourselves that we were not responsible for the deaths of countless men, women, and children. But we were lying to ourselves. We may not have killed them, but we enabled the pirates to do so by working for them. It was hard to leave when, for the first time since becoming vampires, we were able to satisfy our hunger by feeding on the corpses of their victims.*

Hermie shuddered.

When you live like that, it changes you, Del said. *Over the years, my little family began to fall apart. Even my relationship with Lucas changed. I could not love him anymore, maybe because I could not love myself.*

You told me that Hermes saved you and the choir.

But not in time for Lucas, she said.

What do you mean?

Del didn't answer. After several minutes had passed, Hermie felt unreasonably anxious.

Del? Are you there?

I am here.

He sighed with relief.

This part is difficult to talk about, she said. *Difficult to think about.*

Hermie clenched his jaw. *Are you sure you want to continue? I can't stand the thought of you in pain.*

Oh, Hermie. You are so sweet. You are the sweetest boy I have ever met.

Hermie's heart raced. Did he dare hope that Del might develop feelings for him? Or was he destined to remain her friend, however sweet she found him?

CHAPTER SIX

Surprises

Gertie and Taavi flew from the Parthenon and into the dark sky. Gertie took the lead. She led Taavi south of Athens, toward the Mediterranean Sea, where she allowed herself to freefall. With the vampire virus coursing through her, neither the hard impact of the water nor its chilly temperature affected her as she plunged toward the ocean floor. Exhilarated, she looked back with her keen vampire vision at Taavi close behind, grinning.

Using a trick that Jeno had taught her, Gertie propelled herself into the air and then down into the sea, again and again, like a dolphin. She had so many amazing memories of swimming with Jeno just like this, and it felt incredible to be doing it again with Taavi.

She studied the other marine life sharing their space. They passed sharks, rays, turtles, and several species of fish. She felt delighted and unafraid.

After their romp in the sea, Gertie led Taavi to a quiet beach, where she kicked off her socks and shoes and stripped out of her wet clothes.

"What are you doing?" Taavi asked with a laugh.

"What does it matter?" she asked. "You can see through them anyway. They'll dry faster this way."

Holding her shirt and bra in one hand and her jeans and underwear in the other, she held out her arms and spun like the propeller of a heli-copter. Spinning was something she'd often done as a child, to make herself dizzy. Now, using vampire speed, the high was even more spectacular.

She stopped, but the world continued to spin. Barely able to stand, she held her dry clothes out to Taavi as proof of her success.

"Try it!" she cried to Taavi as, struggling to keep her balance, she climbed back into everything but her shoes and socks.

She watched him strip. Even though she'd seen his body through his clothes, there was something sexier about watching him disrobe there on the beach beneath the stars where the water ebbed and flowed and there wasn't a soul in sight.

"Now spin!" she cried.

She grinned with pleasure as he spun around at vampire speed, laughing hysterically. She took a sock in each hand and repeated her method, laughing out loud with Taavi.

They fell together on the sand and continued to laugh as they watched the stars overhead spinning, spinning, spinning.

"I feel drunk," Taavi said.

"I know. I used to do this all the time when I was little."

They lay there waiting for the sky to still. Then Gertie had an idea.

She sat up. "Stay with me tonight!"

"Gertie, I don't know." He flew in the air, knocked the sand from his body, and began to dress.

"It's going to be dawn soon, anyway. You shouldn't risk getting caught in the sun."

He looked into the sky. "I suppose you are right. I lost track of time."

Gertie clapped her hands with glee, though his words made her think of Jeno. Jeno had always been aware of the time. He'd been obsessed with it. To him, immortality was only tolerable with a daily routine in which every minute of the day and night were accounted for.

As she put on her socks and shoes, Gertie said, "When my parents built our house, I was still a vampire, so my suite is in the basement. It'll be perfect for you. Come on. I think I still have some of my father's wine."

She began to run.

"We are running all the way to Athens?" he asked, close behind her.

"Do you mind? I haven't run at super-speed in forever."

"I am game for anything," he said with a laugh.

Hermie turned over on his side and gazed through the portal to the sea, where a school of fish passed by. Sunlight filtered down and glinted on their scales of blue and yellow and green.

Hermie? Del asked. *Are you still awake?*

Yes, he said.

I want to continue. I need you to understand why…why I cannot return your affections.

His throat tightened, and his stomach dropped. He wasn't ready for this, but he said, *Okay.*

Like I said, Lucas and I were happy together for over a decade, but not long after we began to work for the pirates, things changed. I changed, and so did he. I no longer liked the person I was, and I began to despise the person he had become.

Hermie felt sorry for her. *That must have been hard.*

It was.

Delphine was quiet for almost an entire minute before she continued.

*When I told him I no longer loved him, he…..*She hesitated.

Hermie said, *Take your time. I have all day.*

Thank you, Hermie. I have not spoken of this in so long. After I told him I no longer loved him, Lucas tried to change my mind. He begged, pleaded with me not to break off with him. But then…

But then? Hermie repeated. He shook his head and clenched his fists, mad at himself for rushing her when he had just told her to take her time.

But then, after he realized there was nothing he could say or do to change my mind, and without any warning, he...

Her voice trailed off again.

Hermie sighed, trying to remain patient.

He waited until he was starving, nearly drained of blood, when a vampire is the most vulnerable, she said. *Then, he flew from the hull of the ship and into the sunlight, where he...where he became desiccated and...and his body crumbled into dust.*

Hermie covered his mouth, unable to reply.

So, you see, she said. *I am responsible for more than Mina's death. Two souls are in Hades because of me.*

Hermie climbed from his bed and flew down the corridor to the laundry room, where he sat on Del's crate.

Telepathically he said, *Lucas's death is not your fault. He made the choice, not you.*

I caused it. Just like I caused Mina's death.

Her death is on me. She wouldn't have come after you with my sword if I hadn't...

Stop, Hermie. We both know who killed her. And that will always be between us.

No. It doesn't have to be.

Even so, after Lucas's death, I made a vow. I vowed to myself that I would never let another get as close to me as Lucas, because immortality is a long time, and people change, and I could never live with myself if...

He groaned. *Please tell me you won't hold yourself to a vow you made more than a millennia ago.*

I must. We need to focus on our mission. Now, go away, please. Leave me alone.

Hermie sat there flummoxed, unable to accept that this was how things were going to be between them.

Hestie lay beside Poros on top of the covers of his bed. The portal to the sea glistened with sunlight. Although she was feeling lazy, she wasn't sleepy.

"My sister dropped by last night," Poros said.

Hestie readjusted herself, curling closer to Poros, with her head on his shoulder. "I saw her on the top of the center mast."

"She came down and spoke to Captain and me." He played with a strand of her hair. "She wanted to warn us that Poseidon isn't happy. He's planning to block our efforts to interfere with STS."

"We already knew that."

"She thinks he might attack the *Marcella II*."

Hestie sat up. "He wouldn't! Would he? Didn't he swear not to hurt the vampires?"

Poros shrugged. "That's what I asked Athena. She said the vampires were granted clemency for their crimes against Captain and Mina but weren't guaranteed protection."

"Oh, no." Hestie covered her face. "Does Athena know when this attack is supposed to happen?"

"Soon."

Hestie jumped to her feet. "We need to warn the others."

"Captain already has. The vampires can't really do anything in daylight, so they chose to remain in their coffins."

"You mean crates."

"Right. Sorry."

"And Hermie and Jinsoo?"

Poros shrugged again. "I assume Captain told them, too."

Hestie paced the tiny cabin, wringing her hands. "We need to be ready. We need a plan."

She flew from the room in search of Prometheus.

"Wait up!" Poros climbed from the bed and followed.

Hestie found the captain on the flybridge beneath the early morning sun.

"The sooner we leave port, the better," he said with a sigh. "I know they want to train you here, but I'm dying to be in the open sea."

"Aren't you worried about what Athena said?" Hestie asked.

"Of course," the captain said. "But if Poseidon decides to attack, there's not much we can do but fight back."

"Not true," Hestie said. "We can hide. The vampires taught us how to avoid being tracked by flying the ship to new locations each night. We need to move as soon as dusk comes."

"I would be in support of moving," Prometheus said.

Hestie wasn't finished yet. "We also need an evacuation plan for the vampires in case Poseidon attacks us during the day. I can't imagine he wouldn't choose daytime, knowing the vampires' vulnerability. How can we relocate them in their crates? And where should we take them? These are things we need to decide—sooner than later."

Poros and Prometheus exchanged glances.

"She's a sharp one, isn't she?" the captain said with a grin.

"Careful, Captain," Poros teased. "We wouldn't want it to go to her head."

Hestie rolled her eyes. "Whatever. We need to talk about this now. And Hermie and Jinsoo need to be part of the conversation."

Hestie hastened from the flybridge below deck, in search of her brother. As she neared the laundry area, she was surprised to find him sitting on one of the vampire crates—Delphine's crate.

He had tears in his eyes, and his brows were furrowed.

"Hermie? What's wrong?" she asked.

He shook his head but made no reply.

"Well, whatever it is has to wait," she said.

Gertie led Taavi through the predawn sky to her parents' house, just outside of Athens.

"Whoa," he said as they approached. "Is that a house or a hotel?"

Gertie laughed. "It is a bit ostentatious, I'm afraid. But my stepfather employed a lot of people having it built. And he employs a lot of people to maintain it, too. So, I guess you could say it's good for the economy."

"You have servants?" he asked.

Gertie sensed reproach in Taavi's tone.

"Um, well, yes. Come on."

She took his hand and led him over the secure gate and around the side of the estate to the back door, which was usually unlocked. To her relief, the door opened when she turned the knob.

But her relief was short lived, for there in the kitchen staring back at her with his mouth hanging open was Nikita's father, their family's chef.

"Babá? What are you doing here so early?" she asked.

Babá glanced nervously between Gertie and Taavi.

"What has happened, Gertie? What have you done to yourself?"

"This is my friend, Taavi." She turned to Taavi, who was eyeing Babá with suspicion. "Taavi, this is Babá, er, Kyrios Angelis."

"Hello, sir," Taavi said. "It is a pleasure to meet you."

When Babá said nothing in reply, Gertie asked, "Are my parents at home?"

"Oh, well. Your mother is still asleep. She is having visitors for breakfast."

"I *love* having visitors for breakfast," Taavi said with a wink.

Babá gawked.

"He's joking, Babá. What visitors?"

"Detectives."

"Detectives?" Gertie's eyes widened. "Why are detectives coming for breakfast?"

"Perhaps you should speak with your mother. She should be down in an hour or so."

Gertie sighed with frustration. To Taavi, she said telepathically, *I'm sorry. Babá and the Angelis family try to not to be, but they are prejudiced against vampires.*

I think he is merely afraid, Taavi said. *I do not blame him.*

"I'm going to my room," Gertie said to Babá. "I haven't slept all night."

"Are you sure this is wise, Gertoula?" Babá asked, glancing nervously at Taavi. "My baqlawa is nearly ready. Stay and have some."

"I'm sure. No thanks."

She took Taavi's hand and led him downstairs to the basement, to her part of the house. She had another shock when she found someone sleeping in her bed.

She turned on the overhead light. The intruder sat up and blinked. It was Hector.

"What are you doing here?" she asked.

"Gertie?"

His hooded eyes and mussed up hair made her want to crawl into bed beside him, but she checked herself and asked again, "What are you doing here?"

Hector yawned. "Oh, hey, Taavi."

Hector's expression changed as he noticed for the first time that Gertie had been bitten.

Gertie hadn't meant to pry into Hector's mind, but, since he wasn't answering her, she couldn't help herself. His mind revealed that he'd missed Gertie and had come to stay in her room so he could feel close to her. Now, he was wondering why she had the vampire virus in her system. He was becoming suspicious of how close she was standing to Taavi.

"Lajos and I had a disagreement," Hector finally said. "And I couldn't very well kick *him* out. He has nowhere else to go."

"I do not mean to interrupt," Taavi said smoothly. "But I need to sleep as soon as possible. Is there a safe place for me to do so?"

"There's a guest room next door," Gertie said. "You can cut through that bathroom."

"And what about you, Gertie?" Taavi asked. "You need sleep as well."

"I will. Promise. I just need to talk to Hector first."

Taavi nodded and flew from the room.

Gertie folded her arms across her chest and turned to Hector. "Lajos could have gone to Nikita's."

"I thought this was easier," Hector said. "And besides, after your father went missing…"

"My father?"

"Your stepfather, James. He's missing. Isn't that why you're here?"

Gertie collapsed on one of the overstuffed chairs across from her bed. "How long has he been missing?"

"Since yesterday."

Gertie sighed with relief. "Oh, then maybe there's a good explanation. What makes you think he's gone missing? Maybe he had business out of town, or maybe his limousine broke down, or…"

Hector's thoughts gave her pause. Her mother found her stepfather's wallet and cell phone left behind on his dresser yesterday morning. When she questioned his driver, the chauffeur claimed not to have driven James since the previous day. None of his other cars were missing. Gertie's mother called several friends and business associates, but none of them knew of his whereabouts.

Gertie waited patiently for Hector to speak the thoughts she had already read.

When he had finished, she said, "That's why detectives are coming this morning."

Hector nodded. "I feel like this is my fault."

Gertie combed her fingers through her hair and found it full of sand. "Why would you feel like it's *your* fault?"

"Why is your hair full of sand?" His eyes narrowed.

Blood rushed to Gertie's cheeks.

Hector's eyes widened. He glanced toward the bathroom, in the direction that Taavi had gone. "Is there something I should know?"

<u>CHAPTER SEVEN</u>

A Warning

Hestie sat in the ship's galley at the table beside Poros. Hermie and Jinsoo sat opposite them. They had plates of eggs and sticky buns and cups of hot tea and coffee. Prometheus stood at the counter buttering a piece of toast.

Hestie picked at the sticky bun on her plate as they brainstormed for an actionable evacuation plan.

"Selene's cave," Hermie said. "The moon goddess is a friend to vampires, and her cave is high enough on the mountain to be off Poseidon's radar."

"Not a bad idea," Prometheus said before taking a bite of his toast.

"Okay, but how do we get them there?" Hestie asked.

"I wouldn't recommend god-travel," Prometheus said. "It's too easy to trace and too easy to sabotage."

"The vampires could fly there at night," Hermie said, "taking their crates with them."

"But we don't know when or if Poseidon will strike," Hestie pointed out after she'd eaten some of the sticky bun. "What if he strikes while the sun is out?"

Hermie sipped at his coffee. "They could move there tonight, before Poseidon has a chance."

Hestie shook her head. "They could be hiding there for days or weeks, for no reason."

"Not for *no reason*," Hermie argued. "Better safe than sorry."

"Then what?" Hestie challenged. "Do the vampires stay with Selene indefinitely? I think we need an *evacuation* plan, not a preemptive hiding-out plan."

"Why do we need an evacuation plan?" Jinsoo asked with a mouth full of eggs. "Aren't the vamps safe underwater, even when the sun is out?"

"Not safe from Poseidon," the captain said.

Poros sat forward. "I could use my father's chariot. It's just sitting there on Mount Olympus."

"We could go there together today," Hestie said, relishing the thought of riding with Poros across the bright blue sky.

Suddenly, Prometheus dropped his toast and his jaw as he gazed through the window toward the main deck.

Hestie turned to see what the Titan was looking at only to find Poseidon himself hovering in the sky with his trident in hand. Was this the attack they'd been trying to prepare for, already upon them?

The five gods scrambled to the main deck, weapons conjured, to meet the sea lord.

"Well, well, well," Poseidon chided, his sun-bleached hair blowing back from his face in the wind. "You've warded your ship against me, have you?"

"Do you blame me?" Prometheus asked, eyeing the trident.

Poseidon narrowed his turquoise eyes. "No. But, I've come as a courtesy to you, Prometheus, because of all the good you've done while sailing my seas."

Hestie glanced from one giant god to the other.

When Prometheus said nothing, Poseidon continued: "I've come to warn you. I will not tolerate pirate attacks of any kind. I've heard about your little pirate academy. You should all be ashamed."

Hestie balled her fists. "We aren't ashamed. We want to right wrongs. Why should we be ashamed of that?"

"Robin Hood thought he was a good guy, too," Poseidon snarled. "But he and his merry men were outlaws, and so will you be, if you keep company with these vampires."

"We aren't like Robin Hood," Hermie said. "We aren't stealing from the rich to give to the poor. We're stealing from thieves to give back to the rightful owners. There's a difference."

"I'm not sure the vampires share in that distinction," Poseidon accused. "Even so, who decides these matters? Property laws are not always cut and dried. This is not your place, young gods. This is not your purpose."

Hestie had been thinking the same thing for many weeks now. She was the goddess of language and diplomacy between countries. How could she justify becoming a pirate?

Poros took a step closer to Poseidon, and Hestie clutched her sword, ready to defend the boy she loved.

"I'll tell you what," Poros said. "If you can swear on the River Styx that no weapons of mass destruction are being smuggled by Sailfish Trading and Shipping to buyers in the middle east or elsewhere, we'll abandon our pirate academy, as you call it, and go back to bringing modern medicine to the underdeveloped areas of the world. But you'll need to swear."

That's when Hestie noticed that Poros was wielding a lightning bolt. This was the first time she'd ever seen him wield it.

"You forget your place, young god," Poseidon growled. "You may be your father's son, but Athena is our leader now. You have no right to make such demands of me or any god."

"It wasn't a demand," Poros said. "It was an offer."

"One I'm happy to refuse," the sea god said. "You can't possibly understand the delicate balance we gods must keep between countries and the mortals who run them. You're much too green."

"Do the other Olympians agree with you?" Prometheus asked.

Poseidon grimaced. "I'm afraid you'll have to ask them. I haven't been to Mount Olympus. I've been busy rounding up my army of tritons to fight the piracy problems in this area."

"Is that a threat?" Prometheus asked.

"Indeed, it is," Poseidon said. "I'll tell you the same thing I told Hermes: Back off of STS. The Mediterranean has never been safer. Abandon this crazy notion that you know better than I. If you really want to steal from thieves, then join my tritons in fighting pirates, but leave Sailfish Trading and Shipping alone. Trust me when I say that you don't have all the facts."

Hestie was about to ask Poseidon to tell them the facts when, through gritted teeth, Jinsoo muttered, "Why do you have to be such a bully?"

Poseidon frowned. In a less harsh voice, the god of the sea said, "One day you'll learn that being a god rarely makes you powerful and almost never means you're free. Often, we do things because we have no choice."

With those final words, Poseidon disappeared.

"That was cryptic," Hermie said.

"What do you think he meant?" Hestie asked.

"It's just an excuse," Jinsoo said angrily.

Poros made his lightning bolt vanish. "I should get the chariot from Mount Olympus. Maybe while I'm there, I can appeal to the other Olympians for help."

"When will you go?" the captain asked.

"Now," Poros said.

Hestie sheathed her sword. "I'm coming with you."

Gertie had been about to tell Hector what had happened between her and Taavi when her mother entered the room in her pink velvet robe lined with purple silk. Her short blonde hair, the same color as Gertie's, hadn't yet been combed. Gertie jumped to her feet.

"It's true!" Diane said. "You're home!"

Gertie nodded, unable to return her mother's smile.

"Don't worry," her mother said. "We'll find him."

Diane had assumed that Gertie's frown had been caused by her step-father's disappearance, but because Gertie believed there was a logical explanation for it, she hadn't been worried about that. She kept the true cause of her feelings to herself.

For once, she was glad that her mother wasn't the hugging kind. If she had been, Gertie would have fallen apart in her mother's arms. As it was, Gertie stood stoically frowning, fighting back tears of heartache and confusion.

"I'm sure we will," Gertie said.

Diane glanced back and forth between the two teens, realizing for the first time that she'd walked in on a serious conversation. "Well, I need to get ready to meet the detectives. We'll talk more later."

Diane left, closing the door behind her.

Hector climbed from the bed, wearing nothing but his boxers, and stepped into his jeans. As he pulled his t-shirt on, he said, "Are you going to tell me what's going on?"

The vampire virus had completely left Gertie's system, so she could no longer read Hector's thoughts.

As Gertie was about to confess what she had done with Taavi, she had a sudden change of heart. Why should she apologize when Hector was the one who had left?

"Well?" he asked.

She put her hands on her hips. "You broke my trust in you when you left me to figure things out."

Hector gawked at her, as if she had become a vampire again. "How can you say that?"

"I thought I understood. But the truth is, it scared me. How many more times will you need to leave?" Tears pooled in her eyes.

"It wasn't about you and me. You know that."

"If we're a couple, it should always be about you and me," she insisted as the tears spilled down her cheeks.

"I was trying to figure out what I want to do with my life, Gertie."

"It would have been one thing to say you wanted to come home and figure things out. But that's not what you said, is it? You told me to move on—that you didn't want to hold me back."

"Because I didn't want to be selfish!"

Gertie was wracked with sobs. She collapsed in the overstuffed chair. Something hit the side of her thigh. It was a shoe stuck between the cushion and the arm of the chair. She pulled it out and threw it on the floor, taking her frustration out on the shoe. "Not true. It was selfish to cut me out of your life."

"It was only for a few weeks. I came to my senses. I called you to apologize. I wanted to go with you to the ship. You told me not to."

"We already felt broken."

Hector's face was as white as the sheets on the bed. "Gertie, are you with Taavi now?"

"I'm not with anyone."

He fell to his knees on the floor in front of her. "Please don't do this. I'm sorry I broke things off for a while. I promise, if you take me back, I'll never leave you again."

She gazed into his troubled blue eyes, moist with tears. She wanted to believe him. She wanted it badly.

Hermie and Jinsoo sparred on the main deck of the *Marcella II* beneath the bright rays of Helios. Chidori was perched on the railing, tweeting her commentary.

"How do you like your new sword and armor?" Hermie asked as their blades clashed.

"I'm still getting used to it. I can't believe Captain thought of it and that what's-his-name made it for me."

"Hephaestus," Hermie said. "His name is Hephaestus."

"I don't think I can say that." Jinsoo swung his sword wide, and Hermie easily dodged it.

"You have to remember to practice conjuring it, too, so you don't have to wear it all the time."

"I'm still getting used to that, too. It so crazy."

Hermie struck Jinsoo's sword, causing him to back up and reset his stance.

"If Mina were here, she'd talk us out of this," Hermie said.

"She'd want to play *Urban Fighter*, for sure," Jinsoo agreed as he struck his blade against the tip of Hermie's.

"Or sunbathe," Hermie said.

"Or go shopping again," Jinsoo said with a laugh.

Hermie spun around and slammed his sword down hard against Jinsoo's close to the hilt, causing the sword to fall to the wooden deck.

"Oh, Hermie," Jinsoo complained. "I'll never be as good as you."

"Yes, you will. My parents trained me since I was a baby. You just need practice."

They were both alarmed when Chidori shrieked.

Hermie looked up to see over a dozen merfolk on the surface of the sea in the harbor just a few yards away from the stern of the *Marcella II*. They were in a V formation, and the merman at the apex, closest to them, held a conch high in the air.

All of them had green hair, the color of seaweed, and it hung down to their shoulders in a tangled mess. Their eyes were the deepest blue. Although they were humanoid from the waist up and dolphin tail from the waist down, they had shimmering scales on every inch of their bodies and slits for gills at the corners of their jaws. Their mouths were large and full of teeth, and their chests and biceps were huge.

"Those aren't just regular merfolk," Hermie said to Jinsoo. "They're tritons. I wonder what they want. We haven't done anything since Poseidon came to warn us."

Jinsoo leaned over the railing of the ship and jeered at them. "You think you're so sexy, huh?"

"What the heck, Jinsoo?" Hermie cried, pulling his friend by the shirt away from the side of the ship.

"Well, they are kind o' sexy."

The sound of a loud horn carried over the water. Hermie flew up to see the triton leader blowing his conch shell. Jinsoo joined him in the air, above the stern.

"Get back on the ship!" Prometheus shouted from the flybridge.

Before the words had completely escaped the captain's lips, the entourage of tritons leapt into the air, wrapped their enormous arms around Hermie and Jinsoo, and dragged them underwater.

CHAPTER EIGHT

Satyrs and Tritons

Hestie and Poros god-traveled to the gates of Mount Olympus, where they asked the seasons to let them in. Before heading to the outbuilding that stored the chariots, Hestie and Poros entered the great hall, the throne room of the gods.

Hestie was surprised to find her Aunt Jen there talking with some of the other Olympians. They turned to look as she and Poros entered.

"Hello, brother," Athena said from the double throne, where Zeus once sat. "What brings you to this neck of the woods?"

Jen flew to Hestie and gave her a hug. "It's so good to see you, sweetie. How's your brother?"

"Fine, I think," Hestie said.

Poros said to Athena, "I've come for my father's chariot, but there's something else I want to address."

"It isn't here—the chariot," Athena said.

Artemis, who was tightening the string on her bow, said, "Dionysus took it."

"I tried to stop him," Hephaestus said from the opened door of his forge, near the entrance to the great hall.

Apollo, who lightly strummed on a harp, asked, "What is it you wish to address?"

"Are we interrupting something?" Hestie asked, looking from Jen to Aphrodite, who sat on her throne, scowling.

"Yes," Aphrodite said. "But it can wait."

"Morpheus told you about the prophecy—about ballistic missiles and warheads aboard an STS barge heading for Syria, right?" Poros asked.

"Yes," Athena said. "Ares and I are listening for chatter but have heard nothing yet."

Hestie lifted her brows with surprise, glad that the Olympians weren't outright ignoring the issue, as Hermes had suggested.

"Would you let us know the moment you hear something?" Poros asked. "We're working with Hermes and his vampires to prevent the transaction from taking place."

"We have a lot going on," Athena said. "Ares is tied up with another conflict, and Jen and I are working together to rescue children who have been trafficked from Central America. But we'll do what we can."

"No guarantees," Aphrodite said.

Hestie clicked her tongue. "But what if these warheads get in the wrong hands and are activated? Shouldn't this be a priority for the gods?"

"My thoughts exactly," Poros said beside her.

"They rarely do get activated," Artemis pointed out, echoing what Hermes had already told them.

"If I see anything to corroborate the mortal's vision," Apollo began, "I won't ignore it. But, for now, it's just another threat."

Jen gave Hestie a peck on the cheek before returning to the other Olympians and their discussion about the trafficking of children from Central America.

Suddenly, Hestie sensed a warm hand on her shoulder. She turned around to find her mother smiling at her.

"You cut your hair!" Hestie said, pleased by how cute her mother looked with her short, curly bob. Their hair was the same vibrant red, but Hestie's wore hers past her shoulders.

"You like it?"

"It's adorable," Hestie replied with a smile.

"Jen told me you were here," her mother said. "I had to come for a quick hug."

Hestie relished the feel of being in her mother's arms. "I miss you."

"I miss you, too," her mother said. "I've been meaning to visit you on the ship, but I've been so busy." Then she smiled at Poros and said, "Hello, Poros."

"Hi, Therese."

"Tell me how you are," her mother said as they walked from the great hall toward the gates.

"Good," Hestie said. "I've been learning all the ins and outs of being a pirate."

"So I've been told," her mother said with a laugh. "Never in a million years would I have imagined that you or your brother would be doing that."

They laughed.

"We're doing it for the right reasons," Poros said. "Hestie would never do anything morally questionable."

"No, she wouldn't. Nor would Hermie." Then Therese turned back to Hestie. "How is your brother, anyway?"

"I'm not sure. He's still hurting over Mina, and I think he's got an issue with one of the vampires."

"Hmm. Maybe he should come home for a few days—you both could come for a visit."

"Now isn't a good time," Hestie said. "But soon."

And what about you, my sweet girl? her mother asked her telepathically. *How are you, really?*

I'm worried about our mission, but I'm also invigorated by it. I'm fine, I promise.

They hugged once more, and then Hestie's mother left Mount Olympus to return to her duties.

"Where to now?" Hestie, still basking in the warmth of her mother's love, asked Poros.

"To Mount Kithairon, to pay Dionysus a visit."

After Hector had left, Gertie found the bottle of her father's wine, which she kept hidden under her bed, and walked through the adjoining bathroom to her guest room. Taavi, lying flat on his back and straight as a board above the covers, opened his eyes as soon as she entered.

"Did you hear everything?" she asked.

"I tried not to listen," he said. "But even as sleepy as I am, I could not resist."

She uncorked the bottle of wine. "Want some? It's from Dionysus."

"I sometimes forget that he is your father," Taavi said as he accepted the bottle from her.

He sat up and took a long draw before returning the bottle to Gertie. Then he licked his lips. "The very best."

Gertie took a long swig, too. As it always did, the wine of her father infused her with strength, beyond her usual gifts. She felt empowered. Empowered and sleepy.

"Are you comfortable in here?" she asked Taavi.

"No. I was planning to move beneath your bed, once I sensed you sleeping."

"*Beneath* it?"

"I am unused to sleeping in open spaces. I miss my crate."

"You seemed okay sharing my cabin with me on the ship."

"The cabin was nearly as small as my crate. Your rooms here are enormous, bigger than my childhood home."

Blood rushed to Gertie's cheeks. "Why don't you join me, *in* my bed?"

"It would be my pleasure," he said, "if you are sure that is what you want."

"I haven't been sure of much lately, but I'm sure of that," she said before taking another long drag from the bottle of wine. "Come on."

He followed her through the bathroom and into her bedroom, where they climbed beneath her covers. The covers smelled like Hector.

Taavi took one more drink of wine. Gertie corked the bottle and slid it beneath her bed. Then she curled beside Taavi beneath the blankets that smelled of Hector and tried her best to go to sleep.

Hermie found himself in a tangled mess in the depths of the harbor as at least six tritons pulled him, like an undertow, out to sea. He struggled against them, not knowing which way was up or down. Reminding himself to think, he conjured his sword and swung it madly, but the tritons wore armer on their arms, and he could not reach their bare, scaled bodies. Before he knew what was happening, one of them had him by the hair and was dragging him out to sea as others swam beside him in a swarm.

Unable to turn his head, he swung his sword, to no avail. He wondered if Jinsoo had gotten away, or if he, too, was being towed out to sea.

Desperate, he prayed to every god he knew for help.

Cut your hair, his father said to him. *Use your dagger.*

Hermie did as his father suggested, freeing himself from the grasp of the triton. The swarm passed him and swam several hundred yards before realizing he was no longer among them.

That's when he saw Jinsoo being towed by the hair by another one of the massive tritons. Not willing to abandon his friend, Hermie swam toward the herd.

"Hermie!"

Someone cried out to him from the harbor. He turned to see Del and the other vampires swimming toward him.

They risked exposure to the sun to help him and Jinsoo?

Hermie caught up to the swarm of tritons and swung his sword again, slowing them down while the vampires charged. Although they were still outnumbered, the vampires had incredible fighting skills. They wielded their blades like Samurai fighters, and, in a matter of minutes, the tritons dispersed, abandoned Jinsoo, and swam away.

Exhausted, and wanting to help the vampires to avoid the sun, Hermie risked god-travel with the entire group. In less than a second, they were safely back in the hull of the ship in the laundry area.

Hermie rested his hands on his knees and struggled to catch his breath. Everyone else was panting, too.

"Thank you," Hermie said to the vampires once he could speak.

"Yes, thank you," Jinsoo said. "That was scary."

"It was hard to sleep though your screams," Mahdi said with a laugh.

Hermie blushed.

Del wasn't smiling. Hermie could see in her face that she'd been scared for him. A part of him rejoiced that she cared enough.

Jinsoo found towels in the cabinets above the washer and dryer and handed them to everyone.

"How did you leave in the sunlight?" Hermie asked them.

"We can tolerate short bursts," Alastair said.

"As long as we've recently fed," Penny added.

"What did you do to bring on the wrath of the tritons?" Bach wanted to know.

"I have no idea," Hermie said. Then, noticing Taavi wasn't among them, he asked, "Where's Taavi?"

"He did not come back last night," Raimo said. "And he is too far away to reach telepathically."

"He stayed with Gertie," Alastair said. "At least, that is what I hope."

"He prayed to me and told me that," Jinsoo said. "Sorry I forgot to tell you."

"What a relief," Del said.

"Dude." Jinsoo looked at Hermie for the first time. "What happened to your hair?"

The vamps busted out laughing. Hermie reached up with his hand and felt the top of his head. Most of his dark hair grew past his jawline, but the part he had cut now left two inches standing, even wet, at the top of his head.

"I can help you with that," Alastair said. "I'm the barber in the group. I'll have you looking good again in no time."

Hestie and Poros flew over Greece from Mount Olympus to the peak of Mount Kithairon. Helios was already at high noon, and there wasn't a cloud in the sky. The sky was so clear, in fact, that Hestie could see Iris in the distance, flying with her golden wings from her rainbow's arch to refill her pitcher from the sea below. She would later add the water to the clouds, whenever they appeared. Hestie knew that meant rain would be coming in another day or two.

She and Poros landed among trees and a rocky embankment, where the last of the spring snow flowed down the mountainside. They followed the stream in search of Dionysus.

They hadn't gone far when Poros said, "That's not a patch of snow, up ahead, is it? This early in the season?"

Hestie squinted and studied the patch of white in the distance. "That's not snow. It's a white horse, I think."

"It's Pegasus!" Poros cried, picking up speed.

Hestie followed, finally seeing what had alarmed Poros: Pegasus lay on his back, his wings sprawled on the ground, and his legs pointing up to the sky. As they got closer, she saw his eyes were closed, and his tongue was hanging out of his mouth. Dread coursed through her veins, and her stomach lurched.

"Pegasus!" Hestie cried as they approached him.

The winged horse was not alone. He lay among six satyrs and a dozen maenads around a pile of ash and soot—what was left of a bonfire. The sleeping creatures began to stir.

To Hestie's relief, Pegasus opened his eyes and pulled in his tongue.

"What happened to you?" Poros stroked the side of Pegasus's face.

One of the satyrs complained, "Keep yer voice down, will ya?"

"Not until we find out what happened to Pegasus," Poros insisted.

"He got drunk, that's what," another satyr said.

"Now go away and let us rest," another said.

Hestie glanced around the ring of bodies lying on the earth. One of the maenads glared at Hestie before closing her eyes and settling back to sleep.

"Pegasus?" Poros was trying to help the winged horse to his feet. "Where's Dionysus?"

"He needs water," Hestie said. To Pegasus, she said, "Follow me. The stream is this way."

After Pegasus had had his fill of water from the stream, Poros asked, "Can you take us to Dionysus?"

Pegasus nodded. Then he led them further down the stream to a cave in the mountainside.

Beside the cave, Zeus's golden chariot lay on its side with several scratches and dents in it.

"What happened here?" Poros cried, dismay showing in the features of his face. His gray eyes, as fine as his sister's, turned from the damaged chariot to the mouth of the cave, where a soft glow was emanating.

Pegasus remained outside while the two young gods entered. Inside, they found Dionysus lying, asleep, on a feather mattress covered in silk beside a warm fireplace. The god of wine opened his eyes and blinked at Hestie and Poros.

"To what do I owe the honor?" Dionysus asked in a husky voice without getting up.

Like all the gods, Dionysus was beautiful. He resembled Poros, having the same dark golden hair, almost like sand. But while Poros kept his hair short, the wine god grew his past his shoulders, nearly as long as Hestie's. And where Poros had stunning gray eyes like his sister, Athena, the wine god's were dark brown, the color of earth. Even with the dark rings beneath his eyes and his hair matted, Dionysus was beautiful.

"I came for my father's—for *my* chariot," Poros said.

"Oh, it's *your* chariot, is it?" the wine god said wryly. "Even though I'm older than you, brother?"

"I thought you already had one," Poros said.

"I did. It's a long story."

"Oh."

"Take it," the older god said of the chariot. "But it won't do you much good without horses."

Hestie exchanged glances with Poros.

"What happened to it?" she asked. "And where are the horses?"

"The winds won't serve me," Dionysus said. "Those old bags full of air, good for nothing. They didn't mind transforming into black stallions for Zeus, but the *bastard* isn't good enough. They deserted me in the air before we were halfway here from Mount Olympus."

Hestie felt bad for the god but wondered why he had allowed the chariot to fall to the ground. Poros must have been wondering the same thing, for he asked, "You couldn't save her?"

"Who?" the wine god asked.

"The chariot."

"Oh. I didn't let her crash to the ground, if that's what you're thinking. No, she got messed up when I tried to hitch her to the back of Pegasus."

Hestie's brows shot up. "Was he hurt?"

Dionysus laughed. "Not as badly as I was—thanks for asking."

Blood rushed to Hestie's cheeks.

"I don't think this is a good place for Pegasus," Poros said. "If it's okay with you, I'd like to see him safely back to Mount Olympus."

"Fine with me, but Pegasus won't like it. He begged me to bring him along. With Zeus gone, he's been bored to tears."

"I don't get you," Poros said suddenly. "You have so many gifts, and you waste them away, day after day. Aren't you bored of this?"

Dionysus closed his eyes and went back to sleep, signaling that their conversation was over.

Hestie and Poros left the cave to consult with Pegasus. The winged horse hated to speak, but his snorts and whinnies confirmed what the wine god had said.

Hestie had an idea. "What if you come with us, Pegasus? How would you like to live on a ship and help us with our mission?"

Pegasus's face lit up like the moon and he pranced around the trees to show his happiness at having been invited.

"Do you think Prometheus will be okay with it?" Hestie asked Poros while the winged horse danced.

Poros lifted his brows. "Only one way to find out."

CHAPTER NINE

Pegasus

Gertie blinked. She was flying on the back of Pegasus over the deep blue sea. The wind hurled her ponytail behind her and chilled her skin, making goosebumps appear on her bare arms. Hestie, of all people, was riding in front of her, and Gertie was holding onto her waist with both hands.

"What is happening?" Gertie asked.

"You tell me," the young goddess said. "This is where you said to go. We just passed the island of Cyprus, and that's the coast of Syria down there."

Gertie gazed at the coastline, still unaware of why she was there in the sky on Pegasus with a goddess who despised her.

Hestie pointed. "You said the STS carrier would be there, at the port near Latakia, but I don't see it. Do you?"

That's when Gertie realized that she was dreaming.

"What else did I say, Hestie?" Gertie asked. "I'm feeling dizzy and can't remember."

"Maybe you shouldn't have had that wine."

"It usually helps me. It strengthens my gifts."

"You said the STS ship was smuggling the Russian warheads to Syria to be used on other Syrians," Hestie said. "According to your research, the country has been in civil conflict for like a decade. Over 500,000 people have been killed or have gone missing."

"Oh," Gertie said, unable to recall.

Hestie continued: "You said if we came here today, October 20th, you and me, just like this, flying on Pegasus, that we would see the STS carrier from Russia and discover where Poseidon is and what he's been up to. You said we would be able to signal to Hermie when it was safe to board the ship and disarm the warheads."

"Hermie will disarm them?"

Hestie glanced back at her, befuddled. "Yes. You said that, as the god of technology, he was our best chance."

"Did I say anything else?" Gertie asked.

Hestie buried her head in Pegasus's mane and groaned. "Other than the fact that one of us would get badly hurt, no."

Gertie wrinkled her nose, totally confused. "I didn't say which of us it would be?"

Hestie heaved a sigh of frustration. "You said if I knew, it would change the future. Geez, Gertie. What's wrong with you? You're scaring me. Can you please snap out of it?"

Gertie gnawed on the inside of her bottom lip, wishing she had some idea of where this dream was going. Then a memory of something that hadn't yet happened occurred to her. She was sitting beside Hector on the edge of a bed across from Metis in a well-lit cave. Metis was the mother of Athena and Poros. She'd been freed from the belly of Zeus many years ago and was now in hiding—though Gertie wasn't sure how she knew that. Gertie recognized Metis because she looked so much like Athena, with long black hair and stunning gray eyes.

"The sins of the father will be the burden of the son," Gertie muttered.

"What?" Hestie glanced back at her again as they got closer to the port.

"Metis told me that. I can't remember when or why."

Hestie grabbed her head with both hands. "Aye, Gertrude! You're killing me." Then she stiffened. "Wait a minute, was Metis talking about Zeus's sins bringing harm to Poros?"

Gertie wished she knew.

Just then, the STS carrier from her previous dream could be seen making its way to the port near Latakia.

Gertie pointed. "There it is."

"I see it! Pegasus, can you take us closer, just to make sure?"

Pegasus swooped down toward the ship. Gertie remembered everything about it: the five grain bins, the flybridge atop a two-story salon, and the two robust guards whom she had overheard talking. They had said that there were five warheads—one buried in each of the grain bins.

"That's it," Gertie confirmed.

They watched as the carrier docked in the marina. Gertie wished she had the super-vision of a god.

"Do you see anything?" she asked Hestie.

"I see Poseidon!" Hestie said. "He's arguing with someone—I can't see, yet. Pegasus can you fly down just a little closer to the water?"

Pegasus descended and hovered a few yards from the waves. This made Gertie uneasy.

"Maybe this is when we should call Hermie," Gertie said. "While Poseidon is distracted."

"Good idea. I'm praying to him now."

Seconds later, Hestie said, "I see Hermie. He's invisible to mortals, but, trust me, he's there."

"What's he doing?"

"Climbing into the first grain bin. Wow! That was fast! He just gave me a thumbs up and is darting into the next."

Gertie listened as Hestie gave her a play by play. She was relieved when Hestie said, "He did it! He's disarmed them all!"

Gertie was still on edge. She sensed something bad was still to come. She wished she could recall what it was.

"What's Poseidon doing now?" Gertie asked.

A voice from overhead startled her. She looked up only to be blinded by Helios.

"Stay out of it!" the sun god said. "You'll ruin everything!"

Ignoring Helios, Hestie continued to observe Poseidon. Then she covered her mouth. "I see what he's up to. Stay here. I'll be right back."

"Hestie, wait!" Gertie cried, to no avail.

Hestie had disappeared from Gertie's sight.

Then the thing she had been dreading happened. It happened so suddenly, that she was barely aware of it before it was over. A giant monster rose from the sea and wrapped its many serpentine heads around Pegasus. Shrieking and snorting, the winged horse struggled in the air but was overcome.

Gertie closed her eyes and screamed as she was thrown from Pegasus. Within seconds, she found herself in Hermie's arms, his eyes full of tears.

"I couldn't save you both," he said.

Gertie looked down, horrified. Pegasus had disappeared beneath the churning sea. Gertie closed her eyes and groaned with agony. What good was the gift of foresight if she couldn't protect her friends?

She opened her eyes and found herself back in her bedroom in her parents' mansion in Athens. Morpheus stood over her. Taavi was nowhere in sight.

"You can't tell them how it ends," Morpheus warned. "It could change everything."

"Will Pegasus be okay?"

"I don't know," Morpheus admitted.

Gertie shuddered. *The sins of the father will be the burden of the son.* Pegasus was a son of Poseidon. Is that what Metis had meant?

Morpheus sighed. "At least those warheads will be disarmed, and that's what matters most, don't you think?"

Gertie wasn't sure. Was the life of one immortal horse worth less than the lives of countless humans?

She burst into tears.

When she and Poros arrived astride Pegasus and landed on the main deck of the *Marcella II*, Hestie was surprised that not even the captain was anywhere in sight. Helios had just begun his afternoon descent toward the west. Where was everyone?

Through the layers of the ship, she saw, with her god vision, that the vampires were awake, but she couldn't see the captain, Jinsoo, or Hermie.

"You stay here with Pegasus," she said to Poros as the two of them dismounted. "I'll find out what's going on."

Poros seemed more than happy to stay on deck, where he began to show Pegasus around the ship.

"And that's the galley," Hestie heard Poros say as she flew toward the laundry room.

The vampires were hanging out on their crates—all save Alastair and Taavi. Everyone was soaked and wet.

"What's going on?" she asked them.

Del grinned ruefully in a way that Hestie found hard to read. "Why don't you ask your brother?"

"He's in his room," Penny, who was lying on her crate with Sophia, said.

"Alastair's cutting his hair," Mahdi added. "So, you might want to pray to the gods."

"What?" Hestie glanced from one vampire to another, perplexed.

"Oh, Alastair's not that bad," Raimo said. "He cuts *our* hair."

Since all but Alastair wore their hair long, Hestie didn't find that reassuring.

"It's been a while," Bach said. Then he added, "The hair of a vampire grows very slowly."

"You better hope that isn't true of the gods," Mahdi said with a laugh.

The other vampires laughed, too.

Hestie turned and flew to Hermie's room, where she found him and Alastair in the tiny bathroom in front of the mirror, where Hermie's reflection appeared, along with Alastair's clothing. It was unsettling not to see Alastair's face where it should have been in the mirror. Most of Hermie's hair lay in clippings in the sink. Alastair had cut it down to within two inches of Hermie's scalp.

Hestie was surprised by how good Hermie looked. He looked even more like their father.

"Just needed a change?" she asked. "Mom cut her hair, too."

"You saw mom?"

"Yeah. She came to see me on Mount Olympus. I saw Jen, too. They both say hi. Mom thinks we need to go and stay for a few days, when we have the chance."

Alastair stepped back, admiring his work.

"Not bad," the vampire said. "I have not lost my touch, it seems."

"It looks nice on him," Hestie agreed. "But, what's the occasion?"

"Tritons attacked," Hermie said. "I had no choice but to cut my hair, to cut myself loose."

Hermie then went on to tell Hestie what had happened.

"Poseidon didn't waste any time carrying out his threat," Hermie added, after he'd finished his story. "Do you think your trip to Mount Olympus provoked him?"

"I can't think of any other reason," Hestie said. "But, if so, one of the other Olympians must have told him, don't you think? How else would he have been able to react so quickly?"

"Never trust the gods," Alastair said. "No offense."

Hestie recalled each of the Olympians that had been present during her visit and wondered which among them would put her and the rest of the crew at risk by informing Poseidon.

Then she asked, "Where are Jinsoo and Prometheus?"

"Meeting with Clymene," Hermie said.

Hestie frowned.

"What's up?" Hermie asked.

"Poros and I brought Pegasus aboard," she said. "You think Captain will let him stay?"

Hermie's face brightened. "Pegasus is here?"

Without another word, Hermie flew above deck.

Alastair turned to Hestie. "He seems pleased."

"With the haircut or with Pegasus?"

"Both. And he is not the only one. Vampires and horses have a natural affinity for one another. Did you know that?"

She shook her head. "I wonder why."

"Most animals, including humans, fear us on a basic level, even if they are not always aware of it. But not horses." Alastair put the scissors in the medicine cabinet behind the mirror above the sink.

Hestie was saddened by what Alastair had said. She wouldn't like to be feared, she didn't think. She'd rather be loved.

"Legend has it that it was the one gift Athena gave to our kind."

"I'm surprised she gave your kind a gift at all."

"She likely grew to regret it."

"Why does she hate vampires so much?" Hestie wondered aloud.

"In her mind, we destroyed her city. She blames us instead of Dionysus, or the maenads, or even her father, Zeus."

Hestie shuddered. It reminded her of a story her father had told her of Medusa. Athena blamed the victim then, too.

Alastair shrugged. "But, in the beginning, when the first vampires were made into outcasts, ostracized from the rest of the city, Athena gave them horses. This was before anyone knew that vampires could fly."

"Maybe she hoped the vampires would ride away," Hestie said.

"Perhaps. Nevertheless, I have not met a horse that has not liked me. Unfortunately, we do not see too many these days on the open sea."

"Well, once the sun goes down, I'll introduce you to Pegasus."

Alastair smiled warmly. "I look forward to it."

Hermie found Poros and Pegasus in the salon, where the winged horse took up most of the room.

Poros opened his mouth to speak but stopped when Hermie flew directly up to Pegasus and threw his arms around the horse's neck.

"It's so great to see you, boy. How have you been?"

Pegasus gave Hermie a disgruntled snort.

"He's been lonely in my father's absence," Poros explained. "We found him on Mount Kithairon with a hangover."

Hermie's brows shot up. "Pegasus?"

The winged horse hung his head.

Poros stroked Pegasus's mane. "Thank the gods he can fit in here. Otherwise, he'd have no shelter, since he's much too big to go below deck."

"Maybe Captain would allow us to do some reconstruction," Hermie said. "We could widen the portal to the hull and open up two of the empty cabins, combining them into one large stall."

"Hey! That's a great idea!" Poros said.

"What's a great idea?" Prometheus asked as he and Jinsoo appeared with Chidori in the salon beside them. "And why is Pegasus on my ship?"

After Poros had explained why Hestie had invited the horse, Prometheus shook his head.

"My ship is no place for a beast his size," the captain said.

Hermie told him about his idea of changing the interior of the ship.

"How do we know she'll be sound?" Prometheus asked. "I don't want to risk it. Pegasus can't stay."

Morpheus startled them by suddenly appearing beside Hermie in the salon. "I'm afraid he has to."

"I'm the captain of this ship," Prometheus said. "And I don't think it's a good idea."

Unlike some of the other gods, the captain spoke calmly, without anger, as though he were merely stating a fact. But Hermie wondered if Prometheus had something against Pegasus.

"You'll feel differently after you hear what I have to say," Morpheus said.

It was nearly dusk by the time Hermie had finished reconstructing the interior of the ship to accommodate Pegasus. He used state-of-the-art engineering technology to structurally reinforce his changes. Knowing that he would one day be responsible for disarming the warheads that had been looming over them for weeks had dramatically boosted his confidence and uplifted his mood. When he'd finished, he returned to the upper deck—where Jinsoo was feeding Pegasus an apple while Chidori fought nervously for Jinsoo's attention—and offered to give Pegasus a tour of his new stall.

The vampires were waiting for them below deck.

Del's face changed when she saw Hermie. At first, he thought she was happy to see *Pegasus*. But later, after the vampires had each had a turn at petting the white horse, he came to realize that Del was studying *him*.

Poros and Hestie returned from Malta with bales of hay and a sack of oats, and the vampires offered to help spread hay in the new stall. While everyone else was busy, Hermie approached Del.

"Will you come and talk to me, in my room?" he asked her.

Del's cheeks turned pink. "Um…"

"Please? There's something I want to show you."

Del shrugged. "Okay. I guess so."

Hermie led her down the hall to his cabin and invited her to sit in front of one of his computer monitors.

As she took a seat, she asked, "What am I doing here?"

"Have you ever played a computer game before?" Hermie asked.

"Once. There was an arcade in Taranto. I played one game but did not like it."

"What didn't you like about it?" Hermie sat in the chair beside her, in front of another monitor.

She tapped her chin. "Honestly, I do not know. I think I was no good at it."

"Do you have to be good at something to like it?"

"Yes, I think so."

"Will you try to play *Urban Fighter* with me? I think you might like it."

"Oh, Hermie. I do not want to."

"Please?"

Her mouth spread into a grin. "I like your hair. It suits you well."

It was Hermie's turn to grin. He may have blushed, as well. "Thanks, but your efforts to distract me aren't working." He turned on both computers and said, "Let me show you how the controller works. You move this to go forward, back, right, or left. See? And these buttons will move you up, down, and all the way down. These here are for attacks."

Del shook her head. "I do not like this already."

Hermie laughed. "We haven't even started."

He brought up the game and demonstrated how to move around. "You want to shoot the enemy before they shoot you. Ready?"

"I guess so."

He started the game. He was surprised by how tense Del became. He'd never seen her so skittish as she pounded on the buttons and flinched in her seat.

"Oh, no!" she cried. "What am I doing wrong?"

"You're walking into a wall. Use the controller to turn left. You're about to be…"

"I was shot!" she cried, as if it had been real. "What do I do now?"

"Shoot back," Hermie said, trying hard not to laugh at her.

She pounded the buttons with frustration. "I cannot do this. It is too terrifying!"

"Whoa." Hermie stopped the game. "It's okay. We won't play. Don't kill the controller. It's not your enemy."

"Sorry." She covered her face.

"Don't be. I'm the one who should be sorry. You said you didn't like computer games. I should have believed you."

She looked up at him. "Is this your favorite thing to do?"

"Pretty much. I guess that's why it's hard for me to imagine anyone not liking it." Then he added, "It's ironic that you have no fear running head-on into battle, but a computer game terrifies you."

"I do not enjoy doing things where I have no control. I know how to fight in real life. On the game, I do not know what to do."

"Does this mean you don't like to learn new things?" he asked. "Because I could teach you what to do, just as you are teaching me how to be a pirate."

"For most of my life, I had no choice but to learn new things. It was a matter of survival. If given a choice, I would rather avoid it. It makes me feel vulnerable. You understand?"

"I get that you don't like to feel vulnerable," Hermie said. "Especially after your story about Lucas."

"Please do not say his name."

Hermie swallowed hard, wondering if she was still in love with his memory.

"No, Hermie. As I told you, I stopped loving him. I grew to despise him. But I feel so guilty, you see?" Tears welled in her eyes.

"I do see." He used his thumbs to wipe the tears from her face and then didn't think twice about putting his arms around her to comfort her. It seemed like a natural thing to do. But the moment she was crying against his neck, his heart went crazy, and he wondered what the hell he was doing.

Del, however, hadn't resisted. She yielded to her tears and had a good cry against him, her tears wetting his neck. He stroked her hair, happy to finally have a chance to touch it. After a few minutes, she lifted her head, wiped her eyes, and apologized.

"You have nothing to be sorry about," he said gently. "I'm glad I could be there for you."

Then she did something he didn't expect: She kissed him on the cheek.

"You confuse me," he murmured, as electricity coursed through him. "Do you have feelings for me or not?"

"I think the answer to your question is obvious."

"But you said…"

"How I feel about you is another thing that I cannot control. I do not like it. When you were taken by the tritons . . ." Her voice trailed off as she fought tears.

He took a deep breath, trying to calm his heart. He was overjoyed to know that she felt something for him. He could hardly believe it. He bit his tongue, to make sure he wasn't dreaming.

But when he tried to kiss her, she leaned away from him.

"We have to stay focused on our mission," she insisted. "There's no place for both love and war, and there's a war going on."

"But there's nothing to do until October 20th. That's two weeks away. You heard Morpheus."

"We must prepare. We must train. Also, we must be on our guard against Poseidon."

"Del, please, don't be this way."

She stood up and went to the door, where she turned to him and said, "It is the only way I know how to be."

After she left, Hermie sat there, stunned. He couldn't think or feel anything for several minutes. Then he was flooded with a mix of emotions. There was one emotion that stood out above the others. It was anger.

CHAPTER TEN

Attack

Gertie awoke to the sound of rain hammering against the ground outside. She opened her eyes, recalling her dream and Morpheus's visit. Her head ached, probably from the wine.

Where was Taavi?

"I am here," he said.

She scooted to the edge of the bed and hung over the side to look at him.

He flew from the floor to the top of her bed beside her, startling her.

She laughed and said, "You freak! You scared me!"

He propped his head on one elbow and crossed one leg over the other and grinned.

After she'd recovered, she gave him a once over. He could have easily been a supermodel in another life, she thought.

"I heard you and Morpheus talking," Taavi said. "I am happy that the warheads will be deactivated, but will something happen to Pegasus?"

Gertie bit her lip.

"Careful." Taavi grinned and leaned in, as if to kiss her. "You might draw blood, and then I will not be able to control myself."

Gertie rolled her eyes. "I wish. We both know that's not true."

Taavi stood up. "I need to get back. The others will be worried. But before I go, will you answer my question about Pegasus?"

"Something bad *is* going to happen to him, but please don't tell anyone. It could interfere with the mission."

Taavi frowned. "You got it." He kissed her lightly on the forehead. "Will I see you again?"

"Definitely," she said. "According to my dream, I'll be riding Pegasus with Hestie over the Mediterranean on October 20th."

"That's only two weeks away."

"I'm not sure when or how I'll return to the ship, but, yeah, I'll see you soon. Meanwhile, I'm going to find out what I can about my stepfather and STS."

"Say hello to Hector for me," Taavi said with a half-smile.

Gertie wrinkled her nose. "I don't know if he's speaking to me."

Taavi sighed. "Believe me, he is. He wants nothing more than to speak with you."

"Do you think I should?" she asked, trying not to cry.

"Yes, I do."

He kissed her on the head once more and flew from her room.

Hestie leaned against the railing of the flybridge, gazing at the harbor, which appeared to be dancing beneath the starlight with the rain. Iris had filled the clouds, and they were just now beginning to overflow with a steady trickle.

Despite the beauty of the dancing water, Hestie was feeling anxious. Prometheus wanted to move the ship to the Arabian Sea using the vampires' technique of spinning through the air, so as not to be easily tracked by Poseidon and his tritons. Even god-traveling the ship would leave a signature behind that other gods could trace. However, no one wanted to leave without Taavi, and he was too far away to reach telepathically.

From the deck below, Hestie heard Jinsoo talking with Alastair. They were alone on the stern deck outside of the salon, gazing out to harbor, just like her. Chidori sat on Jinsoo's shoulder.

"Why do you call me *cute boy*," Jinsoo asked Alastair.

The vampire laughed. "I think you know the answer to that question."

"But how do you mean? Cute like a kid? Or cute like sexy, hot?"

Alastair threw his head back and guffawed. "I did not know you could be so direct."

"To me, it's the best way to get answers."

"Hmm. I like that."

Chidori flew up and perched on Hestie's shoulder. "You shouldn't eavesdrop."

Hestie grinned and whispered, "I know."

Nevertheless, the two of them remained where they were.

"So, will you answer my question?" Jinsoo asked.

"Why is my answer important to you?" Alastair's eyes twinkled with the moonlight.

"Because I think *you're* sexy, hot, and I want to know if you think the same of *me*, or if you see me as just a kid."

"How old are you?" Alastair asked.

"Fifteen. And you're seventeen, right?"

"My body is seventeen."

"You still haven't answered my question," Jinsoo said. "I wonder why."

"Gods and vampires do not usually get along. And my friends and I were responsible for your sister's death. So, I see no point in telling you that I find you sexy, hot."

Jinsoo rushed across the deck, grabbed Alastair's shoulders, and kissed him.

"Maybe we should go," Hestie whispered to Chidori.

"Yes, you should," Jinsoo said from below.

As Hestie headed for the galley, she noticed Athena in her owl form perched on the center mast. Then, down in the galley, she found Prometheus sipping a mug of something hot.

"Did you see Athena?" Hestie asked.

Prometheus nodded. "She doesn't want the vampires interfering with the business of the gods."

"Oh."

"I told her that warheads getting into the wrong hands was the business of all, not just the gods. Humans have more to lose than any of us."

"I bet she didn't like that," Hestie said.

"No."

"Do you know why she won't support us? Is there something at stake that we don't know about?"

"If there is, she said nothing about it to me." Then he said, "We can't afford to wait on Taavi too much longer. It will take five or six hours to get the ship across land and sea, and my mother is expecting us."

"I could stay behind on the docks and wait for him," Hestie offered.

"That's not a bad idea. Chidori could keep you company."

Chidori chirped her agreement.

"You'd have to be careful of being followed back to the ship," he warned. "There's no point in moving if you lead Poseidon back to us."

"I can handle that."

"Would you mind gathering the others while I finish my coffee?" Prometheus asked.

"Not at all, Captain."

Hestie flew to the hull to inform the others before going up to the stern deck, where Jinsoo and Alastair were still in each other's arms. She cleared her throat.

They pulled apart and scowled at her.

"Sorry to interrupt," she said. "The captain wants everyone up on the main deck."

After Taavi had left Gertie's house, Gertie showered and changed and went upstairs to find something to eat. She found some of Babá's lefto-ver baqlawa and sat down to a plate of it and a glass of orange juice.

She'd been about to text Nikita when her mother entered the kitch-en. Diane looked tired and frazzled, even in her fine clothes and flawless makeup. "There's roasted chicken and veggies from tonight's dinner, if you want it."

"No, thanks. This is fine. Any word from Dad?"

Diane sat across the table from her and covered her face with her hands. "No."

Gertie stopped eating. "What did the detectives say?"

"Not much. They said they'll do what they can."

"They didn't share any theories?"

Diane clicked her tongue and sighed. "They think he ran away."

Gertie's brows lifted. "What? Why?"

"They found no sign of forced entry. No signs of an abduction of any kind."

"Can you think of why he would do that?" Gertie asked.

"He *wouldn't*. He wouldn't just run away without saying anything to me."

Gertie gnawed on her bottom lip, thinking. Then she asked, "Did Dad say anything else to you before he went missing? Anything that stands out now?"

Diane wiped tears from her cheeks. "No. Nothing."

"Do you think he might have left a note?"

Diane furrowed her brows. "I didn't think of that. The detectives looked everywhere and didn't find anything."

"Could Dad have left it someplace that only you would know about? A place special to just the two of you?"

It took less than a minute for Diane to say, "The Hotel Excelsior in Venice. We celebrate our anniversary there every year. He could have left me a message with the concierge, who has become a good friend of ours."

Gertie leaned forward. "Call."

"What, now?"

"Yes, Mom. Call now!"

Gertie watched as her mother took her phone from her trouser pocket and tapped on the screen.

"Concierge, please," her mother said into the phone.

Gertie waited with bated breath.

"Hello, Pablo, it's Diane Morgan…Oh, I've been better. Listen, do you, by chance, have a message for me from James? It seems he's gone missing."

Gertie watched as her mother listened to the man on the other end of the line.

"Okay, thank you…But we were just there…It's hardly the time for me to travel…Okay, thanks again." Diane hung up the phone and shrugged.

"What did he say?" Gertie asked.

"He said he had no message to give me at the moment."

Gertie frowned.

"Our anniversary wasn't even two months ago. We were just there. So why would he insist that I come as soon as possible for a visit?"

Gertie lifted her brows again. "He said that? He said you should come as soon as possible?"

Diane nodded.

"Maybe he has a message but not one he can tell you over the phone," Gertie said. "Maybe Dad was worried that your phone was hacked or bugged or something."

Diane shook her head. "You have a wild imagination, Gertrude. You're not suggesting that I travel to Venice, are you?"

"That's exactly what I'm suggesting."

"But what if your dad turns up here while I'm gone?"

"I'll be here. I'll explain everything to him."

Diane sighed again. "I don't know."

"Mom, has Dad ever talked to you about Sailfish Trading and Shipping, or STS?"

"No, not that I recall. Why?"

Gertie took a sip of her juice. "Never mind."

While Diane made herself of cup of coffee, Gertie wondered about her stepfather and if it were possible that he *had* run away. If he had, had he done so because he *was* guilty of using STS ships for illegal smuggling? Had he somehow learned that Hector had discovered his secret? Is that what Hector had meant when he had said that her stepfather's disappearance was his fault?"

She pulled out her phone and texted Hector: *We need to talk.*

Hermie avoided looking at Del as he joined the crew on the main deck, where they were pelted with rain, to hear the captain's plans. He felt Del was being selfish in her unwillingness to make herself vulnerable to him. She cared more about protecting her heart than considering his feelings for her. It made him miss how easy and carefree his relationship with Mina had been, even if he had never felt as deeply for her as he did for Del.

Tears rushed to his eyes at the thought of Mina. She was such a sweet person. He missed her smile and her laugh.

When Prometheus mentioned that Hestie and Chidori would wait on the docks for Taavi, both Hermie and Poros objected, but Hestie rolled her eyes, saying that she was a big girl with skills and that they disrespected her by questioning her abilities.

This shut up Hermie. Poros needed more persuasion.

"I should stay, too," Poros said.

"We need your manpower," Alastair insisted.

Hestie crossed her arms over her chest and groaned. "We'll be fine."

Chidori added her tweets.

With that settled, the others readied the ship to set sail. Hermie helped Jinsoo to hoist the mains while Poros untied the tether and brought up the anchor. The vampires coiled and stowed the lines. Hermie looked back at his sister and Chidori standing on the dock. He had a bad feeling about leaving them there, but what more could he say without incurring Hestie's wrath?

They sailed the ship from the harbor and out into the open sea.

The crew broke up into teams. Del and Alastair took the top of the center mast with Jinsoo and Prometheus. Bach, Penny, Sophia, and Poros, took the middle. That left Hermie, Mahdi, and Raimo, on the bottom.

"Ready?" Del called from her position near the top of the mast. "Heave, ho!"

Together, they lifted the *Marcella II* about a hundred feet into the air. The massive ship groaned as gravity pulled it in the opposite direction. Hermie hoped the vampires knew what they were doing, because, to him, flying with the ship seemed like a risky undertaking. It would be an understatement to say that they were challenging the laws of physics.

Then Alastair cried, "Heave ho!"

Altogether, they flew clockwise at their top speed, spinning and flying toward the east, away from Malta. It took them nearly six hours as they flew across the Mediterranean, over Saudi Arabia and Oman, and across most of the Arabian Sea to a place a few miles west of Mumbai, India. Hermie was relieved when the ship was safely back on water and he could rest and catch his breath.

But he hadn't rested long when the winds began to wail, and the ship began to toss.

"What's happening?" Jinsoo cried as the starboard side of the ship lifted with a massive swell.

Alastair hovered above the deck, so as not to slide with the tilting ship. "Maybe a storm or an angry god."

Prometheus shouted over the heavy winds, "Do not leave the ship, under any circumstances! It's heavily warded against intruders, but if your feet leave the boards of this vessel, the wards won't protect you!"

Alastair landed on the deck and grabbed the galley door to maintain his balance.

"Do you think this is something more than the weather?" Hermie asked.

"Absolutely," Prometheus said as he ran up to the helm on the flybridge. "We're under attack."

Penny, clinging to the front mast, grumbled, "Poseidon."

"Pray that Lord Hermes comes to our rescue!" Raimo shouted as he slid across the slippery deck and grabbed the railing on the port side just in time.

The rain came down hard, and the sea churned. The starboard side of the ship dipped down only to lift again with another swell. Everyone scrambled to grab ahold of something to keep themselves steady. Hermie found himself moving closer to Del, unable to fight the instinct to protect her.

"What do you suggest we do, Captain?" Poros asked.

With a great groan, the starboard side leveled out. This time, the swell washed over the main deck, nearly knocking Hermie and the other members of the crew into the sea.

"Hold onto the ship and wait it out!" Prometheus shouted from the flybridge. "You vampires should get below deck!"

Hermie held onto the railing and grabbed Del's hand with the other, as she made her way to the portal leading to the hull of the ship. He did the same for Alastair but then noticed the army of tritons emerge from the tumultuous sea.

Poros conjured his lightning bolt and threw it at the tritons. Most of them dodged the strike, but two were paralyzed and lay floating on the surface until another swell washed them underwater. When the survivors next charged, two beautiful goddesses—one silver and the other gold—leapt from the sea and defended the ship. Hermie recognized them as Dione and Clymene.

Hermie was helping the last of the vampires to evacuate the deck, when something else caught his eye: Hestie, Chidori, and Taavi were flying toward the ship, completely unprotected.

We're under attack! he cried to them telepathically. *Hurry to the ship, where the wards will protect you!*

A shriek filled the air as at least twenty of Ladon's one-hundred serpentine heads shot up from the sea.

Poros threw another lightning bolt toward the giant sea monster who once guarded Hera's golden apple tree in the garden of the Hesperides. As Hermie wondered why Ladon would be involved in this conflict, he noticed Poseidon appear with his trident about fifty yards from the ship's port side. The sea god pointed the trident at Hestie, Chidori, and Taavi, causing an explosion of light.

When the light dimmed, three limp bodies fell onto the deck of the ship.

CHAPTER ELEVEN

LOSS

Hermie scooped up Chidori and held onto her with both hands as he knelt at his sister's side on the slick deck beneath the rain and the splashing waves.

"Hestie? Can you hear me?" he shouted.

She didn't move. Had she suffered tremendous pain? Was she *still* in pain? Her skin looked pale and her lips blue. He wondered if her soul had already been taken to Tartarus or if it was still inside her body.

"Hestie?" he said again, more urgently.

Poros fell to his knees and swept Hestie into his arms.

Hermie glanced over at Taavi, whose body had begun to desiccate and crumble into dust from the sting of the trident.

"Oh, no!" Hermie cried, unable to believe his eyes.

"Chidori!" Jinsoo scrambled across the rocking ship to take the limp canary from Hermie.

From the flybridge, Prometheus shouted, "Poros! I need you to fight off Poseidon while the others get below deck!"

"Guard her with your life," Poros said before handing Hestie over to Hermie.

Then Hermie's father appeared.

"Are you here for Hestie?" Hermie asked.

Thanatos shook his head and pointed at Taavi.

Telepathically, Thanatos said, *Hades is here with his chariot beneath the helm of invisibility to evacuate the ship. Help me to get the others to the chariot. I'll guide you to it.*

As happy as Hermie was to see his father, the plan to evacuate seemed flawed. *What about Pegasus?*

He'll be protected by the helm of invisibility, as long as he's tethered to the chariot.

Meanwhile, Poseidon shot his trident at the ship, causing the boards to creek and moan. Thanatos disintegrated into an army and shielded the ship from Poseidon's blows while Dione and Clymene held off the tritons.

Poros threw his lightning bolts at Poseidon and the sea monster, while Prometheus manned the ship, struggling to keep it from capsizing. At the same time, Jinsoo and Hermie helped Thanatos load the invisible chariot with the rest of the crew. To make this easier, Alastair took Hestie into his arms so that Hermie could help bring Pegasus from below deck. Because there wasn't enough room in the chariot for all of them, Hermie, Del, and Jinsoo climbed astride Pegasus with Hermie in the front and Jinsoo in the back.

It was obvious to anyone looking where the invisible chariot was parked, because its passengers did not also become invisible until they entered it. Poseidon acted accordingly, shooting toward them with his paralyzing trident, which Thanatos fought off with his shield. Then Hermes appeared beside Thanatos to block some of the attacks so the chariot could safely take off.

When Del saw Taavi's desiccated corpse—or what was left of it—crumbling and washing away on the deck below, she wrapped her arms around Hermie's waist and sobbed against his back.

I'm so sorry, Hermie said to her telepathically in the chaos.

Hades's two black stallions led the chariot and the tethered Pegasus from the ship and into the night sky.

What about Poros and Captain? Hermie asked Hades telepathically.

Hades did not reply. Instead, he turned the chariot nearly perpendicular to the sea and drove it down into the nearest chasm toward the Underworld.

Hestie blinked and opened her eyes. When she found herself unable to move, she tried to speak, but only a strange sound emitted from her throat. She couldn't even move her lips or her tongue.

"Hestie?" Her mother leaned over her.

What happened? Hestie asked her mother telepathically.

"You were struck by Poseidon's trident, I'm afraid," her mother replied. "But you're safe at home, where you can rest and heal."

What about the others? Hestie asked.

"Hermie and Jinsoo are here," her mother said.

Hermie crossed the room and stood where Hestie could see him. Jinsoo followed. Their eyes were red, as though they'd been crying. Had they been crying for her?

What about the others? Hestie said telepathically to all three of them.

Prim and Katniss, her rats, crawled up her arms and perched on her chest. Then she heard Noodle and Clifford bark and Kitty purr. Her pets brought her comfort.

"Jewels says hello, too," her mother said. "She's in her tank in the other room."

Where's Chidori? Hestie asked.

"She's recovering, like you—though she hasn't yet opened her eyes."

"Mom and Dad don't know if she'll fully recover," Hermie said.

Hestie knew that was true of any struck by the trident. She remembered the stories she'd learned from her parents growing up in Colorado. While most gods and goddesses recovered, there had been two that had not. One was called Diktynna, the goddess of hunting nets. After throwing herself into a fishing net to avoid the advances of the king of Crete, she was struck by Poseidon, who was responding to the frantic prayers of fishermen. For years, Diktynna lay paralyzed in a cave and eventually became part of the mountainside.

The other was a sea goddess named Doris. She was jealous of Amphitrite and wanted Poseidon for herself. Poseidon struck Doris with his trident to thwart her vicious attack on his wife, and Doris never recovered. Poseidon left her at the bottom of the sea, where she eventually turned into a shell.

If gods could be destroyed by the trident, Hestie could only imagine the impact it had on vampires. She was almost too afraid to ask, but she had to know. *And Taavi?*

No one replied. Hestie wondered if she was losing her ability to communicate telepathically.

What about Taavi? she asked again.

"He didn't make it," Jinsoo finally said. "It was awful."

Tears spilled from the corners of Hestie's eyes. It took all her strength to blink them away.

Where's Poros and the others? Hestie asked.

"The vampires are in Tartarus with Hermes," her mother said.

"Now that Hestie's awake, I want to go there, too," Hermie said.

"Why?" their mother asked Hermie.

"Hermes and Alecto are going to interrogate the people we found dead on the STS barge," Hermie explained.

Hestie wished she could be there, too.

What about Poros and Captain? Hestie asked.

Her mother frowned. "They're still on the ship. But Pegasus is here, and he's fine."

How did Poseidon know where we'd be? Hestie asked.

"We don't know," Hermie said.

Hestie closed her eyes. *Athena must have told them. It's the only way.*

"Do you really believe Athena would put you in this kind of danger?" her mother asked. "I can't believe it."

"Maybe she didn't know how far Poseidon would go," Hermie offered.

Hestie looked up at her mother and was surprised by the expression of anger that had crossed her face. Her eyes were narrowed, her brows bent together, her lips pushed together into a straight line, and her cheeks were red, her eyes moist. Hestie had never seen Therese so enraged.

Mom, I'll be okay. Hestie said this to her mother even though everyone knew it was impossible to predict the long-term damage from a direct hit by the trident.

"I'll let you know what we learn in Tartarus," Hermie said to Hestie.

Hestie blinked as her brother and Jinsoo vanished.

Do you know if Poros and Prometheus are okay? Hestie asked.

Her mother's expression softened. "I'm afraid I don't, sweet girl."

Gertie sat across from Hector in her bedroom sitting area. It was Saturday morning, and she was sleepy, because her days and nights were confused. They'd avoided talking about their relationship. As soon as Hector had arrived, Gertie had gotten straight to the point.

"I confronted your stepfather three days ago," Hector said in answer to her questions. "Right after I called you. He claimed to know nothing about the smuggling taking place on STS ships."

"Did he seem defensive? Or angry? Or did he seem surprised?" Gertie asked.

"At first, he laughed at me. Then he got defensive, accusing me of slander and defamation. He shouted a string of curses at me. After that, he told me I was no longer welcome here, and I left."

Gertie could imagine the scene. Although her stepfather was usually calm and business-like, she'd seen him lose it. It was Gertie's observation that James ignored uncomfortable and painful things until they reached a head and exploded from him in an angry tirade.

"I'm sorry he treated you that way," she said.

"I'm more upset by the way his daughter is treating me," he said without meeting her eyes.

"Can't we put our problems on hold for now?" she asked. "I can't handle everything at once. Finding James has got to be my priority."

"I wish I had more to tell you," Hector said. "I have no clue where he could be."

She told him about her mother's trip to Venice. "It may lead nowhere."

"It's worth checking out," Hector said. "Good call."

The corners of Gertie's mouth twitched into a subtle smile. "Thanks."

"No matter what's going on between us," he said, his blue eyes moist, "I hope you know you can count on me to help and to be there for you."

She hoped she could. She desperately wanted to believe she could.

"Look, Nikita's anxious to see you but wasn't sure if you'd want company," he said. "I told her I'd invite you over to the house, to hang out, like we used to."

Gertie gnawed on her bottom lip. She knew Nikita would rather Gertie go to Hector's place, because Lajos was there, and Lajos wouldn't feel as comfortable hanging out at Gertie's. And Gertie would rather go to Hector's too, especially now that her mother was out of town. She could ask their housekeeper, Gabriela, to call her if her stepfather showed up. If that happened, Gertie could be back home within ten minutes.

On the other hand, she was afraid. She was afraid of slipping back into the old, comfortable way she had with Hector. The problem with getting comfortable was that it made her vulnerable. What if he needed to be on his own again? To deal with it *once* was heartbreaking. To be forced to deal with it *twice* would crush her.

Gertie was brought from her reverie by the sudden appearance of Morpheus near the door of her bedroom suite.

Hector flinched and jumped to his feet. "Morpheus! You sure know how to make an entrance."

"I have bad news. Really bad news," Morpheus said with clenched fists.

Gertie stood beside Hector. "What happened?"

"The *Marcella II* was attacked by Poseidon and his tritons last night," Morpheus said. "Ladon, was there, too."

"Is everyone okay?" Hector asked.

"Nearly everyone. Hestie and Chidori were paralyzed. And, well, there's no easy way to say this: Taavi was killed."

Gertie stared back at Morpheus, even as Hector took her in his arms to comfort her. Gertie just stared at Morpheus, unable to believe it.

"I'm so sorry, Gertie," Hector said.

Gertie continued to stare blankly at Morpheus, trying to wrap her mind around it. How could Taavi be gone?

CHAPTER TWELVE

Hades

Hermie flew from his parents' chambers down the winding tunnel along the river of fire toward Tartarus, from which he could already hear the screams of tortured souls. Jinsoo followed close behind.

"This place gives me the creeps," Jinsoo said.

"Really?"

"Um, yeah. It doesn't give you the creeps, Hermie?"

"No." To Hermie, it felt like home.

"Dead spirits screaming, lava flowing, bats and spiders flying and crawling…none of this creeps you out?"

"That isn't lava. It's a river of fire called the Phlegethon."

"Whatever. It's still creepy."

They flew past a bat cave and the chambers belonging to the Furies before they reached a part of the Phlegethon that bordered Tartarus. They flew over the river of fire and up to the black iron gate. It creaked and groaned as Hermie opened it. In the distance, they saw Meg order her falcon to peck out the eyes of a soul strapped to a table. Although souls possessed no physical attributes, such as eyes, they experienced pain as if they did. Hermie recalled Alecto's comparison to the phantom pain experienced by an amputee.

Hermie and Jinsoo made their way past other tables where souls were strapped until they came upon Hermes and the vampires. They stood around a table where Alecto straddled a soul. Hermie recognized the soul as belonging to one of the dead bodies he saw in the STS shipping container. Alecto's red spiky hair had turned into hissing snakes. Blood dripped from her eyes and mouth. Hermie had seen her like this before. Nevertheless, it made him shiver deep in his bones.

And as if the scene couldn't be more gruesome, Alecto's familiar, also a snake, now slithered from the shoulder of the Fury to twist itself around the neck of the captured soul and squeeze.

Alecto had once told Hermie that she enjoyed her work, because it allowed souls to pay for their transgressions. He wondered how she felt about torturing a presumably innocent soul for the sake of learning information.

"Hey," Alastair said to them as they approached.

"Hey," Jinsoo said with blushing cheeks.

Hermie searched the group for Del. It was the first thing he did any time he entered a room where she might be found. The entire group was somber. He imagined they were hurting in the wake of Taavi's death.

He saw her standing between Sophia and Bach on the other side of the table. She met his gaze, giving him a half-smile. He gave her one in return.

"Have you heard from Captain or Poros?" Mahdi asked.

"No," Jinsoo replied. "What about you, Hermie?"

Hermie shook his head.

"Silence!" Alecto commanded.

Jinsoo's cheeks became redder.

Hermes glanced back at them and shrugged, as if in apology for Alecto's behavior.

"His name is Farid Hassan," Alecto said. "He lived in Syria with his wife but was imprisoned by the Syrian government for having sympathy for the rebellion."

"Why was he on the barge?" Hermes asked.

Alecto leaned over the soul, giving it the full force of her fearsome form as her clawed wings expanded from her back and a shriek rose from her throat.

Hermie overheard a string of Syrian words.

"He was being sold to Russia?" Hermie whispered to Jinsoo.

"As payment," Alecto added. "He was being traded for something valuable from Russia."

"The warheads," Hermie said. "Can you ask him if he knows about them?"

"He doesn't know," Alecto said. "Believe me, he'd tell me if he did."

Alecto returned to her beautiful form and unstrapped the soul. "I suppose I'll have to question one of the others now."

Hades appeared near the gate to Tartarus. "While you and Hermes continue with your task, Alecto, I want the vampires to come with me."

"Can I come?" Jinsoo asked.

Hades turned his back without a reply. Jinsoo and Hermie shrugged at one another and followed the lord of the Underworld and the crew of vampires from Tartarus.

"I don't think you should be alone," Hector said to Gertie. "Come to my place. We'll watch movies or something."

Gertie was still reeling from the news delivered by Morpheus moments earlier. Was Taavi really gone?

Hector fingered a strand of hair that had escaped from her ponytail and pushed it behind her ear. She looked up at him, wanting so badly to trust him.

"You need to be with friends right now," he said.

"I know," she said, awkwardly pulling away. "I'll follow you in the Porsche."

"That's not a good idea," he said. "Ride with me, and I'll bring you home when you're ready."

"Are you sure?"

"Yes. Come on. Nikita's anxious to see you."

Gertie slipped her purse strap over her shoulder and led Hector upstairs, where she left a note for Gabriela and Babá, letting them know where she'd be. Then she followed Hector through the front door into the sunny morning air, to the circular drive, where his Mini Cooper was parked.

It felt strange sitting across from Hector as he drove toward his subdivision on the other side of Athens. She had so many happy memories of being in that car with him. She longed for the days when she felt secure in her relationship with him—the days before the doubts had crept in and terrified her. What if she couldn't count on him to be her person?

By the time they reached his house, it was after ten in the morning. Nikita was already waiting in a t-shirt and shorts by the front door when they pulled into the drive. She ran across the lawn and helped Gertie from the car. Then she threw her arms around her and squeezed.

"I'm so sorry for your loss," Nikita said. "Come inside and have some chocolate cake. It's still warm. I just took it out of the oven."

Nikita had inherited her father's habit of using food to both celebrate the good times and to console during the hard times. Unfortunately, Nikita hadn't inherited Babá's talent for cooking and baking delicious food. Gertie wasn't hungry but would have a tiny piece, so as not to seem ungrateful.

Lajos was there waiting in the kitchen when they entered.

"Hey, Gertie," he said. "I'm sorry about your friend."

"Thanks," she said.

"I cut you a piece of Nikita's cake. It's actually not bad."

Gertie chuckled and said, "Thanks," as she took the plate and fork from Lajos.

"What am I, chopped liver?" Hector asked.

Lajos laughed. "You can get your own piece, dude."

With her plate in hand, Gertie followed the others into the living room, where they collapsed on the huge sectional sofa in front of the big screen television, where Lajos had paused his video game. Gertie was surprised when Hector didn't sit beside her, in his usual spot. He respected her space, which was a good thing, she supposed.

"Are you up for a movie?" Hector asked her.

"First, tell me how you like the cake," Nikita said. "It's good, right?"

Gertie said, "It's delicious. Your best yet."

"Quit lying," Nikita said. "It's not *that* good."

"Well, it's not bad," Gertie said with a grin.

"Are you staying in Athens?" Lajos asked. "Or will you be returning to the ship?"

"I saw myself returning," she said. "It was October 20th in the dream. I don't know if I will go any sooner than that."

"Will you go, too, Hector?" Nikita asked.

Hector glanced awkwardly at Gertie. "I'd like to. I'd like to help however I can."

Nikita turned to Gertie. "You should hear some of the songs he's written. They're amazing! I told him he needs to get an agent or something."

"You two should sing them for her," Lajos said. Then, turning to Gertie, he added, "They sound amazing together."

"Let's hear it," Gertie said.

Hector shook his head. "Come on, guys. Let's just watch a movie or play some video games."

"Hector! Gertie wants us to. Come on!"

"But Klaus isn't here," Hector objected. "And Lajos can't hold a tune."

"We can do it without Klaus," Nikita insisted. "Just the two of us."

Hector shrugged and left to get his ukulele. When he returned, he sat on the edge of the sofa near Nikita and began to strum a slow, somber melody.

Then their lovely voices rang in harmony:

Whatever happens to you happens to me.

Whatever dream you dream becomes my dream.

Wherever your heart soars, mine will follow.

Yes, it's true, no matter where you go.

I want you to know.

My heart will follow you.

Gertie listened in awe to the next few verses with tears spilling from her eyes. They were the very words she longed to believe about Hector and his love for her.

When the song was over, Hector said, "It's about you, Gertie. All my songs are about you."

Nikita gave Lajos a smile, but Gertie frowned.

"Did I say something wrong?" Hector asked, alarmed.

Gertie shook her head. "Not at all. Everything you said was perfectly right."

"Mom?" Hestie said—not telepathically.

When her mother's eyes and mouth widened with surprise, Hestie smiled.

Hestie's mother said, "Thank the gods."

"But it was a god who did this to me," Hestie pointed out.

"Figure of speech—although I'm sure Apollo has been doing what he can."

Hestie wasn't so sure.

"Do you need something to drink, now that you can move your tongue?" her mother asked her.

"Yes, please," Hestie said. "How's Chidori?"

Her mother poured water from a pitcher into a golden goblet. "Still no change."

Therese held the goblet to Hestie's lips. The cool water slipped down Hestie's throat and invigorated her. As the water traveled through her system, Hestie felt it. And when her mother wiped Hestie's lips with a cloth, Hestie felt that, too.

Then her father appeared and gazed down at her.

"Thank the Fates," he said. "You're improving. That's a great sign that you'll make a full recovery."

Hestie was less concerned about herself than she was about the others. "Do you know if Poros and Prometheus are okay?"

Her father frowned. "They aren't on the ship. We don't know where they are. They could be hiding. That's what we're hoping, anyway."

Hestie's eyes widened, and her heart raced. What if they'd been taken by Poseidon as his prisoners—or worse? She wanted to sit up, to stand, to fly, to search the ends of the earth for Poros and their captain.

"What if they're still in harm's way?" she said. "Wouldn't they have come here? Have you tried Clymene's cave?"

"I don't know where it is," her father said. "Do you?"

"It's somewhere in the East China Sea," Hestie said.

"Any chance you could be more specific?" her father asked.

"No, but Helios might know."

"I'll pay him a visit," Thanatos said. "Meanwhile, please get some rest, okay, pumpkin?"

Hestie sucked in her lips. "Couldn't we ask Hecate to perform a location spell?"

"I'm sure she will, if it comes to that." Her mother stroked her hair. "Please focus on healing and leave the rest to us."

Again, Hestie said nothing, because she knew that the moment she could, she would leave and go looking for them.

Hermie studied Del as she listened to Hades make his speech about vampire reapers and their importance to the Underworld and to humanity.

"Reaping souls from the dead allows them to feed until satiated while building their self-esteem with a sense of purpose," Hades said. "They retrieve souls from the dark side of the earth so that Thanatos can focus on the bright side."

Hades pointed to the gates, where Cerberus stood guard. Charon entered on his raft with four souls and two vampire reapers.

"The reapers stay with the souls through their sentencing in the House of Judgment and their journey to their final destination, whether that be Tartarus, the Elysian Fields, or Erebus."

"Erebus?" Jinsoo repeated.

"It's a pit filled with water from the Lethe—the river of forgetfulness," Hades explained. "Victims of severe trauma, such as prisoners of war and victims of domestic abuse, go there to recover before moving on to the Fields of Elysium."

"Where is Taavi?" Mahdi asked.

"Can we see him?" Bach wanted to know.

"Nearly every soul of a vampire visits Erebus," Hades said. "I'm sure you understand why."

"No, I don't," Jinsoo said.

Alastair put an arm around Jinsoo's shoulders. "Consider the trauma one must experience when one is denied both life and death. Consider, too, the immense guilt vampires feel from drinking human blood, often obtained in unimaginable ways."

Jinsoo's face turned white as he gave Alastair a nod.

"So, can we see Taavi?" Hermie asked his grandfather.

"Now isn't a good time," Hades said. "Besides, I'm afraid I have some troubling news, something we will need to discuss with the others."

Hermie dreaded to hear what Hades had to say.

"Thanatos returned to the *Marcella II* to help Prometheus and Poros but found no sign of them," Hades said.

Hermie's stomach dropped.

"Where are they?" Jinsoo asked.

The lord of darkness said, "No one seems to know."

CHAPTER THIRTEEN

Making Plans

Hermie and Jinsoo joined the vamps and some of the Underworld gods in his grandparents' throne room. His parents and grandparents were there, along with Hermes, Hecate, Morpheus, and Morpheus's parents, Jen and Hip. Hecate's familiars, a Doberman and a weasel, were also present.

Once they were all seated in a circle around a chunky wooden table, Than, Hermie's father, said, "Helios refused to tell me the location of Clymene's cave, but he insists that Clymene doesn't have them."

Jinsoo covered his face and shook his head. "Poor Captain and Poros. What happened to them?"

"Than and I stayed until Poseidon and his tritons retreated," Hermes said.

Jen glanced nervously around the room. "Do you think Poseidon came back for them?"

"That's anyone's guess," Hades said.

"I wish you would have thought to bring me something from the ship," Hecate said to Than, "something that belonged to them, for my spell."

"Sorry. I wasn't thinking," Than said.

Therese, Hermie's mother, raised her chin. "Maybe they went into hiding. We can't rule that out."

"Or maybe they followed Poseidon back to his castle for a counterattack," Morpheus offered.

Hades frowned. "Not without backup."

"Let's hope not, anyway," Persephone said.

"Poros has the lightning bolt," Hermie pointed out. "Maybe they thought it was enough for a surprise attack."

Hip shook his head. "They would have consulted with the rest of us first, surely."

"I wonder why Ladon was helping Poseidon," Therese said. "Do you think Poseidon is working with the old man of the sea?"

"I was wondering the same thing," Persephone admitted.

"No," Hades said. "My brother would never join up with Phorcys. The two deities despise one another."

"Phorcys and Keto used to rule the sea," Hermie explained to the vampires. "That was before Zeus rescued his siblings from the belly of their father and defeated the Titans."

"We know the stories," Bach said.

"What can we do?" Del wanted to know. "Tell us what to do to help. Can we go looking for them?"

"We need a plan," Hip said.

Hermie lifted a finger. "If some of us draw Poseidon and the tritons away from Poseidon's castle, then others of us could search it while they're away."

Alastair nodded. "Sounds like a pirate move."

"I'm a quick learner," Hermie said with a grin.

"I like the concept," Hades began, "but what would draw Poseidon out?"

"We have Pegasus," Morpheus said. "Isn't he Poseidon's son?"

"Poseidon knows we love Pegasus," Therese said. "He knows we would never harm him."

Jinsoo held his head in his hands and cried, "Oye! We have no choice but to kidnap one of those sexy tritons. It's the only way!"

"It'll take more than one triton to get Poseidon's attention," Hades said.

Del stood up. "We can take them all. Or most of them."

Hades turned to her with a gleam in his eye. "What do you have in mind?"

Hestie gasped when she discovered that she could wiggle her fingers and toes.

"Did you see that, Noodle?" she asked her dog.

He barked and wagged his tail.

Katniss and Prim danced excitedly across her belly. Hestie laughed and sat up.

Clifford and Noodle ran around the room with excitement. Even Kitty, who was usually a lazy girl, jumped from one chair to another with glee.

"Oh, it's all coming back!" Hestie said as she climbed to her feet.

She glanced around, looking for Chidori. The bird was lying on a pillow on the golden table across the room. Hestie went to her bird and stroked her feathers, grateful that her mother had given their pets immortality; otherwise, Chidori wouldn't have had a chance against Poseidon's trident.

"Chidori, don't lose hope. You'll get better, too. I just know it."

Then she turned to her other pets. "Don't tell anyone that I'm better. I have something I need to do first."

The animals promised they'd keep her secret. Then she left her parents' chambers in search of the helm of invisibility.

She felt less fear than desperation. The thought of Poros and the captain being trapped in the belly of another god or thrown into the Titan Pit or ripped to pieces and fed to sharks so that their souls would be forever without their bodies emblazoned her with courage and determination. Prometheus had been like a second father to her, and Poros...Poros had been the absolute love of her life. She knew that with certainty—now that there was a chance that she might never see him again.

As she followed the Phlegethon toward her grandparents' palace, she glanced over the many souls frolicking in the Fields of Elysium on the other side. She wondered if she might see Mina or Taavi among them but didn't see anyone she recognized. With no time to lose, she continued toward the palace and the helm.

She hoped the meeting would keep everyone occupied long enough for her to slip past the throne room. She held her breath as she flew by the doorway and waited until she was several meters down the winding corridor before she breathed again.

Once she neared her grandparents' personal chambers, she flew directly to her grandfather's bedroom. She'd always admired the beautiful gems embedded in the stone walls. They sparkled with the light from the Phlegethon, which flowed in every room of the Underworld save the Seers' Pit. Although Hades's chambers were heavily warded, they weren't warded against *her*. She slipped inside, grabbed the helm, and placed it on her head.

She slowly let out a breath and inhaled another before leaving the room but was suddenly startled when the voice of Hades entered her mind: *I assume you plan to look for them.*

Hestie sucked in air and froze.

You think I'd leave my helm unprotected during a crisis?

Obviously not, she replied telepathically.

If you get caught and anyone asks me, I'll say I knew nothing about it. Do you understand?

Yes, sir. She smiled with relief as she left the palace and headed for the gate. She wasn't sure what she would have done if her grandfather had tried to stop her. She doubted anything short of brute force could keep her from helping the ones she loved.

Be careful, Hestie. And bring Hecate something she can use for her location spell.

Will do, she said.

She flew past Cerberus and over the gate and up through the winding chasm that led to the Upperworld. All the while, her heart pounded madly against her ribs.

"Gertie, wake up."

Gertie blinked. Nikita was bending over her with her cell phone in her hand. Gertie glanced around to find she'd fallen asleep on Hector's sectional. Lajos and Hector were no longer in the room. Through the windows, Gertie saw that night had fallen. How long had she been asleep?

"It's Babá," Nikita said. "He wants to talk to you."

Gertie took Nikita's cell phone and said, "Hello?"

"Gertoula?"

"Yes, Babá. What's wrong?" Gertie said into the phone.

"An Express Mail package just arrived from Italy," he said. "I think it could be important."

"Does it say who it's from?" Gertie asked.

"No. There's no return address that I can see."

"Okay, Babá. Thank you. I'll get someone to bring me home as soon as possible."

Gertie ended the call and gave Nikita her phone. "Where are Hector and Lajos?"

"Lajos is helping with an environmentalist demonstration downtown. He should be back any minute."

"Oh, I bet you wanted to go to that," Gertie said.

"And miss watching you sleep?" Nikita teased.

Gertie blushed. "Sorry. I promise to make it up to you."

"No worries. I really didn't want to go to the demonstration, anyway. You were my excuse."

"Glad I could be of service. Is Hector with him?"

"He's upstairs in his room writing music, I think," Nikita said.

Gertie climbed to her feet and went upstairs to look for him. She found the door to his bedroom open. Hector stood in front of his dresser with a towel wrapped around his waist. His hair was dripping wet, and the fresh scent of soap wafted through the room.

Gertie's breath caught as she was reminded of his beauty. Gods, she missed being in those strong, protective arms against that hard chest. She missed the feel of his smooth skin against hers, of his mouth on hers.

It took a minute for her to realize that he had noticed her.

"Um, um, I'm sorry," she said.

His look was intense when he said, "Don't be."

"Nikita's dad called and said there's a package from Italy. He thinks it might be important."

"Okay, no problem. Let me throw on some clothes, and I'll drive you home."

She nodded and took a step back, into the hallway. "Thanks."

Then she pulled her eyes away from him and returned downstairs to wait.

During the drive to Gertie's house, Hector asked, "Did you sleep okay?"

"Like a rock. Thanks."

"Good. No dreams?"

"None that I can remember." She'd been dreaming of Taavi, but she didn't see the point in sharing that with Hector.

Hector took the next right and said, "If you plan on drinking your father's wine to provoke a vision, I want to stay with you. You shouldn't be alone."

"Thanks." Gertie was reminded that Hector really did care about her and her safety. Why couldn't she believe him when he said he'd never leave her again? She held her hand over her heart to steady it.

When they arrived, they found Babá in the kitchen.

"Ah, Gertoula. Hello, Hector. Here is the package. And dinner is almost ready." Babá handed her a brown cardboard package the size of a shoe box.

It wasn't heavy. In fact, it felt like it was filled with nothing but air. It was addressed to her mother.

"You think I should open it?" Gertie asked.

"If it was sent by Express Mail, then it is urgent," Babá said. "At least, that is how I see it."

"I agree," Hector said. "Open it. I doubt your mom will mind."

Gertie grabbed a pair of scissors from a kitchen drawer and cut through the tape before pulling open the box. Inside was an Italian shoe box. Half-expecting to find an expensive pair of shoes, Gertie opened the lid and was surprised to discover, instead, a notepad from the Hotel Excelsior in Venice—where her mother had gone in search of Gertie's stepfather. She took out the notepad and stared at it, bewildered.

"Does that mean anything to you?" Hector asked.

"No." Gertie thumbed through the pages. Something caught her eye. There was writing on one of them. "Hold on." She thumbed through the pages again until she found the writing. It was a table of numbers and letters in a grid written in James's handwriting. "I know what this is. It's a game we used to play when I was a kid."

"What game?" Hector asked, bemused.

"James called it the cipher game. He'd create a puzzle like this and then give me hints about the key. See how each column is numbered from zero to five?"

"So?" Babá asked from over her shoulder. "What is this puzzle?"

"You need a key, so you know how to rearrange the columns," Gertie said. "Sometimes the key would be my birthday, or our zip code, or something like that. Since the columns only go up to five, I know the key isn't my birthday, because five is the highest number in the key, and my birthday is the ninth of May. There would have to be ten columns for that key to work. It also can't be our New York zip code, which was

10013, because then there would only be four columns—zero, one, two, and three. And it can't be my parents' anniversary, because they were married in August."

"What's the postal code for this area?" Hector asked.

"It's 11521," Babá said.

"I bet that's the key," Gertie said. She found an ink pen from the same drawer where she had gotten the scissors. She tore a clean piece of paper from the notepad and got to work. "The only columns that matter are columns 1,5, and 2. We can ignore the others."

She copied the letters in columns 1, 5, and 2 in their new arrangement. Once she had finished, she read the secret message:

"Don't read this out loud," she read. Blood rushed to her cheeks. "Oops."

"There must be more," Hector said.

Gertie turned to Babá. "Do you think the house is bugged?"

Babá shrugged and glanced nervously around the room.

"Why else would my stepfather not want me to read the message out loud?" she wondered.

Hector flipped through the other pages of the notepad. "Here's another one, on the back of the page. That was clever. He knew you'd find the one on the front before finding this one."

"Well, he couldn't know it for *sure*, but it was *more likely*," Gertie said, not meaning to be a know-it-all. Sometimes she just couldn't help herself.

Hector tore the page loose and handed it to Gertie. This time she was careful not to explain her methods out loud, in case the house was bugged. The fact that there were nine columns numbered zero to eight in this cipher told her that the key was probably her parents' anniversary: 08122002. If she was right, then the only columns that mattered were zero, one, two, and eight. She rearranged those columns, copying down the letters, and gasped when she read the message.

CHAPTER FOURTEEN

Clues

Hestie god-traveled to the *Marcella II* to look for something belonging to Poros and the captain that Hecate could use for her spell. Visiting the ship would also give her a chance to search for clues.

When she arrived, she found herself hovering above the Arabian Sea. The ship had drifted several miles from its last known location. Hestie could see it near the coast of India. She flew to it and immediately realized by its tilt that it had swept onto a sandbar. Using her god strength, she shoved the *Marcella II* from the ocean floor into deeper waters, where she then anchored it, so it wouldn't continue to drift. She also lowered the sails and secured the lines. That's when she noticed Prometheus's hat on the floor of the main deck.

Her heart pounded against her ribs. The only time Captain ever took off his hat was when they went diving, and when that happened, it hung on a hook over the helm on the flybridge. He'd never leave it lying on the floor, where it could be ruined.

She scooped up the hat and fought tears. Her hopes that Poros and Captain had gone into hiding were dashed. Someone had taken them. And, by the looks of it, they'd been taken by force—otherwise Prometheus would still be wearing his hat.

She searched the galley and salon for more clues. Finding none, she went below deck. The vampire crates had slid into the corridor and some of the supplies had fallen from the cupboards—things that had probably happened during the fight with Poseidon and his tritons. Nothing else appeared unusual or provided any hints as to where Captain and Poros may have been taken or by whom. She flew into Poros's room and found one of his socks and then she used her powers to send the sock and the hat directly to Hecate.

While Hecate would perform her spell, Hestie would get a head start on the search for Poros and Captain. The first place she would start was Mount Olympus. She needed to know what Athena was up to.

Hestie trembled beneath the helm of invisibility. Now that she was a goddess, there were worse fates than death that could befall her. As she waited for someone to open the gates, so she could slip inside, she reminded herself that Gertie saw her riding Pegasus on October 20th. Didn't that mean nothing too horrible would happen to her now as she tried to break into Mount Olympus, unseen?

Then she recalled something her Uncle Pete, the god of seers, always said: Only the Fates know for certain what the future holds. The visions of seers can change.

A lump rose in Hestie's throat. What if coming to Mount Olympus beneath the helm of invisibility would change the future and undermine Hermie's chance to disarm the warheads?

She sighed. Second guessing her every move would get her nowhere. In any given moment, she had to act in the way she thought was best. It was all anyone could do.

As she stood there on the ice-capped mountain, waiting, her mind wandered to all the fun times she shared with Poros and Captain and the crew of the *Marvella* and, later, the crew of the *Marvella II*. Although she had a wonderful childhood in Colorado, being on the sea with her new friends felt more like home. Maybe it was because she loved their missions. They infused her with a sense of purpose, a feeling more powerful than anything she'd ever experienced in her life.

She wasn't sure how much time had passed (thirty minutes? an hour?) when the gates opened, and Apollo emerged in his chariot. Hestie dashed inside the gates and flew across the courtyard to the main temple of the gods, hoping for clues.

Hermie couldn't take his eyes off Del as she stood before the Underworld gods and her fellow vampires describing her plan for capturing as many tritons as possible.

"We already know the tritons despise pirates—especially us," she said. "Use some of us as bait and the rest of us as part of an ambush party."

"Bait and ambush," Hermes repeated. "Another lesson in Pirating 101."

"Yes, my lord," Del said. "Those of us acting as the bait will pretend to target a ship in the Mediterranean—preferably a merchant or shipping vessel."

"What if the tritons don't come?" Jinsoo asked.

"Then we wait a while and try again," Del said. "Obviously, we can only operate at night."

"How do you intend to ambush an army of tritons?" Persephone asked.

"We'll need the helm of invisibility, my lady," Del said. "And your chariot, assuming it can operate underwater."

"Indeed, it can," Hades said. "But you haven't answered my queen's question."

"It's a bait and switch method, lord," Del explained.

Hades lifted a brow.

Alastair said, "We appear to be a lookout of one or two, when, in reality, there's a massive amount of us."

Hades picked at his beard. "You're saying that in addition to the pirates boarding the ship, you'll position one or two others as a *pretend* lookout?"

"Exactly," Hermes said. "My V-team has used this method numerous times with the more heavily guarded vessels."

"But they were dealing with mortals," Than pointed out.

"Yeah," Hip agreed. "How will your methods work on tritons?"

"Once the tritons surround the ship and attempt to take the bait, our hidden army will attack," Del said. "The key is to do this covertly, as quietly as possible, picking off the tritons one by one."

Alastair said, "We use invisibility when dealing with mortals, but that won't work with the tritons."

"Which is why we need the helm of darkness," Del explained.

Hades cleared his throat. "It's a good plan."

Del smiled—for the first time in ages, it seemed to Hermie.

Hades lifted his palm. "However, my helm is unavailable at the moment."

"Where is it?" Than asked.

Hades said nothing for five whole seconds. Then he crossed his arms over his chest, leaned back in his chair, and said, "Your daughter took it."

Therese jumped to her feet. "What? When? Why didn't you stop her?"

"Do you know where she went?" Than asked Hades.

Hermie's throat tightened as he thought of the most likely place his sister would go and why.

"I bet she returned to the *Marcella II*," Hermie said. "to get what Hecate needs for a location spell."

"I was going to do that," Hecate said. "Why didn't she wait?"

Just then, Prometheus's captain's hat and a sock appeared on the table in front of Hecate.

"Hestie?" Therese called.

"She isn't here," Hades said.

"Why would she send the items instead of bringing them herself?" Jen wondered aloud.

"I'll go look for her," Than said.

Hades jumped to his feet. "Hold on. You could call attention to her. As it is, she's protected beneath the helm."

Therese covered her pale cheeks with her hands. "But what if she's discovered? Or what if she's already been captured?"

"You need to have more faith in your daughter," Hades insisted.

Hermie glanced from his mother to his father. Were they going to listen to Hades, or were they going to fly after Hestie?

Gertie read over the hidden message on the notepad from the Hotel Excelsior. Then she tore the paper into tiny pieces before throwing them into the flames on Babá's six-burner gas stove.

"What are you doing to my stove, Gertoula?" Babá complained.

"Destroying the evidence. Don't worry, Babá. I know what to do."

"And what is that, exactly?" Hector asked her.

"You'll have to trust me," she said. "I need to freshen up and grab my car keys. I'm not sure how long I'll be gone. I could be back as early as the morning."

"You are going *tonight*?" Babá asked.

"I have to." She headed toward the basement stairs.

Hector followed. "I'm coming with you."

"But I can't even tell you where I'm going."

"It doesn't matter."

He followed her to her room and waited while she freshened up in the bathroom. Then she grabbed her car keys from the top of her desk.

Hector stood up from the overstuffed chair where he'd been waiting. His mouth formed a straight line, and his brows were bent together.

Gertie wished she could smooth the line between his brows with a kiss. Deciding to take a chance, she took a few steps to close the distance between them and whispered in his ear, "Gaia."

When she stepped back to study his face, she saw him processing. Her stepfather's message had read: *Tell Gertie to seek Gaia at night.* Whether the house was bugged or whether immortal eyes were watching, James must have believed that Gaia could help.

Hector had helped Gertie the first time she had ever gone looking for her grandmother. He had taken her to the omphalos, or belly button. It was a cave in Delphi where Zeus used to go to talk to Gaia. Although she was earth and was everywhere, the best place to have a one-on-one conversation with her was at the earth's center, and that place, according to legend, was Delphi. It was a two-hour drive from Athens.

Gertie led Hector back up the basement steps and to the kitchen. As she headed for the back door, Babá stopped her.

"Listen to me," he said. "I can accept that you cannot tell me where you are going or why you are going there, but I cannot let you starve. Today I made your favorite: crunchy rice with lima beans and just a little bit of braised pork added, because I know you don't like a lot of meat. Please eat, both of you, before you go."

Now that she thought about it, Gertie was starving. Babá had already made two plates and put them on the kitchen table with glasses of iced water.

"Thank you, Babá," Gertie said as she took her seat.

Hector sat across from her. "Yeah, thanks, Kyrios Angelis."

As she ate the delicious food Babá had prepared, Gertie thought more about James's message. Why would he want Gertie to go *at night*? Did it have something to do with the vampires? No, because he couldn't have known whether a vampire would be with her. And the message didn't say whether she should go alone or with someone.

Then it hit her: Helios. He had been upset with her in the dream with Pegasus and the Russian warheads. He had told Gertie to stay out of it, that she would ruin everything. By going to Gaia at night, Gertie would avoid being seen by Helios.

But why was the sun god involved with James and STS?

Hestie flew through the great hall. To her disappointment, the only one there was Athena. Hestie had hoped to overhear the gods talking about Poseidon.

The gray-eyed goddess sat on the throne where Zeus once sat. As she combed her long black hair with her fingers, she appeared to be deep in thought. Hestie wished she had the power to read minds. What could the goddess be thinking? Did she know that her brother and her beloved Prometheus were missing? And if she did know, did she plan to do anything about it? Or might she be the one behind their disappearance?

Hestie decided to snoop around. As she was about to leave the great hall to search whatever rooms she could access, Ares, with his vibrant red hair and huge biceps, walked in and said to Athena, "You're playing a dangerous game."

Athena replied, "I have no choice. Playing both sides is my only option."

"We must stop Poseidon. Don't you see? It's the only way."

"You would feel differently if it were Aphrodite's life on the line," Athena accused.

"Perhaps. But it's not. You need to think long-term."

Athena turned toward Hestie with a look of suspicion. She glanced around for several seconds.

"What is it?" Ares asked.

Hestie held her breath.

"Nothing," Athena said. "I'm done talking to you about this. Stick with the plan. The council has decided."

"The council? We're missing half of our players."

"And what fault of that is mine?"

"You didn't consult the council when you sanctioned Poseidon's attack on your boyfriend's ship," Ares accused. "Why must you now?"

"I should have. It was a terrible mistake. I had no idea Poseidon would go that far. I don't care about the vampire, but Hestie might never recover."

Hestie sucked in her lips.

The god of war shook his head. "What were you thinking?"

"I thought I was discouraging them from interfering!" Athena roared. "I meant to protect them, not endanger them!"

Ares grumbled and disappeared.

Then Aphrodite flew into the hall, her long blonde hair flowing behind her, and said, "He's right, you know."

"About which part?" Athena demanded angrily.

"You need to think long-term. Helping Poseidon now won't solve our problem in the long run," the goddess of love and beauty said.

Athena straightened her back. "What would you have me do? Please, give me a better plan. No one else has managed to do so. After Phorcys took Rhode, we tried a rescue mission, and look where that got us. Now he has Amphitrite, too. We can't risk losing more of our people, not while the old man of the sea and father of monsters has become so strong."

Hestie covered her mouth beneath the helm. Phorcys had Poseidon's wife and daughter?

"If those Syrian officials succeed in building their temple for him, all of us will be threatened, not just Amphitrite and Rhode," Aphrodite said.

"The Syrians are desperate to squash the rebellious factions in their country," Athena said. "If we help them, they won't need Phorcys. Then, after the old man of the sea has weakened, we can rescue his prisoners. That's the plan."

Hestie was astonished to learn that some Syrian officials planned to build a temple for the old man of the sea. The prayer and worship of deities by mortals is what gave the deities their power. No wonder the Olympians were afraid.

"You know what Poseidon has agreed to do," Aphrodite said.

Athena sighed. "Like I said, we have no choice. It's highly unlikely those warheads will ever be activated. We've discussed this ad infinitum."

"Ares will never agree to it," Aphrodite said. "I still have followers in Syria. They make a pilgrimage to my temple in Afca every year. I can't betray their trust."

"The council has decided. And who isn't thinking long-term now?" Athena accused.

Hephaestus entered through the foyer. "Prometheus and Poros are missing. Hermes sent the message with Iris."

Athena leapt to her feet. "What? Any idea where they are?"

Iris suddenly appeared beside Hephaestus. "It's true. I've just come from the Underworld."

"They may have gone into hiding," Aphrodite said.

Hestie was tempted to remove the helm and tell them what she knew, but she wasn't sure if she could trust Athena. Athena had sanctioned the attack on the *Marcella II*, the attack that had paralyzed her and Chidori and had killed Taavi. She wiped away tears and flew to the gates of Mount Olympus to wait for someone to open them. When she noticed Iris flying to her rainbow arch, Hestie followed her all the way back to the Underworld, where her family and the vampires were waiting.

CHAPTER FIFTEEN

Down to Earth

Alone in her Porsche with Hector, Gertie found the drive to Delphi awkward for the first hour. Sitting so close to him, in the dark, with nothing else to distract them, like a movie or a video game, made her uneasy. The playlist sounding over her car stereo didn't help matters, because the songs were favorites of his and reminded her of times spent with him, back when they were happy.

She could sense that he had things he wanted to say to her but was holding back. On the one hand, she wished he'd just say whatever it was and get it off his chest. She wanted him to be as transparent with her as possible. It was the only hope they had of ever regaining what they once had. On the other hand, she was afraid of what he might say. If he were to admit that he had doubts about them, it would crush her even more and make it impossible for her to ever have faith in their relationship again.

Some of her uneasiness left her when she glanced over and saw him leaning against the passenger's side window with his eyes closed. She was glad he was sleeping, not only because it killed the tension between them, but also because, unlike her, Hector hadn't slept all day and needed the rest. She listened to the songs playing over her car speakers and let her tears fall freely.

Gertie drove for another hour before the lights of Delphi came into view in the distance. She and Hector weren't going to the modern city, however. Apollo's sacred temple, which led to Gaia's cave, was part of the ancient city and its ruins. It was a place for archaeologists and tourists. Unlike the modern city in the distance, there were no lights, no restaurants, and no hotels lining the road. Except for the light from Selene's silver chariot, the hillside lay in darkness.

Not wanting to drive as far as the museum, Gertie pulled over on the side of the road near the Sacred Path to Apollo's temple, not far from the reconstructed Athenian Treasury. It was one of several statues believed to have been built by the city-states as a form of tithe to the gods.

Gertie parked the car and cut the engine. When Hector didn't stir, she reached over to give his shoulder a shake.

"Hector? Hector, wake up. We're here."

He blinked with heavy lids. "Huh? Oh. Okay."

She stifled a smile. His disoriented expression and sleepy eyes were adorable to her. She wished she felt comfortable enough to move in for a hug.

"You can wait here if you want to keep sleeping," she offered.

"Huh? No. No way. Let's go."

Using the flashlight app on her phone, she led him up the Sacred Path past the Athenian Treasury, toward the famous Sybil Rock, on which the oracles once stood and gave their prophecies. The path continued toward the Stoa, a kind of covered porch where the ancient Athenians once held their market. Beyond that was a stadium and the sacred temple of Apollo—or its ruins.

What the tourists and archaeologists did not know was that Sybil Rock marked the secret entrance to Gaia's cave. Standing at least three meters high and two meters wide, this outcrop of stone jutting from the ground was a natural pulpit for Apollo's oracles. And if one were to climb over the rock and off the beaten path and go up the mountainside for another hundred yards, one would eventually find the mouth of a cave. Hector and Gertie had discovered it together the last time they'd come, with the help of Apollo's oracle.

Together, Gertie and Hector ascended the steep climb toward the opening in the mountainside. It was small and inconspicuous. Although it was likely that archaeologists and others had stumbled upon this narrow cavern, it was unlikely that Gaia had revealed herself to them. She was very particular about making appearances.

The last time Gertie had come here with Hector, Gaia had been waiting for them near the mouth of the cave. Tonight, however, there was no sign of her.

"Grandmother?" Gertie called.

When there was no answer, Getie and Hector continued through the tunnel's descent into the mountain.

Only a few minutes had passed when a figure came out of the darkness glowing like an ember. She had long auburn hair, dark brown eyes, and dark bronze skin. Gertie recognized her as the woman who had basically raised her for the first seventeen years of her life.

"Grandmother!" Gertie cried as she threw her arms around the goddess.

"My sweet girl!" Gaia returned the embrace. "It's so nice to hold you this way again."

Over Gertie's shoulder, Gaia said, "Hello, Hector."

"Hello, goddess."

Although Gertie's back was to him, she imagined Hector was bowing in reverence to Mother Earth. Gertie probably should have done the same, but the goddess was too familiar to her.

"Listen to me," Gaia said, taking Gertie by the shoulders and squaring herself to her granddaughter. "I know why you're here. James sent you, yes?"

Gertie nodded.

"He wants you to know that he's safe. He's gone into hiding."

Gertie glanced back at Hector before returning her gaze to Gaia. "Why, Grandmother? Please tell me it's not because he's a bad man."

"He's a good man who has done bad things," the goddess replied.

Gertie's stomach twisted into a knot. "So, he knew about the smuggling on the STS ships." She thought she might be sick.

"He was doing it to protect his family," Gaia said.

"To protect his family?" Hector repeated. "In what way?"

Gaia released Gertie and sat on a ledge of stone. "It happened last year. I knew about it, too. I'm just as culpable."

"Grandmother, what are you talking about?"

"After you moved to Greece," Gaia began. "That's when James discovered what was happening on those shipping vessels. But before he could do anything about it, a powerful god threatened to destroy him and your family if he didn't keep quiet."

"What god? Helios?" Gertie asked.

Hector gave Gertie a look of bewilderment. "Why would you say that? The sun god wouldn't do such a thing."

"No, I don't think it was Helios. The truth is, I'm not sure who it was. But when James prayed to me about it, I could tell from what he said that it was a god, and I advised him to stay out of the way of the deity."

"So, he kept quiet," Gertie said.

Gaia nodded. "When Hector confronted him a few days ago, James feared the mortal authorities would soon come for him, so I hid him."

"Where is he?" Hector asked.

"He's with Metis. She's watching over him."

"Metis?" Gertie repeated. "Why would the mother of Poros and Athena agree to watch over my stepfather?"

"Because she's in hiding, too," Gaia said. "And because I asked her to."

"I thought she lived with her sisters—Clymene and Dione—in the East China Sea," Gertie said. "That's what Hermie and Hestie told me."

"She did live there, up until the end of the rebellion. After she swallowed Zeus and Hera, it was necessary for her to go into hiding forever."

"But why?" Hector asked. "If the rebellion was over, why did she need to hide?"

"Because Zeus still has sympathizers," Gaia explained. "Metis doesn't want to risk being overcome by those who would do whatever it takes to set Zeus and Hera free."

"I had a dream," Gertie began, trying to recall the details. "I'm supposed to see Metis. The future depends on it. Do you know where she is, Grandmother?"

"I do," she said, "but it's my most heavily guarded secret, the most important secret of this age. Please tell me that I can trust you and Hector with it."

"You told my stepfather the most important secret of this age?" Gertie said, incredulous. "Was that wise?"

"He doesn't know where he is, sweet girl," Gaia said.

Hector covered his heart with his hand. "I swear on the River Styx. You can trust us."

When Hestie entered the throne room, Hades held out his hand and summoned his helm, exposing her to the others seated around the chunky wooden table.

"Hestie!" her mother cried as she flew to Hestie's side. "Thank the gods."

"Quit saying that," Hestie said. "It annoys me."

"Hestie!" her father said with a disapproving tone. "Don't speak to your mother that way. We were worried sick. What were you thinking? Stealing the *helm*?"

"I was thinking that I needed to take matters into my own hands," Hestie said, unapologetically. "One thing I've learned since becoming a goddess is that you can't trust others to help you."

"Don't say that," Jen said. "You can always count on us."

"Hestie, has something happened?" Hermie asked.

Hermes leaned forward. "She knows something."

"Phorcys took Rhode hostage some time ago," Hestie said. "Then he captured Amphitrite during a failed rescue mission."

Jinsoo whispered to Hermie. "Who was captured?"

"Poseidon's wife and daughter," Hermie whispered to Jinsoo.

"Phorcys has threatened to swallow them if Poseidon doesn't do what he says," Hestie explained.

"So that's why Poseidon has been such a butt," Jinsoo muttered.

Hermie turned to Del. "You made a point of teaching us that abductors don't kill, or in this case swallow, their prisoners because to do so would mean forfeiting their leverage."

Del cleared her throat. "That's only true when there's *one* prisoner. If our enemies have multiple prisoners…well, they only need one."

"Hermes, did you know about this?" Hades asked.

Hermes dropped his head. "Okay, okay. Yes, I knew. But I was afraid if *you* knew, you would side against me with the other Olympians."

Hip threw up his arms with frustration. "We have to work together, man."

"You should have told us what we were up against, my lord," Raimo said.

"Would you have acted any differently?" Hermes asked his vampires.

"We might have tried to reason with Poseidon," Alastair offered.

"His wife and daughter are at risk of being swallowed for all eternity by the father of monsters," Hermes pointed out. "There is no reasoning with Poseidon. On the other hand, dozens of innocent Syrian rebels are being captured by their government and smuggled to Russia as payment for weapons of mass destruction. The Furies confirmed this, with their interrogation of the dead Syrians you found."

"What about Helios?" Morpheus asked.

Hermie whispered to Jinsoo, "Poseidon's daughter is the wife of Helios."

Jinsoo cocked his head to the side. "And Helios is?"

"The sun god," Alastair whispered from across the table.

"He's compromised, too," Hermes said.

"What does Phorcys want?" Hades asked.

Hermes shrugged. "I'm sure it has something to do with power."

"It does," Hestie said. "Some Syrian officials have promised to build him a temple."

"A temple for the old man of the sea?" Persephone cried with her brows lifted.

Hestie told them what she'd learned from Athena's conversations with Ares and Aphrodite.

"Good work," Hades said to Hestie. Then, turning to Hermes, he added, "It sounds like Ares and Aphrodite support you."

"They're the minority, I assure you," the messenger god replied.

"I think Athena feels caught in the middle," Hestie offered.

"They all feel that way," Hermes said. "But the council voted to support Poseidon because they were afraid of establishing a precedent."

"What precedent?" Hestie asked.

"The precedent of ignoring the threat of one deity to swallow another," her father clarified.

Hermie lifted a finger. "But what about the precedent of negotiating with terrorists? By giving in to Phorcys's demands, the Olympians encourage future abductions."

"The boy has a point," Hades said. "I was wondering the same thing."

"Athena wants to play a long game," Hermes said. "She's only pretending to appease Phorcys, just long enough to give Apollo and Artemis time to curry favor with the Syrian officials."

"That's what the twins are up to?" Persephone asked.

"As far as I know," Hermes said.

Just then, Hecate entered the room. "According to my spell, Prometheus and Poros are at Poseidon's castle."

"I knew it," Jinsoo moaned.

"Let's stick to the plan," Hermes said.

Hades clapped his hands together. "Agreed. Some of us will bait and ambush the tritons while the rest of us rescue Prometheus and Poros from Poseidon's Castle."

Hermie found Pegasus in the stables with the other horses belonging to the Underworld gods. Swift and Sure belonged to Hades and Persephone. Stormy, Midnight, and Thunder were Hermie's parents' horses. And Hershey and The General belonged to Hip and Jen. Like the others, the winged horse was eating fresh hay in his own stall and seemed content for the time being.

"Hopefully, it won't be long before we get you out of here," Hermie said as he stroked the horse's mane.

Hades's black stallions, Swift and Sure, snorted, letting Hermie know that they were jealous of the attention he was giving to Pegasus. Hermie flew over to their stall and gave them each a quick brushing. They practically purred.

Brushing the horses was therapy for Hermie. He was nervous about his part in the mission to rescue Poros and Prometheus because he hated being underwater. He hated all things slimy and all things with sharp teeth. Going up against Poseidon and his creepy tritons was one thing; but, if Phorcys and the sea monsters were involved, he could only imagine what might happen.

He shuddered. It wasn't death he feared; it was pain.

"I know how you feel," Del said from behind him. "The key is to focus on the prize rather than the process."

"Easier said than done," he said, glancing over his shoulder at her.

"True."

He wondered if Del had come to see him or the horses.

"You," she said.

He put the brush away and left the stall to talk to her.

"I haven't had a chance to thank you," she said, "for helping to evacuate us from the ship."

Hermie shrugged. "I didn't do much. It was my father and Hades."

"You don't give yourself enough credit."

Hermie smiled at her. That was something his mother had often told him, too.

"It's true," she said. "And the fact that you're terrified of pain makes the things you do even more courageous."

He laughed. "I wouldn't say *that*."

She shook her head and took a step closer. "No, you wouldn't."

Was she going to kiss him?

"Is that okay?" she asked.

"But I thought you said…"

"Are you really going to argue with me about this right now?"

"No."

Without wasting another second, he brushed his lips against hers. They were soft and supple and, surprisingly, tasted of oranges.

"That would be my new lip gloss." She smiled up at him, and his heart seemed to stop beating altogether.

"What is happening?" he asked, more confused than ever.

"I just wanted to give you a kiss for luck."

"Thank you." Then he gave her a half smile. Mina had always been direct and blunt about what she wanted from Hermie. Delphina was an enigma. "I wish I could read *your* mind."

To his surprise, she took his hands and said, "Do it."

"I thought you said opening your mind to others wasn't easy for vampires."

"I *want* you to do it."

Hermie swallowed hard and closed his eyes. Like the other time she had opened her mind to him—when she'd wanted him to understand how she felt about Mina's death—he had to dig around to pick up on something. He felt again as if he were trying to listen to a single person in a crowded room where lots of people were talking.

Then he heard it—or saw it, rather. It was a vision of Taavi's desiccated body crumbling from the main deck of the ship and into the sea. He heard the new fear among the many thoughts that were twisted into knots, needing to be teased apart: *None of us knows what the future brings. It is something we cannot control. For this reason, we should live in the present whenever possible.*

Hermie opened his eyes and studied Del's face.

"I was wrong," she said. "I understand that now. I cannot live my life in fear of what the future might bring. I have to focus on the present."

"I suppose that's true."

"I want to live in the present with you, Hermie."

A lump rose to his throat. He wondered if he was dreaming. Was Morpheus playing a trick on him?

Del grinned. "This is not a trick, but I know it is a lot to process, and we have work to do."

He nodded, still unable to find words, still unsure of what her words implied.

She gave his hands a squeeze and dropped them. "Time to go. Ready?"

He took a deep breath, finally able to speak again. "I'm never ready for scary shit, but let's go."

<u>CHAPTER SIXTEEN</u>

Sky and Sea

Gertie's eyes widened, and, for a moment, she wondered if she had heard her grandmother correctly. "Did you say *Greenland?*"

Gaia nodded. "She's with Aether, the god of the upper sky. His cave is in the highest mountain peak north of the Arctic Circle."

"That's a long way from here," Hector pointed out.

"Yes," Gaia agreed, "but if Gertie believes she must see Metis, I know a way that won't take long at all. Would you like me to show you, sweet girl?"

"Yes, please," Gertie said eagerly.

"Follow me."

Gaia stood up from the ledge where she'd been sitting and led Gertie and Hector toward the mouth of her cave, where, moments later, a rainbow appeared. The vibrant colors shimmered and parted, and the beautiful three-foot-tall Iris flew with her golden wings into the cave beside Gaia.

"You called, my lady?" Iris asked.

"How many times have I told you not to call me *my lady*, Iris? We're equals. We didn't free you from Hera just to subjugate you again."

"Old habits die hard, as they say," the rainbow goddess said. "Is there something I can do for you?"

Gaia turned to Gertie and Hector. "This is my most trusted friend. We can count on her to keep our secret—not to mention, she's the fastest, after Hermes."

Iris arched a brow. "What's going on, Gaia?"

"Do you have time to fly these two up to Aether's cave?" Gaia asked the other goddess. "Gertie had a vision, and it may be important, or I wouldn't have bothered you."

"You never bother me," Iris said. "I'm happy to help you however I can."

"Thank you, my friend," Gertie's grandmother said.

Iris turned to Gertie and Hector with outstretched arms. "Come."

Gaia blew Gertie a kiss goodbye as Gertie and Hector each took one of the rainbow goddess's hands. In less than a second, she and Hector were flying with Iris through her magnificent rainbow arch.

Once she'd recovered from the shock, Gertie cried, "This is amazing!" as the vibrant colors shimmered and glowed all around her. She'd been inside Iris's rainbow before but not while flying through it at this incredible speed.

She glanced over at Hector to find him looking just as incredulous as she. The trip was like a combination of the best rollercoaster with the most colorful disco ball.

Then, after maybe thirty minutes had passed, everything stopped, and they were standing on a snow-covered mountain ledge thousands of feet in the air beneath the dark sky.

It was freezing cold and hard to breathe.

"I'll wait for you here," Iris said. "I assume you need a ride back?"

"Yes," Hector said through chattering teeth. "Thank you, goddess."

Hector bowed reverently, so Gertie did the same, even though she felt a little wobbly from the trip and was shivering from the cold.

Hector moved close to Gertie and put his arms around her, to generate body heat between them. Her body relaxed in his arms, and the anxiety, which had made every muscle in her body clench, lessened.

"Hello?" Hector said into the cave, where a dim light danced along the stone walls.

A god with long white hair, a long white beard, silver eyes, and pale skin appeared wearing a white robe made of wool. "Who are you? And why have you come?"

Hector bowed deeply. "Hello, Aether."

"Gaia sent us," Gertie said, bowing when she saw Hector doing so. Showing reverence didn't come naturally to her. "Um, I'm a daughter of Dionysus and granddaughter of Gaia. I have visions. I saw myself speaking with Metis."

The god flew past them to the ledge, where Iris was waiting.

"You can trust them," Gertie heard Iris say.

When the white-haired god returned, he did not seem pleased. He had frown lines around his silver eyes, which seemed to penetrate right though Gertie. As he motioned for them to follow, he mumbled, "The more people who know a secret, the less likely it remains one."

Gertie and Hector said nothing as they followed him inside the cozy cave.

A fire danced in a fireplace made of rock at the very back of a room, which was about twenty feet in diameter. Above the fireplace was a mantle where bowls and pots were stacked. Flanking the fireplace were a couch and a bed with a table between them. Sitting on the couch was a beautiful goddess with long raven hair and startling gray eyes. Her resemblance to Athena was obvious.

"Metis," Gertie blurted out.

Hector bowed reverently, and Gertie followed suit, wondering where James her stepfather, was. Had Gaia misled her?

"It's a pleasure to meet you," Hector said.

"I've been expecting you." Metis motioned to the bed across from her, where someone appeared to be sleeping beneath blankets of wool. Could that be James?

Gertie sat on the edge of the bed, of what felt like a mattress stuffed with feathers. Hector sat close beside her, wrapping his arms around her shoulders to keep her warm. The heat from the fireplace helped, but it wasn't enough to combat the biting cold seeping in from the mouth of the cave.

The god of the upper air took a seat beside Metis. "It would have been nice for me to know that you expected them."

"I wasn't sure when it would happen," Metis said to him. "It might have been years from now. You would have forgotten by then."

"But it wasn't years from now. It was today," the white-haired god complained.

"We can bicker about it later, dear," Metis said turning back to Gertie and Hector. "If you're here, then there's no time to waste. Something I foresaw months ago is already upon us."

Hermie felt apprehensive as he sat between Jinsoo and Morpheus in the back of Hades's chariot, not because they were parked on the bottom of the Mediterranean Sea, or because there was a huge, scary octopus less than a mile away. No, Hermie felt apprehensive because Del was hovering beneath a merchant ship pretending to be the lookout while Raimo, Mahdi, and Penny boarded the vessel above her.

Del usually looked intimidating to Hermie, but right now she seemed small and vulnerable, and it took every ounce of his strength not to swim to her side to defend her against whatever might come.

He had tried to convince the others to let him be the pretend lookout. The vampires were too easy for tritons to destroy. A snap of the neck was all it took. And gods forbid, should Poseidon appear with his trident again…Hermie shuddered as a vision of Taavi's desiccated corpse appeared in his head for the millionth time.

But the others were right when they'd argued that the tritons were more likely to attack if they saw vampire pirates. Their vendetta against the vampires was as old as they were.

And yet, many minutes went by with no sign of the mercreatures. Hermie glanced around at the watchful faces of those in the chariot with him. They sat four to a bench, with Hip astride Swift. It was necessary that everyone be in or touching the chariot or its stallions to be protected by the helm of invisibility, worn by Hades. Hermie was in the back with Alastair, Jinsoo, and Morpheus. In the front, Hades sat between Hermes and Thanatos, who held Therese in his lap. Everyone was on their guard for the appearance of the tritons.

Hermie wondered how long the gods would wait before calling the mission a flop. The tritons were probably busy guarding their prisoners—Prometheus and Poros. He feared the gods and vampires were wasting valuable time. In fact, he hoped they were, because he didn't like his girlfriend being used as bait.

Del glanced back at him, making his heart skip a beat. He knew she couldn't see him sitting there beneath the protection of the helm. But could she sense him? Hear his thoughts?

Be careful, he said to her telepathically.

Hermie was also worried about Hestie and the rescue team. They had gone ahead to Poseidon's Castle to rescue Prometheus and Poros. Jen, Persephone, Sophia, and Bach were with her, along with Hermie's father and Uncle Hip, who were on *both* teams because of their power of disintegration—the ability to be in multiple places at once.

Just when Hermie had begun to relax and believe nothing would happen, the tritons appeared in the distance swimming at their top speed toward Del and the small vessel she was hovering beneath. Hermie's heart picked up speed as all the air left his lungs. It was hard to watch a herd of powerful monsters swimming toward Del and not scream.

Del was immediately captured by two of the tritons while others surrounded the ship. Hermie was supposed to wait to flank the herd on the right with Jinsoo and Morpheus, but he broke protocol and swam to Del's aid. He felt like he was operating on autopilot and was vaguely aware of what he was doing as he slit the throat of one triton from behind and stabbed the chest of the other with his blade.

As he took Del in his arms, he came to his senses and noticed that he'd attracted the attention of the entire herd of tritons. The mercreatures swam toward him and Del with their vicious teeth bared.

Hermie folded Del in his arms, wanting to use his body as a shield around her; however, she resisted, turned her back to him, and pulled out her blades. He did the same, mentally preparing himself for the onslaught.

When the herd reached them, Hermie and Del struck with their blades. The tritons were fast and vicious, like rabid wolves, and their viciousness took Hermie by surprise. He held his breath as he jabbed, swung, sliced.

Hestie followed the rescue team through the Aegean Sea toward Poseidon's Castle. She was grateful that her father and uncle had the gift of disintegration. They were the only beings in existence to have it. Death and Sleep needed to be in multiple places at once, so they could multiply to an indefinite number. Her father once told her that the highest number he'd disintegrated into was three million, but he could go higher if needed. Unfortunately, if even one version of him was wounded or captured, every other version would revert and reintegrate into the wounded or captured version.

Persephone led their team to an outcrop of boulders about a mile away from the castle, where they paused to observe their surroundings. There appeared to be two mermaids guarding the front entrance.

"I'll disintegrate and check the back," her father said. A few seconds later, he said, "Two in the back as well."

"We'll take the front," Persephone said of her, Hestie, and Bach. "Jen and Sophia, take the back. Than and Hip…"

"We know," Hip said with a wink. "We got you."

Hestie's father and uncle disintegrated so that they could accompany both groups—one to the back and the other to the front of the castle.

It wasn't difficult for them to disarm the mermaids of their weapons and bind their wrists with seaweed. The rescue team acted quickly, knowing there would be more guards to face indoors. Together, Hestie and the other gods pried open the castle door and were immediately stunned by what they found inside.

Two vertical body-sized tubes were filled with water and chained to the palace floor. Large electric eels swam in circles along the outside of the tubes, rubbing against the metal chains. Inside the tubes floating upright with their eyes closed and their arms as lifeless as puppets were Poros and Prometheus.

Tears filled Hestie's eyes as a feeling of dread filled her heart. The sight of Poros looking dead as he floated in his glass coffin was enough to make her want to wail out with desperation. She hurt for Prometheus, too; but, deep inside, she knew it was the sight of Poros and the thought of losing him that made her want to punch something, to destroy something.

She looked around the room, expecting guards, but saw none.

"I've seen this before," her father said, the bubbles from his mouth momentarily obscuring her view of him. "The electric eels against the metal create a powerful forcefield of electricity."

"What do we do, Dad?" Hestie asked as she treaded water beside him and tried not to panic. "Are they dead?"

"No. They're alive. Probably paralyzed by the trident," he said.

Hestie gasped and choked on the sudden intake of water.

Bach's voice spoke inside Hestie's head. *Vampires cannot hear underwater. Remember to communicate with us telepathically. What should we do?*

Jen swam up to get a closer look. *Oh my gods.*

Hip conjured a spear and threw it at one of the tubes. When the spearhead hit the tube, it caused an electric flare that propelled the weapon away. It shot across the room and struck a back stone wall.

Should we destroy the electric eels? Thanatos asked everyone telepathically. *It would be a shame, since they're innocents and, unlike the tritons, can't come back.*

"We need Mom," Hestie said suddenly. To the vamps, she said, *My mom can use her arrows to make the eels cooperate. It's her special gift.*

Good thinking, her father said. *If the eels swim away, we can break the tubes without the danger of an electric explosion.*

"Should I bring her, or will you?" Hip asked his brother.

"I'm already on it," Than replied.

"Don't risk god-travel bringing her here," Persephone said. "Use the chariot." *And the rest of you, stay on your guard. This could be a trap. I don't like how quiet it is around here.*

"I'm anxious to hear what you have to say," Gertie said to Metis. "But, first, I have to know, is that my stepfather, James?" She pointed to the lump beneath the wool blankets.

"Yes," the goddess said. "I gave him an herb to help."

"What she means to say is that he was annoying us, so we put him out of our misery," Aether said with a chuckle.

"The herb is safe," Metis added gently before giving Aether a look of irritation. "Now, trust me when I say that time is of the essence. The sins of the father will be the burden of the son."

Gertie had the strangest feeling of déjà vu. "I remember you saying that to me—or, in my vision of the future, I recalled you saying that to me. What does it mean?"

"Listen to me, Gertie," Metis insisted. "Poseidon has created a diversion to lure Hades and his family from the Underworld. While they're away, Poseidon will lead Phorcys, Keto, and their family of sea monsters to the Titan Pit, where they will release all Titan prisoners who pledge allegiance to Phorcys. Hydra is already waiting for her parents to help them overcome Cerberus. Cerberus is one of their children, too; but, unlike Hydra, the three-headed-dog is loyal to Hades."

Gertie turned to Hector, trying to take it all in. "Oh, my gods. What do we do?"

Metis leaned forward. "You need to return to the Underworld with Iris, take your bull form, and stand with Cerberus against the sea monsters."

"You want me to fight the monsters?" Gertie thought she was being asked the impossible.

Metis nodded. "While Gertie heads to the Underworld, Hector must dive from Iris's rainbow into the Aegean Sea and inform Hades and his family of Phorcys's true plan. I have no other way to get them a message without giving away my location to my enemies, and the priority for Iris is to get you to the Underworld."

"What about Aether?" Hector said. "Wouldn't it be faster if he took the message to Hades?"

Metis frowned. "He refuses to involve himself in the conflicts of the gods. His name should be Aloof."

"Neutral," Aether said. "I remain neutral."

"Aloof, indifferent, unmoved," Metis complained.

"I let you move in, didn't I?" Aether said to Metis.

Metis turned to Gertie and Hector. "You know what to do. Now, go!"

Gertie stared blankly at Metis, still trying to process all she'd been told.

"Go!" Metis said again.

Hector took Gertie's hand, and she stumbled behind him to the ledge, where Iris was waiting.

"I heard," Iris assured them "Take my hand."

Iris pulled Gertie and Hector through her rainbow across the world back toward Greece and the Aegean Sea, the home of Poseidon's Castle. As they flew, Gertie continued to process what she'd been told. The sea monsters were attempting to infiltrate the Underworld? Their goal was to free any Titans pledging allegiance to them? How could the gods have allowed this to happen? Wasn't there anyone in Hades protecting that realm?

Less than thirty minutes flew by when Iris parted the glorious colors and shoved Hector into the air. Gertie screamed as she watched Hector tumble toward the sea, flailing his arms and legs, until he hit the water and disappeared beneath it.

Before Gertie could object, they were flying through the rainbow again.

"Wait!" Gertie cried, but Iris didn't stop until they were near the gates to the Underworld, where Cerberus, the three-headed-dog stood guarding the entrance to Hades.

"Transform," Iris said. "I sense the monsters at our backs."

"I can't just turn," Gertie said. "I-there's a process."

"Then you better get started, pronto," Iris said, looking over her shoulder.

That's when Gertie saw them. Hydra led the sea monsters through a narrow chasm, swimming in the Acheron toward Cerberus and the tall iron gate. Gertie ran along the bank ahead of them, focusing on her bull form and praying to her father, Dionysus, to please find it in his heart to help her.

CHAPTER SEVENTEEN

Help

Hermie was relieved when he and Del managed to thwart the first line of attack by the tritons, and even more relieved when he was faced with—not another triton, but his father. Hip and Than had amassed an army and, with the help of the other gods and vampires, had picked off the herd from behind.

As the gods and vampires returned to the chariot, victorious, Hermie apologized again and again for not sticking to the plan. He was mortified not only because he had let down his team, but also because he had exposed his deep feelings for Del to the rest of them, including his parents.

"You were the perfect bait," Hermes said once they were all back in the chariot and preparing to head to Poseidon's Castle. "It couldn't have gone any better."

"But the next time you disobey my orders," Hades said, "there will be consequences."

Hermie was relieved that no one was angry with him. As they piled into the chariot, he offered Del his lap and was glad when she accepted. Most of them were doubled up, so no one gave him any funny looks as he circled his arms around her slender waist.

He was pleasantly surprised when Hades drove the chariot up into the sky rather than through the water. Everything seemed to be going his way. Next, they would rescue Poros and Captain, and all would be well again, until October 20th, when he was destined to disarm the warheads.

He sucked in his lips, trying to stifle the enormous grin that wanted to cross his face. He'd rather not broadcast his jubilance to the others, though he suspected he was doing so unwittingly to the vampires. Oh, well. Why should he care if they knew? He was in love, he was happy, and he would soon be a hero.

Then his father told them what he saw in Poseidon's Castle: tubes powered by electric eels holding the paralyzed bodies of Poros and Prometheus.

"We need you and your arrows," Than said to Hermie's mother.

"What the hell is that?" Hades said from upfront, where he held the reins.

"That's Hector," Morpheus said. "Did Iris just push him out of her rainbow?"

"I think so," Therese said.

Hermie gasped at the sight of Hector tumbling toward the sea.

"Should I go after him?" Alastair offered. "I'm the fastest flyer."

"That title belongs to Hermes," Hades said. "Even so, we should all stay beneath the helm, in case this is a trap."

Hades turned the stallions and directed the chariot in what felt like a nosedive toward the flailing body of Hector. Hermie felt his bottom leave the seat of the chariot. He held on to Del and to Jinsoo beside him, who was gripping the side of the chariot with both hands. Hermie tried not to show on his face the terror that he felt in his stomach. He hated the feeling of falling, even though he knew he could fly.

"Lord Hades," Morpheus cried. "Please let me take my chances and go to Iris. Something must be wrong."

"What does your father say?" Hades asked as they neared the water's surface.

"Go to her," Hip said from where he sat astride Swift. "I'll follow."

Hermie's winged cousin took off, along with another version of Hip. Hermie gritted his teeth and clung to Del as they prepared to plunge into the sea.

Gertie ran along the bank of the Acheron River toward Cerberus, who growled at her as she approached. Her anger at the situation, at this *completely helpless* situation, was involuntarily expressed by Gertie with a snort. She reached out with her arms, which became forelegs, and she felt the rocky bank pounding against hooves. It was a strange feeling that she might never get used to, but she was grateful for it; for, in her bull form, she was as big as Cerberus if not as powerful.

"I'm here to help!" she said to the three-headed beast.

The sea monsters were on her heels. Cerberus took a chance on her and opened the gate to let her through just in time. He snapped the gate shut, and the two of them held it closed—Cerberus with his forelegs and Gertie with her bull horns—as the sea monsters bore down on it, hissing and shrieking and seething with hate.

Gertie had never seen Cerberus growling and barking so ferociously and up close. He was a force to be reckoned with as he shoved his weight against the gate. Gertie, beside him, bore down, too, snorting and growling at the sea monsters.

Echidna, a goddess with a serpent tail, swung her tail hard against the gate repeatedly. Ladon and his one hundred serpent heads came up behind her and did the same, causing the iron hinges to break. Chimera, who had the heads of a lion, a goat, and a serpent, grabbed one of the bars between her lion's teeth and pulled, again and again, until the door of the gate broke free. Hydra hissed and shoved Gertie aside with her giant dragon head as Phorcys and his monstrous mermaid wife broke through.

Gertie heard a voice shout from behind her, "Fall back!"

She turned to see Charon, the old ferryman, standing on the bank of the River Styx, beckoning to her and Cerberus.

Still in her bull form, Gertie scrambled behind Cerberus and Charon along the riverbank toward Tartarus, where the three Furies and Hecate stood ready with their spears and their familiars. The Furies' hair had turned into hissing snakes. Meg's falcon was shrieking, and Tisiphone's white wolf growled. Alecto's wings were out, and she and her snake were ready to strike.

Hecate, too, looked fierce with her spear in one hand and a blade in the other. Her black Doberman stood beside her baring her teeth.

Gertie, Cerberus, and Charon joined them, and together they formed a line stretching from the Phlegethon to the River Styx as the sea monsters attacked. The Furies and Hecate launched their spears at the sea monsters while Cerberus clawed and snapped. Gertie struck blindly with her bull horns at the mass of creatures and screamed with pain when Chimera bit through her flesh.

Phorcys broke through their line and dove into the River Styx. Keto, his vicious mermaid wife, followed. They were swimming for the Titan Pit!

Then, when Gertie thought that things couldn't get any worse, Poseidon appeared behind the sea monsters bearing his trident. He pointed it toward her and her allies and shot his paralyzing beam at them. Gertie and her allies scattered.

Not sure which way to turn, Gertie ran toward the Titan Pit after the old man of the sea and his wife. Poseidon flew past her, shooting his trident and barely missing her.

From a distance, she saw Phorcys and Keto at the pit door. The deadbolts and adamantine chains would surely prevent them from opening it. If they didn't, the state-of-the-art security system installed by Hermie last year should stop them. So, what were they doing? She stopped in her tracks to listen and observe. They were shouting at the prisoners within to join Phorcys in overthrowing the Olympians!

She recalled from her books that monsters did not have the power of telepathy afforded to other deities, which explained why the Titans didn't know that Phorcys and Keto were coming. Gertie could hear them on the other side of the door, asking questions. Phorcys growled messages of overthrowing the Olympians.

The old man of the sea said, "Poros, the most powerful, is paralyzed. So is his keeper, Prometheus. Poseidon is at my mercy, as I hold his wife and daughter prisoner. Zeus and Hera have been swallowed. The other Olympians are divided. Now is the time to regain our reign. Follow me, and I will lead the old gods to victory!"

Then Gertie saw Poseidon aim his trident at the locks and chains on the pit door. Little by little, his powerful beam seemed to be wearing down the locks. Meanwhile, behind her, the other monsters were fighting their way toward Gertie. Morpheus had joined the ranks of her allies, but one more god wasn't enough to hold back the sea monsters.

What should Gertie do? Should she attack Poseidon, who would likely paralyze her? Or turn back to face the other monsters? Or should she wait for the Titan door to be breached to face the onslaught of prisoners? Gertie prayed to her father, to Hades, and to the other Underworld gods in a desperate plea for help. What chance did she and the others have against a mob of angry Titans?

Hermie held on to Jinsoo and Del as Hades drove them in a straight line toward the sea. Even with god vision, the black sea beneath the starless sky looked like a sheet of slate with nothing beyond it. Out of habit, he held his breath when the horses and chariot penetrated the surface. Then he blinked as his eyes adjusted to being underwater. Above them in the distance, Hector's body flailed. The chariot sped toward him. Hermes reached out and grabbed Hector by the shirt before dragging him into the already crowded vehicle. Then the stallions pulled them out of the sea and back into the dark sky. Hermie finally breathed again.

Hector coughed and gagged and shivered.

"Hector, what happened?" Jinsoo cried in a shrill voice from where he sat on Alastair's lap.

"What's going on, man?" Hermie wanted to know.

"Are you okay?" Mahdi asked from underneath Bach.

The presence of Hermie's Uncle Hip made Hector yawn; but it was his father's presence that put Hector's life in jeopardy.

Realizing this at once, the two gods risked exposure and left the chariot to hover at a distance beneath Selene's chariot, so Hector could explain himself.

"Metis told me to warn you," Hector began through chattering teeth.

Gertie felt paralyzed with indecision. Poseidon's trident was wearing down the locks on the door to the Titan Pit, while Phorcys preached to the Titans waiting on the other side. His mermaid wife stood guarding her husband and the door, her fierce eyes trained on Gertie in her bull form. As Gertie prepared to charge the door, she glanced back again at her allies and saw something that gave her renewed hope. Her father, Dionysus, had joined the battle in defense of the Underworld. He swung his sword and sliced off Chimera's serpent head. This caused Keto and Phorcys to shriek and scramble to defend their monstrous children. Gertie was overwhelmed with shock and gratitude. Her father had answered her prayers!

When she glanced back at the door to the pit, however, she was horrified to see the locks breaking and the door creaking open ever so slightly. The fingers and hands of prisoners slipped through the small opening, reminding Gertie of a scene from a zombie book. She took a deep breath and charged the door with her horns leading. Then she thrusted with her full force against the door, ramming it shut. In the next instant, she felt a sharp pain course through her body. Her legs and head convulsed for many seconds before her mind went blank and everything was dark.

Hestie was alarmed when, in the distance, Hades's chariot dashed by at the speed of light. Weren't the gods on the other team going to stop to help?

She was relieved when her father appeared with her mother.

"Why didn't the others stop, too?" Hestie asked as her mother began shooting her harmless arrows into the electric eels and telling them to swim away. Her arrows worked on animals like Cupid's did on people. They made their target fall in love with Therese and want to do her bidding. Unfortunately, they only worked on mortal animals and not on immortal monsters.

"Poseidon and the sea monsters are attacking the Underworld," her father explained. "Oh, my gods. It's worse than we thought."

"The gate is broken, and Cerberus is gone," Hip added.

"The sea monsters," Than cried.

Suddenly Hestie's father and uncle disappeared.

"What?" Persephone cried.

"Oh, no," Jen said with a pale face. "I'm going to see what's happened."

"You're going to risk god-travel?" Persephone asked her.

Jen nodded and vanished.

"Stay focused," Persephone said to Therese, who had also turned pale.

"What do you think happened?" Hestie asked, afraid of the answer.

"One of two things, as you know," Persephone said as Therese got the last of the electric eels to leave the castle.

Please, tell us what's happening, Bach said telepathically.

Hestie nodded. *My father and uncle have either been injured or captured while helping the others to stop the sea monsters, who have apparently infiltrated the Underworld.*

Hermie held onto Del and Jinsoo as Hades drove the chariot with lightning speed from the dark sky above the Aegean to the gates of the Underworld.

When they arrived near Cerberus's post, Hermie was shocked to see the tall iron gate busted off its hinges and lying on the bank of the Acheron. Cerberus was gone. There wasn't a soul in sight.

He followed the other gods from the chariot along the Acheron to where it met the Styx.

"This way!" Hades, leading the charge beneath the helm of invisibility, cried.

They flew along the River Styx past Tartarus. Hector ran along the bank below.

Along the way, Hermie saw Chimera's decapitated serpent head and three of Ladon's one hundred heads floating in the River Styx. Then they passed Tizzie's injured wolf lying on the bank of the Phelegethon being guarded by Meg's falcon. As they approached the abode of the Furies, they came upon Cerberus, who was whining due to a severed leg.

"Hold tight, boy!" Hades called from somewhere beneath the helm.

Up ahead, Phorcys, Keto, Echidna, Hydra, and what was left of Ladon and Chimera screeched and flailed and fought with claws, teeth, and tail against Hecate, the Furies, Morpheus, Charon, and, of all gods, Dionysus.

That's when Hermie saw them: On the other side of the battle, the Titan prisoners were attempting to push open the door to the pit. The only thing stopping them was the limp body of an enormous bull.

"Gertie?" Hector cried as he ran through the battle to Gertie's side.

Hermie conjured his sword and rushed alongside Del and the others to fight but stopped short when he saw his father and uncle lying on the rocky bank of the Styx.

Hestie's mother shot one of her arrows at one of the tubes. A tiny crack appeared in the glass. She shot at the other, creating a crack there, too.

Hestie rushed to the tube containing Poros and picked at the crack. It was like peeling a hardboiled egg. With trembling fingers, she managed to make an opening large enough to pull Poros's limp body free. Her mother did the same with Prometheus, while Persephone and the vampires kept watch.

"Oh, Mom! He won't wake up!" Hestie cried as she cradled Poros's head. "Now what do we do?"

"No realm is safe," Persephone said. "Do you think we can trust Selene? Helios is her brother, after all."

"Better not risk it," Therese said. "What about your mother's winter cabin?"

Persephone nodded. "Good idea. Since we have no chariot, shall we risk god-travel?"

"I think so," Therese said.

Together with Poros and Prometheus in their arms, the three goddesses god-traveled with the two vampires to Mount Parnassus, where Demeter lived in the fall and winter.

They arrived just outside Demeter's door.

"Where are we?" Bach asked.

"Demeter's winter cabin," Hestie, holding Poros in her arms, replied.

Demeter opened the door. "What's this?"

"Hestie will explain," Persephone said as she and Therese carried the limp body of Prometheus indoors, where they laid him on a couch. "Therese and I must go."

"Mom, I'm scared," Hestie said as she followed her mother inside with Poros.

"I know," her mother said. "And that's okay. Fear is part of life. But so is hope. Hold onto that."

"You wait out there," Demeter said to the vampires.

Hestie turned to her great-grandmother with a look of reproach.

"I will not have those filthy creatures in my home," Demeter said.

"You don't know anything about them," Therese insisted.

"There's no time to argue," Persephone said. "The vampires will leave with us. Hestie, stay here and be on your guard, in case we were followed."

Hestie nodded as her mother and grandmother left for the Underworld with Sophia and Bach.

"Lay him here," Demeter said, pointing to a bed in an adjoining room. "And tell me what has happened."

Hermie ran to his father's side. "Dad!"

Charon caught up to him, sheathed his sword, and said "I'll take him and his brother to the throne room. You keep fighting."

Del put a hand on Hermie's shoulder. "Your father will be okay. Focus on the fight."

Hermie nodded but felt sick.

As Charon flew away with the limp bodies of Hermie's father and uncle, Hermie noticed that Hades had taken Poseidon's trident and was threatening to paralyze a Titan who was attempting to exit the pit. Poseidon was nowhere to be seen, and the sea monsters were fleeing toward the broken gate, chased by most of the vampires, Hecate, Hermes, the Furies, and Morpheus.

Hermie's Aunt Jen appeared in the chaos.

"The Titan Pit!" Hermie cried to her.

Hermie, Del, Jinsoo, and Jen rushed to aid Hector, who was using his blade to slice off the fingers of any hands that breached the door. All at once, they pushed the door closed and held it shut as Hades used his powers to mend the broken chains and locks.

Once the door was secure, they huddled around Gertie, who lay on the ground in her bull form.

"Is she alive?" Hermie asked.

"I hope so," Hector, who was crouched beside her, said.

"Where's Hip?" Jen asked.

"Charon took him to the throne room," Hermie said.

Jen vanished.

Dionysus appeared, sweating and panting, and knelt beside Gertie. "Don't tell me I was too late."

CHAPTER EIGHTEEN

Shattered

Hermie stood in the throne room of the Underworld near the table where his father and Uncle Hip were laid out. They were breathing but still paralyzed from Poseidon's trident. Their skin was pale, and their lips were blue, reminding Hermie of how Hestie had appeared after she'd been struck. Del stood beside Hermie with a hand on his shoulder. He should have been overjoyed by her touch, but he felt numb and on the verge of tears. No one knew for certain how the trident would affect a god. Hestie had made a full recovery, but there was no guarantee that their father or uncle would. Chidori had yet to make a peep.

Jen and Morpheus stood on the other side of the table trying to awaken Hip. If Hermie could speak, he would do the same with his father, but he was still processing everything that had happened.

On the other side of the room, Gertie lay in her bull form on the chunky wooden table surrounded by Hector and a few gods and vampires. Hoping that she wasn't permanently trapped in her bull form, they were relieved that she was at least breathing. Hector had prayed aloud to all the gods present to please help her. His eyes were full of tears as he stroked Gertie's hide and tried to awaken her. Hermie felt for them, but the only person he could really focus on right now was his father—though, in the back of his mind, he also worried about his mother and sister. They still hadn't returned with the rescue team.

There were others wounded who were awake but in need of healing: Cerberus huddled in one corner, where Hecate was reattaching his severed leg, and Tizzie's wolf lay nearby with broken ribs. Everyone else had suffered wounds that had already healed. Hermie had had a few gashes from his fight with the tritons, but they were already gone—at least he thought they were. He couldn't really feel anything at the moment.

To Hermie's relief, his mother and grandmother flew into the room with Sophia and Bach. Hermie had been about to fly into his mother's arms but stopped short when Hecate beat him to it and updated the new arrivals on all that had happened. Having to hear it over again only made Hermie feel worse.

Then his mother rushed to his father's side while Persephone updated the others on Poros and Prometheus.

"Than! Than, can you hear me!" His mother caressed his father's chest, hoping to wake him, to no avail.

When his mother finally wrapped her arms around him, Hermie broke into tears.

"He's going to be okay," she said of his father, though there was no way she could know for sure.

"Is Hestie okay?" he asked.

"She's fine. She's with Poros and Prometheus."

"They should be here," Hecate said, "for when Apollo comes. I'm happy to retrieve them if you tell me where they are."

"I'll go with you, my dear," Persephone offered, and the two goddesses left.

Hades said, "I need to secure my realm. The Furies are guarding the gate, but I need to mend and ward it and check the other entrances. We also need to comb every nook and crevice for enemies that may have been left behind either because they were maimed or killed or because they're planning something. I know you're tired and hungry and worried about the injured, but I need as many of you as possible to help."

"I'll get started," Hermes offered before he vanished.

Then Athena rushed inside the room with a face full of tears. "Forgive me. I don't deserve it, but please forgive me. I made a terrible mistake. I hereby step down as the leader of the Olympians. I'll do whatever I can to help you." She glanced around the room. "Where is Prometheus?"

"We need Apollo," Hades said. "Bring him here, and I'll tell you what happened to Prometheus."

Athena nodded and disappeared.

Then Hermie's mother turned to his father and said, "Come back to us, Than! Please, come back to us!", causing a resurgence of Hermie's tears.

Del put her arms around Hermie. He wanted to be strong, but he was scared. Why had this happened? Why had any of it happened? And where should they go from here?

Del cupped his face and said, "You know where we go from here. In one week, you are going to disarm those warheads and save a bunch of lives, remember?"

Vaguely, he did.

"We have to stay focused," Del said. "Our mission is not over."

Hermie looked into her deep, dark eyes and nodded. "You're right. We have to stay focused."

He wiped his eyes and turned to Hades. "What do you need us to do to secure the realm?"

"Follow me," Hades said. Then he stopped and turned to Dionysus. "Thank you for your help. It was most unexpected."

"I did it for my daughter," the god of wine replied.

Hades gave him a curt nod and then turned to Jen and Therese. "Guard the wounded, and trust no one."

Hades glanced once more at Dionysus before he turned to leave.

Hermie and Del followed the lord of the Underworld, along with the vampires and most of the gods. Even Cerberus limped behind, anxious to return to his post.

"I need someone to ward the entrance where Hydra once guarded," Hades said.

"I can do that," Morpheus offered before flying away.

"I'll need to recruit another monster," Hades muttered. "I'm very disappointed in Hydra."

"Might I recommend Amphisbaena?" Athena said, appearing near the broken gate just as they had reached it.

"I'll consider it," Hades said. "Where's Apollo?"

"With the injured," the goddess of wisdom replied. "And Prometheus?"

"He should be arriving in the throne room at any moment."

Athena vanished.

Hermie noticed that she hadn't asked after her brother and found it sad. The only family that seemed to care about Poros was Captain.

Hestie lay sobbing into a pillow beside Poros's paralyzed body on the bed in one of Demeter's rooms. She had every reason to believe that he would recover; however, she couldn't help but imagine the worst. She lifted her face from the pillow and tried to be strong. She stroked his hair and said his name, again and again.

Seeing Poros weak and vulnerable was difficult for Hestie, and yet it had made her understand something about herself and her feelings for Poros. Her love for him had become unconditional. Even if this would be his permanent state and he could never hold her in his arms again or do things with her, if he remained bedridden and helpless for all eternity, she would love him. She would care for him forever because she loved him more than anyone or anything in the world.

"Please wake up," she said. "Open your eyes and let me know you can hear me."

To her surprise, he did open his eyes. He couldn't speak, but he communicated with her telepathically.

Where's Captain?

"Oh, Poros!" she cried, throwing her arms over his chest.

Just then, there was a knock on the front door. Demeter opened it and welcomed Hecate and Persephone into the house. Hestie watched through the doorway of the adjoining room where she lay as Demeter embraced them and said, "Thank the Fates, you're not harmed!"

"Yes, we're fine, my dear," Hecate said.

"We've come to take Prometheus and Poros back to the Underworld," Persephone explained. "Apollo is coming to work his healing powers on them."

Hestie turned to Poros. "Did you hear that? Apollo will heal you! I just know it!"

Where's Captain? he asked again.

She stroked his cheek. "He's on Demeter's couch."

Once the gate to the Underworld was repaired and warded and Cerberus was back at his post, the Furies and other Underworld gods split up to check the many secret entrances and to refortify them with wards. Since Hermie and Jinsoo hadn't learned how to make wards, they and the vampires were tasked with searching the realm for enemies that may have been left behind. Hermie and his group split up into pairs. Hermie was grateful to be partnered with Del.

"We need to feed soon," Del said as she flew beside Hermie toward the Fields of Elysium.

"I'll go with you, when we're done here," he offered.

"That's not necessary," she said. "You're needed here."

The thought of allowing her out of his sight, where he couldn't protect her, rattled him.

"I survived for centuries before I met you," she said with a laugh.

Blood rushed to his cheeks. "I know."

He studied the murky waters of Erebus and found nothing but the dead soaking there.

They continued their search over the Elysian Fields, where Hermie caught a glimpse of Mina sitting among the purple flowers. She looked happy, as did the other souls frolicking and lounging about her. She smiled up at him as he flew overhead, and, for a moment, he thought she recognized him. His heart leapt. He waved. When she turned away, unmoved by his enthusiasm, he was reminded of the truth: she had not recognized him. Not at all.

"I'm sorry," Del said somberly.

"You have nothing to be sorry about."

"I'm sorry for your pain."

"I'm okay. More than okay. It's my father I'm worried about."

"Hermie!" Jinsoo's voice carried over the Phlegethon from the direction of his parents' chambers. "Come quick!"

Hermie gave Del a look of alarm as the two of them sped toward Jinsoo. He stood at the entrance to his parents' abode.

"Look what I found!" Jinsoo cried.

When Gertie opened her eyes, she was alarmed to find that she was still in her bull form.

"Gertie?" Hector raised his brows. "Oh, thank the gods!"

She blinked. Both Hector and Dionysus were gazing down at her with anxious looks on their faces.

Because she couldn't yet move her mouth, she prayed to her father, *Why am I still a bull?*

"Drink this," he said, tipping a bowl of wine near her snout.

She lapped it up and was relieved when she felt herself transform back into her human form.

But she still couldn't move. She lay on her side. Her arms stretched in front of her, and one leg rested on the other. She was in the same position she'd been lying in as a bull.

"Apollo is coming to help you," Hector said. Then, chuckling nervously, he added, "I was ready to become a cow to be with you."

That made her laugh, and she was shocked when her chest moved.

"That's a good sign," Dionysus said. "Have another sip of wine."

"Hold up," Apollo said as he approached. "Don't give her too much of that, or she might slip back into a coma."

Gertie wished she could speak so she could defend her father. He was only trying to help, and the wine *had* helped.

Apollo lay his hands on her shoulders, and she felt their healing warmth course through her.

"Will she recover?" Dionysus asked.

"We'll have to wait and see," Apollo said. "I healed her spine, so, if she does recover, she'll be able to move her limbs."

Gertie gave Apollo a prayer of thanks before he left her side.

Then Dionysus leaned closer to her and, to her surprise, stroked her hair. "I'm sorry I haven't been there for you, Gertie. It's taken me a while to realize it, that I've become the same selfish father to you that my father was to me. I've been driven by self-pity and self-loathing. I see that now. I promise to do better by you and to love you, as a father should."

Tears flooded Gertie's eyes. For the first time in her life, she could think of nothing to say.

"Chidori!" Hermie cried at the sight of his yellow canary perched on Jinsoo's finger. "Oh my gosh! How do you feel?"

She chirped that she was perfectly fine and anxious to know about the rest of their family and friends. Together, they finished searching their quadrant of the realm, and finding nothing unusual, returned to the throne room to meet up with the others.

Hermie was further delighted to discover that his father and uncle had sat up. His mother and aunt were helping the gods to their feet.

"Dad!" Hermie nearly knocked his father over with a hug.

<u>CHAPTER NINETEEN</u>

Epiphanies

Gertie began to feel the pressure on her hand where Hector was holding it and the occasional brush against her shoulder by her father, Dionysus. She tried to wiggle her toes and fingers but couldn't tell if they were moving. She wanted to ask Hector and her father to check for her, but her lips and tongue and teeth wouldn't cooperate. So, she sighed and closed her eyes again, wondering if she'd be a vegetable for the rest of her life.

But then she recalled her dream of flying on Pegasus with Hestie on October 20th. Didn't that mean she was destined to recover? Or had her act of bravery at the Titan Pit sabotaged the future? Had her decision to throw herself against the door to the pit changed everything? What would happen to the warheads?

Her paralysis wasn't the only thing overwhelming her. Gertie was still digesting the words of her father. She didn't know how to feel about them. Should she believe him? Even if he meant them now, would he mean them forever? Or would he break her heart and leave her disappointed again?

It occurred to her that her fear of being hurt by her father was the same fear that she felt about Hector. Why couldn't she open herself up to them? Why couldn't she trust that they meant what they said?

Whether the blasts from the trident had jolted her brain, or whether her paralysis had given her time to think, Gertie was beginning to understand the answer. She knew why she couldn't have faith in their love for her. As much as she wanted to blame them for letting her down in the past, it wasn't about *them* at all. The root of her fear had become apparent to her.

She was terrified that she was unlovable.

It all made sense to her now. That's why her first love had been a vampire. If nothing else, Gertie had known that she could offer Jeno blood. And when Hector had left her to figure out what he wanted to do with his life, she'd turned to a vampire again. She'd done it because she knew that even if she was worthless in every other way, her blood made her valuable to Taavi.

Taavi's words came back to her as more tears formed in her eyes: *You must remind yourself constantly that you are good enough, that you have gifts, that you have worth and deserve to occupy the space you live in.*

She'd tried to compensate for her unlovability by being an expert at all things, to prove her worth to everyone she encountered. But the one person she hadn't proven it to was herself.

That wasn't completely true, because she knew that she was smart and strong and brave. She believed in herself as a warrior. What she couldn't believe was that anyone could *love* her. And she believed this because no one truly *had* before Hector.

Hector had loved her, and he still loved her. It was hard for her to believe and to accept. More tears spilled down the side of her face as she took Taavi's advice and told herself, again and again: She was worthy of Hector's love. She was worthy of the love of her father. She was good enough, she had gifts, and she deserved to occupy the space she lived in. Even if she never recovered, she was lovable.

Maybe one day, she'd believe it.

Hestie narrowed her eyes at Athena, who was leaning over Prometheus, where he lay on a table beside Poros.

"This is your fault, you know," Hestie muttered to the goddess.

"I know," Athena said as tears streamed down her cheeks. "And I'm sorry."

Hestie was flummoxed. She'd never known the goddess to admit that she was wrong. Did this mean that she and the Olympian council were allied with the Underworld gods again? Or had Athena and Apollo defected?

She was pulled from her reverie when her brother entered the room with Jinsoo and Chidori.

"Chidori!" Hestie cried.

The bird flew from Jinsoo's fingers and perched on her shoulder before giving Hestie kisses.

"I'm so happy that you're better!" Hestie said.

After hugging their father, Hermie flew to her and pulled her hair.

"I'm glad to see you in one piece," he said.

"Same," she said with a grin.

Hermie stared down at the limp bodies of Poros and Captain. "No change?"

"Not yet," Athena said.

Hades entered the throne room with Persephone at his side. He cleared his throat. The others in the room grew silent as they waited for him to speak.

"I'm pleased to inform you that the Underworld is once again secure."

The room exploded with applause.

Del came up behind Hermie and said, "We're going with Hermes to feed. I'll be back soon."

"Why is Hermes going?" he asked.

Hestie was wondering the same thing.

Over Del's shoulder, Alastair said, "He thinks we should stick to traveling by chariot for now, just to be safe."

"I'm coming with you," Hermie said.

"I want to go, too," Jinsoo said.

Chidori tweeted a string of chirps begging to be taken into the fresh air.

Hermes beckoned them to come. "I could use some extra sets of eyes and ears."

Hestie stopped her brother. "Before you go, will you charge my phone? I need it for something important."

Hermie touched her phone with his finger. "That should do it."

"That's so cool," she said, still unused to his powers.

He grinned. "I know."

Hestie watched as he and Jinsoo left with Chidori and the vampires. Then she said to Athena, "I'll be right back."

Hestie went off to be alone in one of the winding corridors near the light of the Phlegethon to make a video on her phone asking her fans to pray for Poros and Prometheus. "They're badly hurt," she said into her phone camera as she fought tears. "And your prayers could make a huge difference."

She said goodbye in thirty different languages before ending the video and uploading it to Youtube. Then she made her way back to Poros.

The other gods in the room were talking to Apollo, so Hestie took the opportunity to ask Athena a question.

"Have you and Apollo joined Team Hermes? Or are you still Team Poseidon?"

"For someone so smart, you aren't so smart," Athena said.

Hestie put her hands on her hips. "I don't understand."

"We were never Team Poseidon, as you call it," Athena said. "This wasn't about supporting Poseidon over Hermes. We were only buying time until we could build up enough leverage to thwart the old man of the sea. You and Hermes and your vampire friends kept getting in the way."

"It seems to me that Hermes and my vampire friends helped to save your reign."

Hestie suddenly realized that the other gods had stopped talking and had turned to listen to her and Athena.

"Perhaps," Athena said. "But Amphitrite and Rhode are still missing, and that temple in Syria may still be built for Phorcys." Then she asked, "What's happening to Poros?"

Poros's skin had begun to glow.

"I don't know," Hestie said, alarmed. "Apollo? What's happening to him?"

A bright flash of light pulsed from Poros's body, causing Hestie and the others to jump back in surprise. Hestie's heart ramped up as she covered her mouth.

Please, she prayed to the other gods. *Please let Poros be okay!*

From the east coast of Sicily, where he guarded the entrance to La Luna Rossa, or The Red Moon, the pub in Syracuse where the regulars knew the vampires, Hermie saw a fork of lightning in the night sky. It appeared in the east, over Greece. But there was something strange about the lightning. It came from the ground. The lightning was striking *up*, not down.

"What the hell is that?" Hermie muttered to himself.

He felt the ground shake beneath him. In the distance, the Ionian Sea began to churn.

The Ionian Sea was the home of the sea monsters. Were they up to something?

Hermie called out to Hermes telepathically. In less than a second, the messenger god was at his side.

He pointed to the lightning and the sea. "What is that?"

"We better get back," Hermes said. "Help me round up the others."

Hermie followed the older god into the pub and called to Jinsoo and Del telepathically. Hermie had hoped to avoid seeing Del in the arms of Lorenzo, the mortal she usually fed on when visiting La Luna Rossa, but there they were, in the hallway near the restrooms. Del fed from his neck while Lorenzo pressed her body against him. To her, he was food. But it was obvious that, to Lorenzo, she was more than a drug.

Hermie grabbed her arm. "We need to go."

"Hey, it's the kid again," Lorenzo said in Italian. "Get lost."

"It's urgent," Hermie said to Del, ignoring the mortal.

"I'm not finished yet," she said with a pout.

Hermie rolled his eyes. "Then hurry."

He left to search for the others because they were ignoring his telepathic pleas. Hermes had better luck. He put his fingers to his teeth and blew a sharp whistle that made everyone in the pub stop what they were doing to look around.

"I need my V Team, now!" Hermes shouted.

The vampires obediently wiped the blood from their mouths, left their donors, and hustled after Hermes to the chariot parked near the docks.

Hermie and Jinsoo followed.

Hermie said nothing as he sat with Del in his lap, partly because he was worried about what might lie ahead, and partly because he had begun to wonder if maybe Lorenzo wasn't the only one who enjoyed the feeding sessions.

From the corner of his eye, he noticed Del's brows lift with surprise.

Of course, I enjoy eating. Don't you? she asked him telepathically.

As a matter of fact, he enjoyed it very much, especially when there wasn't kimchi involved. But it was never necessary for him to embrace his food or to be held by it. While he was eating it, his food never pressed a boner against him.

Enough, she said.

If you don't like it, stay out of my head, he said.

Del harrumphed and folded her arms as Hermes turned the chariot into the narrow chasm leading to the Underworld, where the entire realm was alight with a golden hue.

Hestie put her arms around her mother's waist as she watched Poros with trepidation. The light emanating from him had expanded as far as she could see. The ground beneath them trembled. Poros's body had risen from the table where Prometheus had just opened his eyes for the first time since becoming Poseidon's prisoner.

Poros was as bewildered and anxious as the rest of them. Although he couldn't speak, he was sending prayers to everyone there: *What is happening to me?*

When Hermie and the others returned, they watched the spectacle before them with the same awe and trepidation as the rest.

Poros floated through the room until he reached Hades's throne, where he landed gently in a seating position with both arms outstretched. Then the helm of invisibility flew across the room and landed in his lap.

"What are you playing at!" Hades growled.

Poros stared dumbly back as the trident lurched out of Hades's grasp and flew to Poros's left hand.

"What in the name of the Fates is going on?" Hades shouted.

The other gods murmured among themselves when, without Poros moving a finger, his lightning bolt appeared in his other hand. All three gifts from the Fates—the helm, the trident, and the lightning bolt—were now possessed by Poros. What did this mean?

Hestie turned to her mother. "Do you know what's happening?"

Her mother shook her head as she continued to stare in the direction of Hades's throne.

The gods and vampires speculated in whispers without taking their eyes from Poros.

The bright light emanating from Poros's body dimmed as three beings flew to his side. They resembled little old ladies, but they were said to be the most powerful beings in existence because only they knew with certainty what the future held. They were known as the Fates.

Hestie knew who they were because of the stories her parents had told her. Clotho was known as the spinner. She wore half of her long gray hair in a bun on the crown of her head and the other half down her back. Tall and thin and wearing a pink velvet pantsuit, she spoke with a throaty voice and was the least patient of the three sisters. She was the first to speak.

"Poros, son of Zeus," Clotho said. "You have a choice. Either accept the yolk of leadership that is your true destiny or watch the Olympians fragment until they are overthrown."

Hestie wondered what Clotho had meant by "the yolk of leadership" being his "true destiny." Was she saying that he had no choice but to take his sister's place?

Poros licked his lips and seem relieved to have the use of his mouth again.

"What is happening?" he asked aloud.

"We already know what you will choose," Clotho said. "Nevertheless, you must still make the choice."

"Accept the burden of leadership," Lachesis said. "Or reject it, knowing that the Olympians will suffer for it."

Lachesis, if Hestie remembered correctly, was known as the weaver. She was short and plump with short curly hair. She wore a bright blue shawl over a blue velvet dress.

"Why does it have to be me?" Poros wanted to know. "Why can't my sister lead instead?"

"Your sister has a different destiny," Lachesis explained. "She cannot fulfill it while leading the council. Your resistance to lead has already caused the Olympians to fragment."

Hades made his way to the front of the room, where Poros sat on his throne. He turned to the Fates. "*I* was chosen to lead. In a democratic election, my fellow Olympians chose *me*. I'm the one who abdicated to Athena, not Poros."

"They would have chosen Poros," Atropos said. "Had he made himself a contender."

"That seems highly doubtful, given his age," Hades said.

"Which of us knows what the future holds?" Atropos asked. "You or me?"

Hades made no reply.

If Hestie remembered correctly, Atropos was known as the cutter. Hestie thought she was the cutest of the little old ladies with her white hair in a bob with bangs that curled under. Her bangs reached the top of her black-rimmed glasses that framed her crystal blue eyes. She wore a lavender velvet blazer over a white blouse with a denim skirt.

"I don't know the first thing about being a leader," Poros said.

"My point precisely," Hades said.

Prometheus surprised everyone by sitting up and climbing to his feet.

Athena gasped as tears sprang to her eyes.

"Sure, you do," Prometheus said to Poros. "You've been the leader of my crew for years."

"Captain!" Poros tried to get up from the throne but seemed to be trapped there. "You feel okay?"

"Fine," he said. "Believe in yourself, Poros. I do."

"But I want to sail the seas with you. I want to continue our mission of bringing medicine to areas in need."

Hestie wanted that too, but she would do whatever it took to be with Poros.

"You can still do that," Clotho, the tall one, said as she pinched a speck of lint from her pink trousers.

Atropos pushed her spectacles up higher on the bridge of her nose. "While your father led, he had plenty of time to do other things."

"I'm living proof of that," Dionysus said from the back of the room. "If our father had time to have affairs and make mischief with Hermes, then you can't do any worse from Prometheus's ship."

Hermes chuckled. "Hear, hear."

"You will need to attend council meetings and help to enforce laws established by the council," Lachesis, the short and plump one, added. "That's where things have gone wrong. You haven't been there."

"No one should have all three gifts," Athena said. "Isn't that too much power?"

"Don't you know your brother at all?" Atropos asked Athena. "The last thing he wants is power. Who better than he to make the custodian of our gifts?"

"I don't want them," Poros said.

"My point exactly," Atropos said.

"Can I give them away?" Poros asked.

"That's up to you," Clotho said. "All that is required of you to fulfill your destiny is that you accept the burden of leadership. How you go about it is completely up to you."

"Whether or not he leads and how he goes about it is *all* up to him," Lachesis said. "He like everyone, has free will. We just know what he will choose."

"And yet we still have to ask him to choose," Atropos said. "We can't tell him what to do."

Poros picked up the helm and tried to stand up.

"You can stand once you decide," Clotho said. "And can you hurry it up? I want to get back to the arcade."

Poros turned to Prometheus, who gave him an encouraging nod.

"I accept," Poros said.

The three Fates vanished.

Poros finally managed to climb to his feet. Hestie could tell that he was nervous as he stood before the gods and vampires staring back at him.

"I promise to lead as best as I can," he said. "But I'm counting on all of you to help. The more we work together, the better, in my opinion. That's what Captain always taught me."

"You had an excellent teacher," Athena said.

Hestie was surprised that Athena wasn't more resentful of having been dethroned. Was she trying to score points with her brother with her compliment? Or was she being sincere?

"I want Hades to have his helm," Poros said. "It belongs to him."

Hades lifted his hand, and the helm returned to him. He didn't offer any thanks. He showed no gratitude at all. He seemed more resentful than Athena, even though he had abdicated, and she was the one being forced to step down.

Poros raised the trident. "I want Captain—er, Prometheus—to have the trident."

"No, no, no. I don't want the trident," Prometheus said. "Give it to Poseidon. It would be a wise gesture to unite the Olympians."

Poros nodded. "That's great advice. I'll be counting on you to give me more of that in the future."

"What of the lightning bolt?" Hermes asked.

Poros chuckled nervously. "I guess I'll hold onto that for a while and see how it goes."

"What will be your first order of business as the new leader of the Olympians?" Apollo asked.

Poros chuckled again. "I don't suppose *you* can tell me? You *are* the god of prophecy, after all."

Everyone in the room laughed.

"Seriously, though," Poros began, "I think the first thing we need to do is to reunite the Olympian Council on Mount Olympus and come up with a plan to save Amphitrite and Rhode. And thanks to a vision from our friend Gertie, I know what we need to do."

Dionysus stepped forward and said, "You should thank her for more than her vision. She's the main reason the Titan prisoners remain in their pit."

"That's true," Hermes said. "We all owe Gertie a great deal of thanks."

Hestie looked across the room at Gertie, who lay on the chunky wooden table still paralyzed. The girl may be an annoying know-it-all and an attention whore, but she was certainly brave.

She was pulled from her thoughts when Athena said to Prometheus, "I'm so happy to see you fully recovered. I look forward to visiting you again on your ship."

Prometheus frowned. "I know it was you who gave our position away to Poseidon."

Athena lowered her chin. "Yes, but…"

"You are the reason one of my crew was killed," he said.

Athena reached out to touch his cheek, but he grabbed her hand and asked, "How could you imagine that I would look forward to a visit from you?"

Hestie averted her eyes as the goddess of wisdom turned ghostly pale before turning to leave.

"Where are you going?" Hades asked Athena as she was fleeing.

"Home."

Athena didn't wait for his reply.

Hestie noticed Poros watching his sister leave. He wore a look of disappointment. Hestie could only imagine how conflicted he felt about everything.

"Let's meet on Mount Olympus in two days to discuss our plan," Poros said.

As most of the Olympians cleared out of the throne room, Hestie approached Poros.

"Leadership looks good on you," she said.

He frowned. "I disagree."

"You're not having second thoughts, are you?" she asked.

"And third and fourth and fifth thoughts, too, but let's not discuss them here."

"Where, then?"

"On the ship. I want to return as soon as possible."

CHAPTER TWENTY

Frustrations

Hermie was happy to be back in his cabin aboard the *Marcella II* and even happier to be playing *Urban Fighter* with Jinsoo.

"I got you good, Hermie," Jinsoo said. "You need more practice."

"Just you wait."

The vampires were back in their crates getting some much-needed rest. Gertie and Hector, who had begged Prometheus to bring them back with them, were also resting. Even Captain was asleep in his room.

Only the four young gods were restless. Hermie could hear Poros and Hestie arguing in Poros's room down the hall. He wasn't paying attention to them. He had a lot on his mind, and he could tell, by Jinsoo's nervous chatter, that Jinsoo was feeling the same.

"Game over," Jinsoo said, victorious.

"Enjoy the feeling while you can. It may be the last time you experience it."

"Oh, shut up. I beat you plenty of times."

"You know when I told you that your English was getting better?"

"Yeah. I remember."

"Well, I was wrong," Hermie said. "I don't think you know what the word *plenty* means."

"You love to talk, don't you? Why don't we play again, and see?"

"I have a better idea," Hermie said.

"Sword fight?"

Hermie laughed. "No. I'm sick of fighting. Aren't you?"

Jinsoo shrugged. "Not really."

"I was thinking we should ask Pegasus to give us a ride. I bet he's bored."

"Great idea! That way, you can avoid getting beat by me a second time!"

Hermie laughed. "You're funny, Jinsoo."

"Hey, I know! But listen, Hermie. Before we go, I want to ask you a serious question."

"Okay. Go ahead."

"Do you think it's possible for a god and a vampire to, I don't know, fall for each other? And is that even allowed?"

Hermie felt the blood rush to his cheeks. "Why do you ask?"

Jinsoo's cheeks reddened, too, and that's when Hermie realized that Jinsoo wasn't talking about Hermie and Del. It suddenly occurred to Hermie that Jinsoo was falling in love with Alastair.

"Oh, I get it," Hermie said. "Well, I don't think there are any laws against it. And I *do* think it can happen. It's just that…"

"What?"

"Have you seen them feed?"

"That doesn't gross me out. Does it gross you out, Hermie?"

Hermie scratched his head and got up from his desk. "Maybe a little. It's not *that*, though. When they feed, well, it seems intimate. You know what I mean?"

"Oh, like kissing?"

"Yeah. Like kissing. I think, when you're not a vampire, that might be hard to live with, knowing that the person you love is practically making out with another person all the time. Does that make sense?"

Jinsoo frowned. "Yeah. That makes sense."

"Come on. Let's go for a ride."

Jinsoo followed Hermie from the room, but Hermie could tell that he'd ruined Jinsoo's happy mood.

"Why did you accept, if you don't want to lead?" Hestie asked Poros from where she sat opposite him on his bed.

"It felt like I didn't have a choice."

"But the Fates said it *was* your choice."

"It didn't feel like much of one." Poros jumped up from the bed and stood facing the portal to the sea. "It was a lot of pressure. Everyone was looking at me, expecting me to accept. The Fates even said the Olympians would fragment until they were overthrown unless I accepted."

Hestie flew from the bed to stand behind him. The ship was moving fast, returning to the Mediterranean Sea. Colorful marine life flashed by the portal as the ship sped past it.

"That doesn't make sense," Hestie said. "Think about it."

"That's all I've been doing, Hestie."

"The Fates say that we have free will. They claim that they don't control us but only know what we will choose because they can see the future. If that's true, then how can they see *two* possible futures? Wouldn't they see *the one and only* future, not two possibilities?"

Poros turned to her with his brows furrowed above his stunning gray eyes. "Hold on. Say that again."

"When I was young, my parents told me that I had free will," Hestie said. "They explained the difference between predetermination and foreknowledge. Predetermination means that no one has a choice. It means we are destined to go down a predetermined path. Foreknowledge is not the same thing. A prophet can have foreknowledge of what you will do without causing it."

"I see what you're saying. It just seems ridiculous—me being the leader when there are so many more experienced gods, like my sister. I don't want to be the power monger my father was. He only cared for himself."

"You will never be like him."

"I want to be like Captain."

She squeezed his hand. "You already are."

"Everything about my father makes me sick. The idea of sitting on what was once his throne makes me…angry."

"I believe in free will, Poros. And if you don't want to be the leader, then you can choose not to be."

"But what about the fragmenting of the Olympians?" he asked as he sat on the edge of the bed.

She sat beside him. "I don't trust the Fates. They could be lying about that."

"What?" he whispered. "How can you be so cavalier about them? They're the most powerful beings."

"I don't know if that's true," she said. "Their hands seem *tied*. They know things but can't seem to be able to do anything about it. In fact, they seem like the most miserable beings in existence. Think about it. The only happiness they've managed to find is in games of chance."

"Because their futures are the only futures they can't see," Poros said.

"That's every reason why they should do more. They could be helping mortals, like we are. Instead, they live the reclusive lives of hermits and dole out occasional warnings. I think it's lame of them."

"It must be horrible," Poros said, "to know everything that will happen, to be aware of every tragedy that befalls every living thing. I can only imagine how paralyzing, how debilitating such knowledge might be."

"Fine, I feel sorry for them. But I still don't trust them. And I think you've got to stand up for what you feel like you must do, what you want to do with your life, Poros. It's not like you'd rather drink wine and dance every night like Dionysus. You want to help people. You want to serve. You are the most selfless person I know. That's why I think it's wrong that the Fates are trying to manipulate you into doing something you clearly don't want to do."

Poros smiled and cupped her face. "You're really something."

"I know."

"You've given me a lot to think about."

"Good."

She was glad when he kissed her. If he hadn't done so, she would have been even more frustrated with him than she already was.

But then, after a scrumptious, warm, wet kiss, he stood up and said, "I'm going to abdicate to Athena."

"What? No! Taavi's dead because of her."

"No, Taavi's dead because of Poseidon."

"She sanctioned the attack."

"She didn't know what lengths Poseidon would go to."

"She should have. He's desperate to get his wife and daughter back."

"Okay, she made a mistake. Zeus made millions of mistakes and look how long he led the Olympians. Doesn't she get to make one or two? Are you suggesting that I would never make a mistake as the leader? You must know how impossible that is."

"She hates the vampires. We can't trust her."

"I've already thought of that. I have a proposal to remedy that."

Hestie crossed her arms over her chest. "Okay. Let's hear it."

"As a reward for her bravery, I want to make Gertie the goddess of vampires."

Hestie's mouth fell open. "You can't be serious. She's already such an annoying little show-off. Can you imagine her as a goddess?"

"Yes. And I think she'd be brilliant."

"You'll need the approval of the council."

He nodded.

"What if she doesn't want that?" Hestie said.

Poros laughed. "I'm pretty sure she won't say no."

"Well, I still think you should ask her."

"I will."

"She hasn't recovered, Poros. What if she never does? I mean, I hope that won't be the case, but what's the point of making her suffer eternally?"

"Hmm. Good point. Well, if she doesn't recover, we can find another to swear an oath to protect the vamps. Is that your main complaint against my sister, that she won't care about their wellbeing?"

"How can you defend her? She doesn't even seem to care that much about you."

He frowned.

"I'm sorry. I shouldn't have said that."

"No, you're right. None of them do. The Olympians are my relatives, either a brother or sister, or an aunt or uncle, and none of them seem to care. Only Captain…"

She put her hands on his shoulders. "And me, and Hermie, and Jinsoo, and the vampires."

"I know."

"The others just need more time. They hardly know you."

"Maybe."

"Oh, Poros."

Hestie put her arms around him and kissed him. "Once they know you, they're going to love you as much as we do."

"I hope so."

"Well, maybe not as much as *I* do."

He lifted his chin and looked at her. "You love me a lot, huh?"

She smiled, feeling a little embarrassed now. Maybe she'd admitted too much too soon, but there was no going back. She nodded.

"I love you a lot, too," he said with a grin.

She laughed with relief.

He held her tight, his chin resting on her shoulder, her chin resting on his.

"I really do," he said.

She smiled as tears slipped down her cheeks. "Me, too."

Gertie lay beside Hector in what had been her cabin on the *Marcella II*. She still couldn't turn her head or speak. She was glad that Hector was finally getting some sleep. He'd been stressing over her for nearly two days.

Fortunately, he had managed to mask his stress and fear when he'd called Gertie's mother to let her know where they were. Hector had also told Diane that James was safe. Gertie would explain everything when she came home, though Hector couldn't say for sure when that would be.

Diane hadn't been completely pacified by the call, but at least she wasn't in the dark.

When Gertie's father, Dionysus, arrived with a bottle of wine, she sighed with relief.

You came, she said to him telepathically.

I told you, Gertie. You can count on me from now on.

Hector sat up, as if he had spidey senses. "What are you doing here?"

"Gertie asked me to come," the god of wine replied. "She asked me to bring her this."

Hector leaned over Gertie, so he could meet her eyes. "Apollo said it could make you go back into a coma."

Gertie prayed to her father: *Please tell him that I know what I'm doing and that your wine has healing properties for me, because I'm your daughter.*

"She told me to tell you to trust her," Dionysus said.

Hector groaned as her father poured some of the wine into a goblet. Dionysus then poured the wine from the goblet into her mouth. Although some of it spilled down her chin and neck, she swallowed some of it down and felt it moving through her system.

More, she said to her father telepathically.

He gave her more.

"Are you sure this won't hurt her?" Hector asked her father.

"No, I'm not," he said.

More, Gertie said to her father.

When Dionysus held the goblet to her lips for a third time, Hector said, "Wait!"

Hector looked into Gertie's eyes and asked, "I think you should listen to Apollo. He's the god of healing."

To her father, Gertie said, *Please tell him that if he really loves me, he'll trust me.*

"I'm not going to tell him that," her father said.

Dionysus put the goblet to her lips, and she drank, able to use her mouth and tongue for the first time since she'd been struck.

"It's working," she said.

"Gertie! You can talk!"

"Do you want more?" her father asked.

"No thanks," she said. "But thank you. Thank you so much. I think I need something else."

"What?" Hector asked.

Gertie took a deep breath. "The bite of a vampire."

Just then, Penny entered. "If I bite you, will you guys stop talking? It's bad enough that we have to listen to Poros and Hestie at the end of the hall."

"I promise," Gertie said.

Penny flew to Gertie's side, bit her wrist, and drank.

It took a few minutes, but the familiar feeling of euphoria finally swept through Gertie. Then she felt her senses become heightened. She sat up in the bed as Penny withdrew.

"It worked!" Hector cried.

"Good," Penny said. "Remember your promise."

Penny flew from the room.

"I'll leave this here," Dionysus said as he put the bottle of wine on the bedside table. "Call me if you need me."

Her father disappeared.

As Hector was about to speak, she put her finger to his lips.

Using the power of the vampire virus, she said into his mind: *No more talking. Let me tell you what I want to do instead.*

Then she told him telepathically in vivid detail.

The look on Hector's face made her want to guffaw, but she covered her mouth and stifled her laughter to keep her promise to Penny.

CHAPTER TWENTY-ONE

A Memorial

It was dusk when Poros and Pegasus returned to the *Marcella II* after the meeting on Mount Olympus. The captain and the other members of the crew were gathered on the main deck, waiting. The deck had been decorated with candles and a few flowers plucked from a nearby island. Everyone had tears in their eyes, including Gertie, because the purpose of their gathering was to say goodbye to a friend.

Poros filled them in on how the meeting went. He'd been successful in convincing the gods to give his sister, Athena, another chance.

"There's one other thing," Poros said to them. "I had a recommendation. The vampires have had lords, like Dionysus, Hades, and Hermes, but those gods have mainly found ways that vampires can serve and have a purpose. And those gods have other duties and distractions that prevent them from making you guys and others like you a priority."

"What are you saying, Poros?" Del asked.

"I told the others that we need a god whose main duty is to watch over the wellbeing of the vampires," Poros said. "The gods created you, and you're their responsibility, whatever my sister might think."

The faces of the vampires brightened, even on this sad occasion. Gertie was grateful that there was a god who cared about the vampires as much as she did.

"That is so thoughtful of you," Alastair said.

"I am overwhelmed," Mahdi admitted. "Few seem to care."

"I think it's a great idea," Gertie said. "It's about time."

"That's really cool, man," Hector agreed.

Gertie squeezed Hector's hand.

"I thought I heard you talking about something like this the other night," Penny said, "but I did not want to get my hopes up."

"What did the council say?" Prometheus asked. "Did they support your idea?"

"They did," Poros said.

"What? That surprises me!" Bach said.

"I cannot believe my ears," Raimo said.

"They were especially pleased by the name of the person who I think would be perfect for the job."

"Who?" Hermie asked.

Poros grinned. "Gertie."

Gertie covered her mouth, unsure if she had heard Poros correctly.

"The gods were impressed by what Gertie did to prevent the Titans from escaping the pit," Poros said. "They've agreed to allow me to give her immortality and make her the goddess of vampires."

Gertie didn't know what to say. It was like a dream come true. She turned to Hector. Although he smiled back at her, she could tell he was conflicted. He'd once told her that he wanted to live a human life. Would she have to give him up to become a god?

"Take some time to think about it," Prometheus said. "Immortality is no easy concept for a mortal to understand. Take some time and feel confident in your answer before you give it."

"As always, that's excellent advice, Captain," Poros said.

But Gertie could feel the hopes and dreams of the vampires all riding on her shoulders now, along with Hector's hopes and dreams for their human future together.

"Thank you for the honor," Gertie said to Poros. "I will let you know as soon as I've made my decision."

Hermie was happy for Gertie and the vampires. He smiled at Del, who stood across from him in their gathering circle. She smiled back, but he could tell she that was upset with him. He knew he'd upset her with his comments about Lorenzo, and he needed to apologize. However, if he were to be honest with himself, he was scared that he might never feel comfortable with her feeding habits. It killed him to imagine her in the arms of another man, even if, to her, that man was more like a hamburger than a lover.

What if, one of these days, that man is less like a hamburger than a lover? What if one of these days, she falls for her food?

He noticed her laugh and shake her head. Was she responding to his thoughts?

What else would make me laugh? she said to him telepathically.

I'm scared, he said in his mind. *I'm scared of getting hurt.*

And you don't think I'm scared? Why can't we be scared together?

Prometheus's voice interrupted their telepathic conversation. He said, "We gather together this evening to remember our friend and brother Taavi Galanis. We pray that his soul finds its way to the glorious Fields of Elysium, where he will be happy and peaceful for all of eternity. We also pray that our memories of him will comfort us and that soon our grief will be replaced by peace."

"Amen," Poros said.

"Amen," Hermie and the others said.

"How about a song to commemorate the occasion?" Prometheus asked the vampires.

Alastair began in his rich bass voice:

While you live, shine.

Have no grief at all.

Life exists only for a short while,

And Time demands his due.

Then the others joined in harmony:

The rain descends, and from high heaven
A storm is driven:
And on the running water-brooks the cold
Lays icy hold:
Then up! Beat down the winter; make the fire
Blaze high and higher;
Mix wine as sweet as honey of the bee
Abundantly;
Then drink with comfortable wool around
Your temples bound.
We must not yield our hearts to woe, or wear
With wasting care;
For grief will profit us no whit, my friend,
Nor nothing mend;
Think not on what we have lost,
But rejoice that we once had.
For grief will profit us no whit,
Nor nothing mend.

When they'd finished, Gertie said, "That was beautiful."

"It really was, guys," Hector said. "Thanks for that."

"Indeed," the captain said. "Thank you. Would anyone care to say a few words about Taavi before we light a fire in his memory?"

"He kept me sane," Bach said. "He was always so happy."

"True," Raimo said. "And he and Mahdi together, they should have had their own show."

Mahdi wiped his eyes. "I will miss that."

Gertie cleared her throat. "He taught me something important, something I needed to learn. He told me that you must remind yourself constantly that you are good enough, that you have gifts, that you have worth and deserve to occupy the space you live in. He taught me how important it was that I learn to love myself." She sniffled and wiped her eyes. "Thank you for that, Taavi."

They were silent together for a few moments. When no one else had words to share, they walked through the galley and salon to the stern deck, where Prometheus had a block of wood he'd already soaked in lighter fluid. He struck a match and set flame to wood. As the wood was engulfed, Prometheus said, "Taavi Galanis, may the perpetual light of the Underworld shine upon you and bring you peace."

The captain lay the burning wood onto the sea. The vampires, gods, and demigods watched the little funeral pyre float away beneath the darkening sky until it was no longer visible, even to those with super-human vision.

When the memorial service was over, everyone returned to the galley for wine and food. Hestie took the opportunity to pull Poros aside and ask, "How do you feel, now that you've officially abdicated your leadership position?"

"I know it was the right thing to do."

"Good. I'm proud of you."

"I wouldn't have been able to do it without you, Hestie," he said. "I've never known anyone to talk about the Fates and gods the way you do, so irreverently."

"I don't mean to be irreverent—really. I believe that we can't count on anyone but ourselves in this world. Well, I know there are *some* we can count on, like everyone aboard this ship and my parents. But I don't think we should trust the gods and the Fates to be there, to guide us, or to protect us. I think we have to do those things for ourselves, as much as we possibly can."

"I don't know if I agree with you completely, but I admire you for being so strong," he said. "You're an inspiration to me."

She blushed. "Thanks. How did your sister take it? Was she happy?"

"She was shocked," he said with a laugh. "But she didn't hesitate to take back her throne. I think she was born to lead. She's new at it. She'll get better with time."

"I hope you're right."

"Gertie surprised me with her hesitation," he said, suddenly changing the subject.

"Me, too. And what she said about Taavi, well, I had no idea she didn't love herself to the moon and back."

"Really? That was an easy thing for me to spot. That's why she tries so hard."

Hestie took a sip of her wine, feeling a bit like a jerk. "I guess I've misjudged her."

"We all make mistakes," Poros said.

Hestie scoffed. "Touché."

"The irony is," Poros said, "I think you might be more like Athena than you think."

"What? How can you say that?" she was on the verge of getting angry.

He lifted his hands in the air. "Forget I said it. Never mind. I didn't mean it as an insult. I love and admire my sister."

"Let's change the subject," Hestie said, before popping a cheese cube into her mouth. "Tell me about tomorrow's plan. Are you sure it's the right move?"

"Can one ever be sure of such things?" he asked. "But it seems like the right move. Do you not agree?"

She shrugged. "I just don't want anything to get in the way of Hermie disarming those warheads. If Phorcys gets wind of your plan…"

Poros put a finger to her lips. "Better not talk about it here, just in case there are spies nearby."

She nodded and kissed his finger.

"Mmm," he said with a grin. "Maybe we should go back to my cabin for a little dessert."

"Yes, please. I'm nervous about tomorrow and need a distraction."

"I'm at your service, my lady."

CHAPTER TWENTY-TWO

Intervention

The morning of October 20th, Gertie tip-toed from her cabin, so as not to awaken Hector, and crept to the stall Hermie had built in the hull of the ship.

"Hi there, Pegasus," she said as she entered. "How about a brushing? Does that sound good?"

Pegasus nodded his head.

She found a brush and moved its bristles across his white hide. She wavered with indecision over whether she should warn him about what lay ahead. She didn't know him well enough to guess if the information would prevent him from going on the mission. If she told him, would he freak out and refuse to go? Also, the anticipation of what lay ahead would be terrifying for him. Maybe it was better for everyone, including him, if he didn't know.

She sighed.

In her vision, Helios had been directly above her, which meant that she and Hestie should be flying with Pegasus over the island of Cyprus by noon.

"There you are," Hector said with sleepy eyes and uncombed hair.

He looked hotter than hot.

"Good morning," she said, trying to hide her feelings of dread.

"Good morning. I'm sorry I fell asleep after, you know."

"That's okay. Did you sleep well?"

"Yeah. You?"

"So-so. I have a lot on my mind."

"That's the understatement of the year."

Hector moved around to the other side of Pegasus to stroke his fur.

"Today's mission has to succeed," she said. "It will save thousands, maybe even millions, of lives."

"I know you're scared, but you're also brave. I have no doubt that you'll do what has to be done. You've proved that time and time again."

She smiled up at him as tears welled in her eyes. "Thanks, Hector. That means a lot to me."

"I also think you deserve this honor that Poros and the Olympians want to bestow on you."

Gertie took a deep breath and slowly exhaled. "I'm trying not to think about it."

"Why? I thought you'd be ecstatic."

"Come on, Hector. You know why."

"Are you saying that you'd have to choose between us and immortality? You couldn't do both?"

Gertie stopped brushing Pegasus and walked around the other side to get a better view of Hector's face. "Don't you remember what you said to me just a few months ago? You said you'd never want to be a god because you would never want to put your kids through what you went through as a kid. You said you want your kids to have the kind of childhood you always dreamed of, with little league and, I don't know, picnics, or whatever."

"Weren't you listening to the song I wrote you, Gertie? I said that my heart will follow you wherever you go. I know this is what you want. I'll live with it for as long as I'm alive, so long as you won't mind being married to an old man one day."

Tears spilled from Gertie's eyes as a smile cracked her face in half. "Seriously?"

"Yeah."

She threw her arms around him.

Then she stepped back and said, "I have an idea, but I want to run it by you first."

"Uh-oh. What?"

"What if I make it a condition that I'll only become the goddess of vampires if the gods grant you immortality, too?"

Hector lifted his brows and raked a hand through his messy blond hair. "Wow. Uh, do you think they'd even go for that?"

"It couldn't hurt to ask. The question is, is that what you want?"

"Um, gosh, Gertie, can I have a minute to think about it?"

She wished she had the vampire virus running through her veins so that she could read his thoughts. Was he leaning more one way than another? She couldn't read his face.

"Take as much time as you need," she said.

"Good morning," Hermie said from the door to the stall. "Are you ready for this?"

Gertie glanced at Hector, who still seemed to be grappling with her proposal, and turned to Hermie. "I'll meet you guys on deck. I need a moment."

Hestie stood with Poros and Captain on the main deck with a stomach full of knots. Poros was about to fly to Mount Olympus, where he would join the other gods in their surprise attack on Phorcys's castle. And she was about to fly away with Gertie on Pegasus so she could signal to Hermie when to board the STS vessel carrying the warheads.

Today was the long-awaited day they'd all been preparing for. It was the day that would hopefully save the future.

"Be careful," she said to Poros.

"Same to you," he said.

She kissed him on the cheek. "Good luck."

He squeezed her hands. "Good luck. I'll see you later this afternoon."

She hoped he was right, but she didn't say that. She didn't want to express her fears and worries. Today was a day to be strong.

Prometheus offered Poros his hand. "Good luck, Poros."

Poros took his hand and shook it. "Thanks, Captain. I'll see you soon."

After Poros god-traveled away, Prometheus turned to Hestie. "Ready?"

"Ready."

"That makes one of us," Hermie said as he arrived from the lower deck with Hector and Pegasus.

Hestie put her arms around the horse's neck. "Pegasus is ready, too. Aren't you boy?"

The horse gave her a nod.

"He likes adventures, just like me," she said.

"Awesome," Hermie said with a hint of sarcasm.

"You already know you're going to be the hero of the day," Hestie said. "What are you worried about?"

"Oh, I don't know," Hermie said. "Failing to fulfill a prophecy, letting everyone down, causing the deaths of millions. Not a whole lot, I guess."

Gertie emerged from below holding a bottle of wine.

"Would anyone like a drink for courage, before we go?" Gertie offered.

"No thanks," Hestie said.

Hestie doubted wine would give her courage. It was more likely to make her sleepy. She almost said so aloud but realized how it would sound: snarky and judgmental.

Gertie took a swig and offered the bottle to Hermie.

"I'm okay," he said.

Gertie shrugged and gave the bottle to Hector. "Will you put that away for me?"

"You bet," Hector said.

"Who rides in front?" Hestie asked Gertie awkwardly.

"You do."

Hestie mounted Pegasus. With help from Hector, Gertie mounted behind her.

"Good luck," Prometheus said.

"You've got this," Hector added.

Hestie and Gertie waved as Pegasus took off into the bright, clear sky and headed for the coast of Syria.

"Gertie, there's something I want to tell you," Hestie said. "I owe you an apology for the way I've behaved around you. I'm sorry I've been such a jerk."

Gertie didn't say anything. Hestie supposed she wasn't sure if she was ready to forgive Hestie. Hestie thought it best to leave it alone.

Gertie tightened her grip on Hestie as they neared their destination.

"What is happening?" Gertie asked.

"You tell me," Hestie said. "This is where you said to go. We just passed the island of Cyprus, and that's the coast of Syria down there."

Hestie scanned the shoreline but didn't see the ship they were supposed to find.

"You said the STS carrier would be there, at the port near Latakia, but I don't see it. Do you?"

"What else did I say, Hestie?" Gertie asked. "I'm feeling dizzy and can't remember."

"Maybe you shouldn't have had that wine."

"It usually helps me. It strengthens my gifts."

"You said the STS ship was smuggling the Russian warheads to Syria to be used on other Syrians," Hestie said. "According to your research, the country has been in civil conflict for like a decade. Over 500,000 people have been killed or have gone missing."

"Oh," Gertie said.

Oh? Was that all Gertie had to say? Maybe Hestie's apology had been premature. Had Gertie really gotten too drunk to be of any use on the most important mission of their lives? Unbelievable!

"You said if we came here today, October 20th, you and me, just like this, flying on Pegasus, that we would see the STS carrier from Russia and discover where Poseidon is and what he's been up to. You said we would be able to signal to Hermie when it was safe to board the ship and disarm the warheads."

"Hermie will disarm them?"

Hestie glanced back at her, trying to keep the fear and anxiety from taking over. "Yes. You said that, as the god of technology, he was our best chance."

"Did I say anything else?" Gertie asked.

Hestie buried her head in Pegasus's mane and groaned. "Other than the fact that one of us would get badly hurt, no."

"I didn't say which of us it would be?"

Hestie heaved a sigh of frustration. "You said if I knew, it would change the future. Geez, Gertie. What's wrong with you? You're scaring me. Can you please snap out of it?"

"The sins of the father will be the burden of the son," Gertie muttered.

"What?" Hestie glanced back at her again as they got closer to the port.

"Metis told me that. I can't remember when or why."

Hestie grabbed her head with both hands. "Aye, Gertrude! You're killing me." Then she stiffened. "Wait a minute, was Metis talking about Zeus's sins bringing harm to Poros?"

Hestie began to worry that her advice to Poros to ignore the Fates might have repercussions. Maybe that's what Metis was trying to warn Gertie about.

Gertie pointed. "There it is."

Hestie scanned the coastline and was relieved when the STS ship came into view.

"I see it!" Hestie said. "Pegasus, can you take us closer, just to make sure?"

Pegasus swooped down toward the ship. It appeared exactly as Gertie had described it: five grain bins, the flybridge atop a two-story salon, and the two guards.

"That's it," Gertie confirmed.

Hestie watched as the carrier docked in the marina.

"Do you see anything?" Gertie asked.

"I see Poseidon!" Hestie said. "He's arguing with someone—I can't see, yet. Pegasus can you fly down just a little closer to the water?"

Pegasus descended and hovered a few yards from the waves.

"Maybe this is when we should call Hermie," Gertie said. "While Poseidon is distracted."

"Good idea. I'm praying to him now."

Seconds later, Hestie said, "I see Hermie. He's invisible to mortals, but, trust me, he's there."

"What's he doing?"

"Climbing into the first grain bin. Wow! That was fast! He just gave me a thumbs up and is darting into the next."

Knowing Gertie lacked god vision, Hestie described to Gertie what Hermie was doing.

When Hermie had given her a thumbs up for the fifth time, Hestie said, "He did it! He's disarmed them all!"

"What's Poseidon doing now?" Gertie asked.

Hestie sensed Helios getting closer. She avoided looking up at him as he said, "Stay out of it! You'll ruin everything!"

Ignoring Helios, Hestie continued to observe Poseidon. Then she covered her mouth. "I see what he's up to. Stay here. I'll be right back."

Hermie had just disarmed the last of the warheads and had been about to search the docks for Poseidon and Phorcys when he heard Gertie scream.

He flew toward her and was horrified by what he saw. Ladon's one hundred serpent heads had grabbed Pegasus from the sky and had pulled him under the sea, and Gertie was flailing through the air, about to land into the middle of it.

He god-traveled to Gertie and caught her in his arms, but he was too late for Pegasus. Tears fell down his cheeks as the beloved white horse was dragged so far beneath the water that Hermie could no longer see him.

"I couldn't save you both," he said.

"But maybe it's not too late," Gertie said. "Before we left, I woke up Bach and convinced him to bite me. I have the vampire virus coursing through me. I've just been waiting for it to take effect."

"What about the sun?"

"That's why I drank so much of my father's wine, because it protects me from the sun when I'm a vampire and heightens my powers."

She jumped out of his arms before he'd had a chance to process all she'd said.

Hovering in the air beside him, she said, "Come on! There's no time to lose!"

"You have no weapon!" he shouted as he conjured his.

"I'll have my bull horns!"

She plunged into the sea.

Gods, she was brave, and he had no choice but to be brave, too. He dove into the water after her.

CHAPTER TWENTY-THREE

A Final Battle

Gertie was having trouble shifting into her bull form as she sank into the sea, closer and closer to the ocean floor. With her vampire vision, she saw Ladon below. The monster's serpent heads were twisted around the body of the winged horse. Because vampires couldn't hear underwater, she couldn't tell if Pegasus was crying out. In fact, she couldn't tell if he was alive.

What did Ladon intend to do with him?

Gertie continued her attempts to transform by moving her legs through the water, as if she were running, and by reaching out with her arms. However, nothing was happening except that she was wasting valuable time and appearing ridiculous.

Hermie swam past her with his sword drawn. Was he really going to take on Ladon alone?

Since her attempts to shift were failing, she swam after him.

While she swam, she reached out to the vampires telepathically. *Can you hear me? It's time. Ladon has Pegasus at the bottom of the sea between Cyprus and the coast of Syria.*

She only hoped Bach had managed to convince the others to be ready. She hoped they'd risk exposure to the sun to help save Pegasus.

Not all of Ladon's one hundred heads were wrapped around Pegasus. At least eighty of them were still free and threatening as Hermie swam toward them, swinging.

When Ladon wrapped another of his heads around Hermie's waist, Gertie screamed through gritted teeth.

Then it happened. She shifted. Her scream became a snort. With her massive weight, she raced to the bottom, where she rammed her horns against the thick, serpentine necks. Although it was difficult to maneuver in the water, her bull form had other advantages. With her feet on the ocean floor, she could better leverage her weight and charge.

It was utterly satisfying when her horns succeeded in piercing the necks of the monster. She snorted with glee and charged again, managing to get her horns into the center of Ladon's body mass, where Pegasus was being held. As she charged into the center, some of the necks holding Pegasus loosened, and the horse bucked against the beast with a mighty force.

Pegasus was alive!

"Pegasus!" Gertie cried, though she couldn't even hear her own voice.

That's when the vampires appeared with their blades drawn. Seeing them swimming toward the battle made Gertie's heart leap with love for them. She really wanted to serve as their protector one day.

Relieved and encouraged by their arrival, Gertie fought relentlessly against the necks holding Pegasus. Between her horns piercing and Pegasus's hooves bucking, Pegasus managed to get completely free of the monster.

But there were too many heads for their small number, and Hermie, along with Penny and Bach, were trapped in some of them.

Gertie told Pegasus telepathically to swim to safety.

After ramming her horns into as many necks as she could, Gertie tried another tactic. She opened her mouth and bit one of the serpentine necks, crunching through layers and layers, nearly biting the head free.

Ladon screamed.

As she prepared to bite the monster again, she saw something coming toward them from the west. One thing she did not have as a bull was peripheral vision. She turned her head and was overjoyed to see the Olympian gods in their chariots rushing to the scene. Within minutes, all one hundred heads of Ladon were either bound or cut off, and Hermie, Bach, and Penny were freed.

Gertie shifted back into her usual form, exhausted and relieved.

Hermie came up to her and said something, but she said, "Vampires can't hear under water. Can you tell me telepathically?"

You are the bravest person I know, he said.

Hermie caught up to Del as the vampires and gods piled into the half dozen chariots parked on the ocean floor. His parents with Jen and Hip; Hades with Persephone, Hecate, and Alecto; Athena with Hestia; Ares with Aphrodite and Hermes; Apollo with his sister; and even Hephaestus in his horseless, mechanical chariot.

With Hephaestus were Poseidon, Amphitrite, and Rhode.

Hermie and Del climbed into his parents' chariot. His mother and father embraced him.

"You were so brave," his aunt Jen said.

"Are you okay?" his mother asked.

"Unbelievably, I am," Hermie said.

His mother and father chuckled. Del shook her head and smiled.

"I think he takes more after me than he does you," Hip said to Hermie's father.

"And how is that possible?" Jen wanted to know.

"Genes, right, Hermie?" Hip asked with a glance back.

Hermie just laughed.

As they sped back toward the ship, Hermie asked Del telepathically, *Is it hard to see Poseidon among us?*

If you and the captain and the rest of his crew could forgive me for killing Mina, then I should be able to forgive Poseidon for killing Taavi.

Hermie circled his arms around her waist and kissed her cheek. As they reached the surface, he used his body to shield her from the sun, but to his surprise, Helios was nowhere to be seen.

"It can't be nightfall already," Hermie said as the chariot flew toward the *Marcella II*.

"Helios is hiding behind some really thick clouds," Hestie said from Apollo's chariot. "Because he knows the vampires helped to save his wife."

"Come here, sweet girl," their mother said.

Hestie flew into their parents' arms.

"We're so proud," their father said.

"Come see us soon," their mother said.

All six chariots hovered above the ship while the crew of the *Marcella II* returned to the main deck, where Pegasus was already waiting.

From Hephaestus's chariot, Poseidon said, "Please accept my sincere apology for my attacks against you and for the death of your friend. I was out of my mind, and I will do whatever I can from this day forward to support you."

Alastair, who hovered in the air just above the main deck, turned to Poseidon. "Thank you, Lord Poseidon. I speak on behalf of my fellow vampires when I say that we forgive you and are grateful for your future support."

"I am glad to hear it," the lord of the sea said. "I also owe many thanks to Hestie, who helped me overcome Phorcys and rescue my wife and daughter."

"Gertie was part of that effort, too," Hestie said.

Hermie glanced at Gertie, whose eyes widened with surprise at having heard her name mentioned in a positive way by Hestie.

Hermie said, "We also have Gertie and the vampires to thank for rescuing Pegasus."

"You had a hand in that, too," Gertie said.

Hermie smiled.

"Have you accepted Poros's offer, Gertie?" Hades asked.

Gertie's cheeks turned red. "I'm thinking it over and will have a decision soon."

"Good idea," Persephone said. "There's a lot to consider."

"Look at the young lovers below," Aphrodite said to Ares. "Something cheerful to think of on a difficult day."

Hermie let go of Del's hand, feeling embarrassed. Was Aphrodite talking about them in front of everyone?

Hermie noticed that Jinsoo had no problem holding Alastair's hand. He chastised himself for being such a coward.

Del chuckled beside him.

"Does anyone know why Ladon attacked Pegasus?" Jinsoo asked.

"I do," Apollo said. "For more leverage. Phorcys intended to steal something else precious to Poseidon, to keep him under his control."

Hermie flew to Pegasus and wrapped his arms around him.

"Where is Phorcys now?" Hermie asked.

Artemis said, "He's tied up with the rest of his family at his castle, until we figure out what to do with them."

"Speaking of which," Athena began, "we should return to Mount Olympus and make a decision. The sooner the better." She turned to Poros, who had joined the others on the ship. "Are you coming, brother?"

"I'll leave you to it," he said. "But I hope to see you soon."

"Father?" Hector cried from the deck of the ship.

Hermie couldn't recall which god was Hector's father, but he figured it out when Hephaestus stopped, backed up his chariot, and gazed down at Hector.

"Hello, Hector," Hephaestus said. "I'm pleased to see you contributing to the efforts of Prometheus and his crew. I'm very proud of you, son. If you're around tomorrow, I'll return for you and take you back to Mount Olympus to see my forge."

With that, Hephaestus drove off, leaving Hector gaping.

As soon as the chariots were gone, Hestie threw her arms around Poros.

"What a relief!" she said against his neck.

He held her tight in his arms. "Thank the gods."

She pulled away and wrinkled her nose. "*We* are the gods, Poros. Thank *us*."

"And them."

"Okay. You're right. And them."

"How long will Helios stay hidden?" Penny asked.

Hestie turned around to face Penny and the other vamps. "All day. We have the whole day to celebrate."

"Let's shake it off," Mahdi suggested.

"Taavi would have liked that," Raimo said.

"Let's do it," Del said. "Will you join us, Hermie?"

"I can't sing, but okay," Hermie said.

"Jinsoo? Alastair asked. "You will play along, yes?"

"You bet, Alastair!"

The vampires, gods, and demigods sat in a circle on the main deck.

"Who starts?" Hestie asked.

"I will," Mahdi said.

Hestie glanced up to the flybridge, where Prometheus watched the activity below him. She was pleased to see him wearing a smile on his face, but she wondered if he would ever find it in his heart to forgive Athena, as the rest of them had."

Alastair, who sat between her and Jinsoo, whispered, "He has a very forgiving heart. I'm sure he already has."

Hestie returned the vampire's smile and joined in the game.

After a day of singing and celebrating with the gods and vampires, Morpheus appeared on board to return Gertie and Hector to Gertie's home in Athens. It was hard to say goodbye to her friends. She didn't want to leave. But she was anxious to see her mother and stepfather, who, according to Morpheus, had returned home with Iris's help. She was also eager to see Nikita, Lajos, and the rest of the Angelis family.

Everyone was waiting for her and Hector when they arrived. After a day of celebrating with the crew of the *Marcella II*, she and Hector spent the evening celebrating at her home. Babá had made a delicious spread of food for all, including not one, but two cakes.

In a private moment in his study, away from the others, James told Gertie and Hector that he may have to face criminal charges for the part he played in STS, but he urged them to tell the gods that there was more work to do.

"People are being smuggled out of Syria against their will and sold to corrupt business owners in Russia," he said. "I have nightmares about them every night. If you and the gods hadn't captured that monster who was threatening me, I don't know what I would have done, but this can't continue. It just can't."

Gertie crossed her arms over her chest. "Don't worry. Hector and I will tell them, and we'll do all we can to stop STS, once and for all."

She turned to Hector. She wasn't sure what he would decide about becoming immortal, but she knew that, whatever he decided, they would fight the fight together.

THE END

Thank you for reading my story. If you enjoyed it, please consider leaving a review. Reviews help other readers to find my books, which helps me.

Please visit my website at www.evapohler.com to get the next book, *Guardians of the Sea*.

What doesn't kill you makes you stronger.

After enduring Delphine's dangerous training regimen, the young gods and demigods embark on a mission to take down the corrupt shipping company once and for all, to liberate victimized communities up and down the Mediterranean and nearby seas.

But unforeseen conflicts cause the young gods and demigods to question the nature of their mission, their purpose, and their relationships with one another.

In the face of impossible choices, how important are love, loyalty, and friendship? Moreover, how far should one go to defend those who can't defend themselves? Should one sacrifice everything?

Read the surprising conclusion of *The Vampires and Gods Series.*

For lovers of Greek mythology, paranormal romance, and action adventure stories.

CHAPTER ONE

The Boy on the Bus

I hadn't realized you packed *that* coat," Gertie's mother complained as Gertie and her parents were leaving their room at the Hotel Excelsior in Venice. "It's not one of your best."

It was a gray puffer coat that tied at the waist and had a soft flannel lining.

"Then it's a good thing you won't have to look at it," Gertie muttered.

Her father glared at her but didn't comment. Instead, he went ahead of her through the lobby to the front desk to check out.

On the way to the ferry, in the back of the limo, Gertie sat across from her parents and said, "It's still not too late to change your minds."

"We're not having this discussion again," her father said. "End of story."

"Don't worry, Gertrude. You'll have the time of your life."

Somehow, Gertie doubted that.

"I know *I* did," her mother added. "I'm jealous of you, actually."

Gertie frowned. "You're welcome to go in my place."

Her mother leaned forward and patted Gertie's knee. "Everyone's frightened of trying new things."

She flinched, unused to being touched. "I'm not," she lied. "I just like my own bed."

"It will be there for you when you get back," her father said. "You're seventeen, now. It's time for you to venture away from the nest."

"Happy Birthday to me," she muttered beneath her breath.

Gertie tried to ignore the fact that they were more excited for her to go than she was. She'd never heard of two people more eager to become empty-nesters than her parents. And it wasn't like she was the last in a long line of siblings. She was an only child—an independent one at that. Why couldn't she stay in her room and be left alone?

She wasn't surprised when they didn't get out of the limo and walk her to the ferry. Instead, they had their driver do it. They had offered plenty of excuses—it was too windy out for her mother's asthma and too sunny for her fair skin. Plus, her father had a heart condition. And so on and so forth.

Once she was onboard and inside her cabin, she sat on the bed and cried. She hated her parents for making her do this. They had told her to enjoy the scenic boat ride along the Adriatic Sea, but she was determined to spend it all indoors. She rummaged through her bag, found her e-reader, and read until she fell asleep.

It was dark the next day when she got off the ferry in Patras to board the bus to Athens. So much for seeing the sights.

The wind blew strands of her blond hair into her mouth, her eyes, and the sweaty crease of her neck. It wasn't cold—was actually quite warm—but she was glad to have her coat as she pulled her bags behind her.

Gertie expected more people to be riding the bus, but there were only three: an older couple sitting together in the front seat and a boy her age near the back. He was cute and was looking at her with interest. She sat two seats in front of him, without returning his gaze.

"People like you don't usually ride the bus at night," he said after a few minutes. His Greek accent was thick and sexy.

She glanced back at him. "People like me?"

"Young and wealthy."

"Well, if you want to rob me, go for it."

He laughed. "I don't want to rob you."

"The bus driver seems to think so," she said. "He keeps looking at us in his mirror."

"He's bored and has nothing else to do."

She didn't reply but pulled out her phone and logged on to Goodreads.

"You must be pretty hot," he said after a while.

"I beg your pardon?" She felt a blush coming on.

"In that coat. It's eighty degrees."

"Yeah. I didn't have room in my luggage." She spoke without turning back to face him, while scrolling through Goodreads on her phone. She wanted to update her status on where she was in her book.

"Where are you going?" he asked.

"Athens."

"I guessed that much. Are you going to visit relatives?"

"Nope."

"Then you must be one of those visiting students," he said, moving to the seat behind hers.

He smelled like soap.

"Yep. You nailed it."

"I did what?"

"I'm sorry. That's just an expression." She glanced back at him. His face was so close, that she could see the big round pupils in his dark brown eyes. His dark curly hair fell around his face, nearly touching his shoulders, which were bare except for the one-inch strap of his blue cotton tank. The muscles in his arms were solid and well defined. If he weren't so cute, she might be uncomfortable.

When she looked into his eyes, she found it difficult to pull away. He was mesmerizing.

Her phone vibrated, stirring her from her stupor. It was a text from her mother, asking if she had landed yet in Patras.

"On bus to Athens," she texted back.

When the boy said nothing more, she rummaged through her bag for her e-reader and returned to the world of her book.

Not thirty minutes had passed when she felt the boy lean on the back of her seat and ask, "What are you reading?"

"*Interview with the Vampire*, by Anne Rice."

He gasped.

She spun around to face him. "Have you read it?"

"No, no. Is it good?"

"So far, yes. I'm loving it." Then she added, "I've always been fascinated by vampire stories."

The corners of his mouth quirked. "Is that so?"

"What's so funny?" She narrowed her eyes. "I don't believe in them or anything; I'm just interested in the mythology."

"I see."

She didn't like that he was laughing at her, so she turned around in her seat to face the front and continued reading. It was difficult for her to get back into the novel after that. She kept seeing the boy's face in place of the words.

Only a few minutes had passed, however, when the boy leaned forward and asked, "So what interests you? About the vampires?"

"A lot of things." She glanced back at him. "Their superpowers, for one: invisibility, flight, mind control…"

"Don't forget x-ray vision," he said, giving her a once over.

"Yeah. Right." She laughed. "You're thinking of Superman."

He laughed, too. "What else?"

She turned in her seat and rested her back against the bus window so she could face him. "I guess the idea of conquering death is interesting to me."

"Are you afraid of death?"

"No. Not really. But I suppose I'm curious about it."

"In what way?" He leaned closer.

"Well, don't you wonder if there's life after death? Do we go to heaven? Or do we go to sleep? Or do we just stop existing? Not that it matters. I just wonder, that's all."

"If it doesn't matter, then why do you wonder about it?"

"It *matters*. I just meant we're going to die regardless of what happens." She twisted the belt of her coat. "Like my grandma. She just died. And so I wonder if she can still hear me and stuff, you know?"

He sat back in his seat and studied her, like he was assessing her.

She blushed. "What?"

He shook his head. "So, what else about vampire *mythology* do you find interesting?"

"I don't know." She twisted the belt in the opposite direction. "The combination of power and powerlessness, I guess. It makes them tragic."

"Powerlessness?"

"They can't help what they are. They don't usually choose to become vampires."

"But they prey on humans, yes?" he asked.

"In the story I'm reading right now, a vampire is trying to live on the blood of animals, but it's very difficult for him."

"Thee moy." The boy cringed. "I can imagine."

"I once read that vampires are a reflection of us. We created the mythology to represent ourselves."

He leaned forward again, his arm almost touching her. "Explain."

She bit her lip, searching for the right words. She must have been thinking hard, for she drew blood. The boy leaned in, and for a moment, she thought he would kiss her.

The bus hit a bump, and she fell back against the window, hitting her head. The boy eased back in his seat. She rubbed her head and turned to face the front.

"You okay?" he asked from behind.

She nodded without looking at him.

"So, tell me," he said, leaning on the back of the seat. "How are vampires a reflection of humans?"

"Deep down inside, we're all monsters."

"You really think so?"

She nodded. "And yet we have so little control."

"Power and no power."

She glanced back and gave him a subtle smile. "Exactly."

He said nothing in reply, so she turned to her book. After several minutes, she was finally able to get back into the story. A few times, she wondered about the boy behind her, but she didn't see any reason to try to talk to him. She would be leaving this country in one year, to never return, so what was the use of making friends?

She could hear her mother's voice in the back of her head reminding her that she had no friends at home, either, but it wasn't Gertie's fault that everyone at her private school in New York was fake.

At some point, she must have fallen asleep. When she opened her eyes, she saw the boy leaning over the back of the seat looking down at her with a mouth full of fangs and blood.

She cringed and opened her eyes—for real this time. She glanced back at the boy, but he was gone.

<u>CHAPTER TWO</u>

The Host Family

When she arrived at the station in Athens, she found a boy holding up a sign with her name written on it: Gertrude Morgan. She almost didn't see the sign, because the boy holding it was so beautiful. He was flanked by another boy about his age—eighteen or nineteen, but shorter—and a girl, either the same age or younger.

The girl had studs in her nose and cheek and had spikey, short hair. All three wore summer shorts, flip flops, and t-shirts with graphics of what appeared to be bands. Gertie realized the outer two were related, both having the same brown hair and brown eyes and petite build. They looked nothing like the boy in the middle, who towered over them and was breathtaking, like a Greek god.

"Gertie?" the girl asked as Gertie came to a halt in front of them.

"That's right."

She was astonished when the girl nearly plowed her down with an embrace. "I'm Nikita! It's so great to finally meet you!"

Nikita was the name of one of the members of her host family. She and Gertie had been texting and emailing the past two weeks about the trip—what to bring and what to expect. Surely this girl wasn't one and the same.

"You're Nikita?"

The girl frowned. "This is Hector, our friend. And that's Klaus, my brother. I'm pretty sure I told you all about him. He's been dying to meet you."

"Okay, Nikita," Klaus said. "You don't have to make me sound so eager."

"It's nice to meet you," Gertie said, still a little shocked. They didn't look like the private school kids back home.

"Our parents and little sister are waiting in the car," Nikita said. "Can you boys help her with her bags?"

The two boys took her rolling suitcases—one apiece—and Nikita took one of her shoulder bags, and then they followed the boys through the station to the sidewalk outside. Gertie found herself studying the lines on the back of the taller boy named Hector.

When they reached the car, Gertie had another shock. It was a two-door coupe meant for four passengers, but there were already three inside.

They weren't inside long. Just as Nikita had done, the man, woman, and child, all thin and petite and dark-haired like their other family members, climbed out and hugged her. The mother even kissed her on her cheek.

"We're so glad to have you join our family," the mother said, cupping Gertie's face in her hands. "Look at you, Gertoula! You're so beautiful, koreetsi mou!"

"It's Gertie," Gertie said.

"Of course, Gertoula! I mean Gertie."

"Mamá puts oula and itsa and aki on the end of everyone's name. Even Babá's!" Nikita explained. "She calls him Babáki mou!"

"Yes, Nikitsa, koreetsi mou!" her mother said, and turning to Gertie, said, "So you call me Mamá, too. Yes?"

"And I'm Babá," the father said affectionately. Then he picked up his little girl, who seemed seven or eight years old, and said, "And this is Phoebe."

"Mamá calls her Phoeboula, so don't get confused," Klaus said.

"Hello," Gertie said to the girl.

The girl smiled but said nothing. Then Gertie remembered what Nikita had said in her text about the fire three years ago. Their baby brother had died. Phoebe hadn't spoken since.

Babá and the boys put her luggage in the trunk of the coupe before piling into the car. Phoebe sat in the front seat, without a seatbelt, and Nikita climbed on her brother's lap.

"Should I call a cab?" Gertie asked.

"No, no!" Babá said, holding the door open for her. "There's room for you."

Hector climbed out. "Take my place. I need to head home anyway. I'll take a cab or the bus."

"No, Hector. I promised you baklava," Mamá insisted.

"I'll come by for some tomorrow," Hector said. He waved goodbye and then raised his hand for a cab.

Gertie climbed in beside Klaus. Nikita shifted from her brother's lap and squeezed between them. No one wore their seatbelts. Gertie wasn't even sure the old coupe had them.

The car smelled like onions, mold, and sweat, but Gertie resisted pinching her nose as they drove through the streets of Athens from the bus station. Mamá and Babá spoke animatedly about their country, the American school, the ruins, and many other topics during the thirty-minute ride. When they pulled up in front of a dilapidated apartment building, Gertie thought they were playing a joke on her.

It wasn't a joke.

Babá and Klaus dragged the heavy suitcases up the three flights of steps to the apartment. Apparently, there were no elevators. When Mamá opened the door and flipped on the light, at least a dozen roaches scrambled for cover.

"Get them!" Babá called.

Nikita dropped Gertie's bag and rushed in behind her brother, stomping like winemakers in a vat of grapes. Phoebe joined them, enthusiastically, like it was a game.

"Good! Well done!" Babá said as they scooped up the dead bugs with their bare hands and threw them in the garbage can across the room.

Gertie was afraid to step inside.

"Come in! Come in!" Mamá said. "It's not much, but it's very comfortable. No? Let me take your coat. You won't need that here but maybe a few days out of the year."

Gertie kept her coat. "That's all right. Thank you."

The furniture was shabby, but tidy. The kitchen across the room was neat but very outdated. The lighting was poor, which Gertie thought was probably good.

"I'll show you where to put your things," Nikita said. "Let's go."

"And then come back here for my baklava, so Gertoula has a proper welcome," Mamá said.

As they turned down a narrow hall, Nikita said, "That's my brother's room, and my parents have a room down the hall. There's the bathroom, and here is my room, where you'll be staying."

Gertie's face paled. A family of five shared a three-bedroom apartment? The living area and kitchen were tiny, so Gertie had hoped there were bedrooms to escape to. How did everyone fit?

"You can have Phoebe's bed. She'll sleep on a cot with Mamá and Babá while you're here."

"I don't want to be any trouble," Gertie managed to say.

"You must be joking!" Nikita said. "We're all so happy to have you. It's all Mamá and Babá have been talking about. It's been the American girl this and the American girl that for two weeks!"

"I don't understand why they are so happy to have me," Gertie said.

Nikita shrugged. "They are very proud of our country and relish the opportunity to show it off to a young, impressionable American. In other words, they have plans for you every day between now and the start of school. Tomorrow, we go to Crete, Babá's favorite island."

Gertie took in a deep breath. A tiny apartment filled with people and daily activities galore. She wondered when and how she would have time to be alone to read and relax.

She wanted to call her parents and tell them she was sick.

"I'm not feeling well," she said to Nikita. "Can I go straight to bed?"

Nikita's eyes widened. "Oh, no. You just arrived! Mamá and Babá and Klaus and Phoebe—they will all be so disappointed. They've been anxious. I'm sure Mamá has some medicine to make you feel better. Come with me."

Gertie hesitated, so Nikita waited for her in the doorway as Gertie looked around the small bedroom, with its plain white walls and short metal beds. Two scratched-up wooden chests of drawers took up all the wall space between the beds, and there was no on-suite bath—just a small closet without a door, stuffed to the gills with clothes and books.

Gertie stepped closer to the books. "You like to read?"

"Oh, yes. Klaus and I both read voraciously. This is only a small part of our collection. We have many more books downstairs in the basement."

"There's a basement?" Gertie wondered if that might be her getaway.

"It's not very pleasant, but yes. I'll show you tomorrow. Right now, Mamá wants us to eat her dessert."

CHAPTER THREE

The Basement

Gertie had hoped to sleep in, but the walls were thin and the rooms too close to keep the apartment quiet much later than nine o'clock, so she crawled out of bed and asked to use the shower. Because the shower in the main bathroom didn't work, Gertie was forced to use the one in Mamá and Babá's room. Nikita warned her, however, that the toilet in that bathroom was broken, so she should use the one in the hall. So, between the two bathrooms there was only one working shower and one working toilet, but plenty of roaches.

"When do we leave for Crete?" Gertie asked Nikita once she had finished dressing and had put on her shoes.

"Not until tonight." Nikita plopped on the rickety bed across from Gertie's. "Want some breakfast?"

"No, thank you. Why tonight?"

"Well, mainly because Babá works all day, but also because it's better to take the ferry while you're sleeping, so you don't waste time."

Great, Gertie thought. Another long ferry ride. She wondered how many people would be sharing her cabin.

"Babá wants us to lunch at his café," Nikita said.

"He owns a café?"

"No, no. He's the cook. He wants to show off his culinary skills. So, what do you want to do until then? Hector offered to drive us wherever we want to go. Maybe you want to see the Parthenon?"

"Maybe." She wouldn't mind seeing more of Hector. "But what I'd really like to see is the basement. Before we go sightseeing, will you show me the rest of your books?"

Nikita frowned. "I don't know."

"Please? You were okay with it last night."

Nikita stood up and crossed to the door. "Okay, but don't touch anything."

Gertie followed her out.

When Klaus heard where they were going, he wanted to come too. Mamá begged Gertie to eat something, but Gertie said her stomach was upset.

"Don't touch anything that doesn't belong to you down there," Mamá said to her children as the three teens waved goodbye.

The stairs to the basement were not well-lit, so Gertie held tightly to the railing as her eyes adjusted to the darkness. Once they had made it all the way down, Klaus pulled a chain above his head, and a single bulb illuminated the cavernous room. It was a fairly massive basement, with the dimensions of the building broken up into many nooks and crannies, and entire rooms closed off with heavy wooden doors.

"Our books are over here," Nikita said.

Gertie followed Nikita through a maze of boxes and crates toward a wooden bookshelf against the back wall. Along the way, Gertie noticed two chests in the middle of the room resembling antique coffins. One was as large as a man, and the other half its size.

"Are those what I think they are?" Gertie asked. Heavy chains and padlocks wrapped around the middle of both coffins.

"Of course," Nikita said. "But they don't have dead bodies in them." She laughed—nervously, it seemed to Gertie. "Just a bunch of old stuff."

"How old are these?" Gertie touched the top of the one nearest her.

"No!" Klaus grabbed her hand. "Don't touch that."

Gertie lifted her brows with surprise. "Why not?"

Klaus was still holding Gertie's hand. He dropped it, blushed, and averted his eyes.

"There really are bodies in them, aren't there?" Gertie said without inflection.

"Yes," Klaus said. "So leave them alone."

Nikita narrowed her eyes at her brother. "He's joking."

"Why are they kept down here?" Gertie asked. "Instead of a cemetery?"

Klaus turned to Nikita. "We should tell her."

"Shut *up*, Klaus!" Nikita gave him a threatening glare.

"Tell me what?"

"She's going to find out sooner or later," Klaus insisted.

"We are *not* having this conversation. It will gross her out." Nikita turned to Gertie. "Just ignore him. He wants to frighten you with old stories about the dead, but they are *just* ghost stories."

"I love ghost stories," Gertie said, brightening. "I'm especially fond of vampires."

Nikita clapped a hand to her forehead and closed her eyes. "Can we just look at the books and leave?"

Gertie moved closer to the bookshelf and read the titles along the spines. Many of the books were in Greek, but at least a third of them were in English. Of the English books, most were children's classics, such as *The Secret Garden, Charlotte's Web, Huckleberry Finn, Little Women, Island of the Blue Dolphins,* and *Treasure Island*—all of which Gertie had already read. They also had the Harry Potter books, all Rick Riordan books, most of Tolkien's works, and—of all things—all ten books of Anne Rice's *The Vampire Chronicles.*

"Have you read these?" Gertie asked.

"We've read everything down here," Klaus replied.

"I'm on the first one." Gertie plucked the dusty paperback from its place on the shelf and cracked it open. "I have it on my e-reader."

"You're welcome to borrow anything you see," Klaus said.

"Any *book* you see," Nikita qualified. "Most of this stuff down here doesn't belong to us."

"Which one of you is the vampire lover?" Gertie asked, as she returned the book to its shelf.

Before the siblings could answer, a loud noise, like the sound of a thud, startled all three of them.

And it came from the smaller of the two coffins.

All three looked first at the coffin, and then at each other with shocked and terrified eyes. No one breathed for a full five seconds.

Then Klaus said, "Let's get out of here."

The teens scrambled up the basement stairs.

In the doorway, Gertie said, "The light."

"Leave it," Klaus said. "Let's go."

<u>CHAPTER FOUR</u>

The Parthenon

After lunch at Babá's café, where the only thing Gertie recognized was the gyro (so that's what she ate), Hector drove Gertie, Nikita, and Klaus to see the Parthenon and other ancient sites.

He drove a red and white Mini Cooper—not what she expected for a boy of his stature because he seemed too big for it. But it was in good condition, and the four of them fit comfortably. Klaus and Nikita insisted that she take the front seat, so she had the better view of the sights as they drove toward the acropolis.

"Why didn't you take your car to the bus station last night?" she asked Hector out of curiosity.

"Mr. and Mrs. Angelis didn't want me to waste my gas when we were going to the same place."

"That's their way," Klaus said.

"Mamá and Babá can be very persuasive," Nikita added.

"So, what made you decide to come to Greece?" Hector asked.

Gertie shrugged. "I didn't decide. My mom did."

"Is she from Greece?" he asked.

"No. She came to school here for a year, just before she married my dad. She loved it so much that she wanted me to come, too."

"You'll love it," Nikita said. "Greece is the most beautiful place in the world."

Gertie wished she cared more about seeing beautiful places, but the truth was, she'd rather read. The adventures in books were always so much more interesting than the ones in real life—though she had to admit that if Hector lived in New York City, she wouldn't mind having an adventure with him. Too bad he lived here.

"It's especially beautiful at night," Klaus said. "We have to take her to the rock to watch the sunset."

"Don't we have to catch the ferry to Crete?" Gertie asked.

"At ten-thirty," Nikita said. "We have plenty of time."

"It can be dangerous here at night," Hector said. "But I guess if we stay together, we'll be all right."

"Dangerous how?" Gertie asked. "You mean like muggers?"

Hector glanced in his rearview mirror at the siblings in the backseat, but they kept their mouths clamped shut.

"Just stay with *me*." Hector reached over and patted her hand, sending shocks of energy up her arm. "And you'll be fine."

Hector squeezed the car into a spot on the side of the road, and then they walked in the summer heat up toward the acropolis. The first thing they came upon was the Theater of Dionysus wedged in the southern slope of the hill.

"Dionysus?" Gertie perked up. "I thought the Parthenon was a tribute to Athena."

"That happened after," Hector said. "This area was first occupied by a cult of Dionysus. This is where drama is said to have been born."

Although Gertie wasn't a fan of sightseeing, she was a fan of the ancient Greeks and their mythology. She loved it almost as much as she did vampire lore.

"There used to be a temple for him here, too," Nikita added. "But it got moved when they built the Parthenon."

"Some people believe that Dionysus continues to hang out here, beneath the acropolis, in the secret caves," Klaus added.

"Secret caves?" Gertie asked. She'd much rather see the secret caves than the broken old buildings.

Nikita and Hector both rolled their eyes at Klaus.

"Come on." Hector continued along the path.

Gertie caught up to him. "Can we go see the caves?"

"They're closed off to tourists," Hector said. "And they're danger-ous, so no."

When they passed the area leading up to the Parthenon, Gertie stopped. "Don't we want to go this way?" It was the way everyone else was going.

"Later, before sunset," Nikita said.

"I want to show you the Temple of Hephaestus," Hector said. "It's the best-preserved ancient temple in the world."

"And it's special to him, too," Klaus added.

Hector sighed and Nikita shook her head.

"Special how?" Gertie asked.

"Let's go get something to drink." Nikita slapped her brother on the arm. "It's too hot out here."

As they continued down the path, passing an enormous amphithea-ter they called the Odeon, Klaus said, "You guys are only postponing the inevitable."

Gertie stopped just as they were turning onto a pedestrian street. "What are you talking about, Klaus? What are they not telling me?"

Nikita stepped in front of her brother and squared herself to Gertie. "Hector was born there. He's embarrassed by the story, but Klaus doesn't know how to keep his mouth shut."

"Oh." Gertie followed them along the street toward a stretch of shops and cafés.

The teens were shining with sweat by the time they sat down and or-dered drinks. Gertie asked for a Coke. Hector ordered a Frappe. Nikita and Klaus ordered water and insisted on paying the bill. But Hector pulled out his wallet and handed money to the waitress before either of the other two.

"You should let me pay for everything," Gertie said after the waitress had left. "My parents gave me a credit card with unlimited credit."

Nikita and Klaus turned red.

"But you're our guest," Klaus said. "We want to pay."

"Yes, but…" Gertie was about to say that her parents had so much more money than theirs, but she bit her lip. "You are already having me in your home. I want to give something back."

The Angelis kids smiled. *Faux pas* averted.

"Maybe next time," Hector said.

They took their drinks with them as they walked down the road toward the temple. It was a fifteen-minute walk, but the heat shining down on them and reflecting up from the pavement made it seem longer.

"Helios is bright today," Hector said.

Gertie smiled. "The sun god, right?"

"She knows Helios!" Klaus said laughing. "This is great."

"I know about all the Greek gods and goddesses," Gertie said. "I love them almost as much as I do vampires."

Hector flinched at her last statement but then tried to cover it up. As they walked further, however, he couldn't seem to resist asking, "How can anybody love vampires?"

"I meant I'm interested in the lore. I love reading stories about them." She told him about *The Vampire Chronicles* and some of the other novels she had read that had made her want to read Anne Rice. "Klaus and Nikita have the whole collection in their basement." Then she added, "That basement is pretty creepy, by the way. We'll have to ask Babá to get me the rest of the books." She laughed.

But Hector's face was serious when he asked, "What happened in the basement?"

"We heard a noise," Gertie said. "In one of the coffins."

"It was probably just a rat," Nikita said, avoiding Gertie's eyes.

"But that coffin is heavily chained," Gertie objected. "How would it have gotten inside?"

"Rats can eat through just about anything," Hector said. "Oh, look. See the temple over there?"

They couldn't get to it from that side, so they had to go around to the east for a few more minutes. Once they reached the ruin, Gertie thought it was worth the walk. It looked exactly as it must have once appeared in ancient Greece, except for a few cracks. Standing in the same spot where others once stood thousands of years ago was surreal.

After they walked around and read some of the plaques, Hector returned to the front of the temple and sat on the ledge looking out over the landscape below.

"See that jumble of rocks down there?" he asked.

Gertie sat beside him and looked down the hill at a maze of stones in the grassy hillside.

"That's the ancient agora," he said.

Nikita and Klaus joined them on the ledge.

Nikita said, "It was like the town square of ancient Greece."

"It's where our ancestors would go to have fun," Klaus said.

Hector laughed. "Like all they did back then was party."

They all laughed.

"They had to have fun some time," Klaus said.

As an American, that was one thing Gertie didn't have: because her ancestors were immigrants, she couldn't walk around in her hometown and reflect on the ancient past of her heritage. She had to go to another country to do that.

Gertie really wanted to ask Hector to tell the story about the day he was born, but she didn't know him well enough, and she didn't want to embarrass him. She supposed she would have to coax the details out of Nikita later.

They spent the rest of the afternoon walking around the acropolis and then had some dinner at one of the cafés. Gertie was able to convince them to let her pay with her credit card. At seven in the evening, they climbed the hill up to the Parthenon. Most of the other tourists were leaving to catch their buses and ferries and taxis, but there were still some milling about and enjoying the drop in temperature on the now windy hill.

They walked around inside, all three of them inundating Gertie with information, and then Klaus called everyone outside.

"Let's climb down to the rock," he said. "The sun is close to setting."

"Don't you mean Helios is about to sink in his cup?" Gertie teased.

"Wait," Nikita said. "First Hector should tell Gertie about his great-grandfather. It happened right here."

"What happened right there?" Gertie asked.

"Oh, okay," Hector said. "But first, look over there. That's where Athena and Poseidon had their famous contest over who would become the patron god of this city. Have you heard the story?"

Gertie nodded. "That's where it happened, huh? Poseidon gave them a salty river and Athena the olive tree. So, where's the olive tree?"

"They're all over this area," Hector replied. "We have the best olive oil in the world."

"Now you sound like Babá," Nikita said.

"But it's true," Hector argued.

"Can we go to the rock now?" Klaus asked.

"Wait, his great-grandfather's story," Nikita prompted. "Go ahead, Hector."

Gertie was beginning to get the feeling that Nikita was in love with Hector.

"Oh, right," Hector said. "Well, during World War II, the Nazis occupied Athens."

Klaus came over and put an arm around Gertie. "And his great-grandfather was guarding the Greek flag when the Nazis ordered him to take it down."

Klaus was the same height as Gertie, and he looked at her, eye-to-eye with a cute smile on his face. She hadn't noticed his deep dimples before. Was he flirting with her? Or just being friendly, like Mamá and Babá and Nikita?

"So did he take it down?" Gertie asked Hector.

"He did," Hector said. "He took it down, put it on, like a badge of courage, and jumped to his death, right down there."

"He was standing on this very spot. Right, Hector?" Nikita said.

Hector nodded.

"Can we go to the rock now?" Klaus, who still had his arm around Gertie, asked.

"Let's go," Hector said, leading the way.

They climbed down from the flag platform onto a dimpled, raw ledge of rock jetting out from the acropolis just below the Parthenon. According to Nikita, teenagers liked to come hang out here some evenings, sometimes with an iced chest of beer or bottle of wine to share—always in groups and never alone. Tonight, there were no others, and the few tourists above them were already making their way down along the path on the other side of the hill.

Every part of Athens was visible from this spot except the west, but the view of the sun dipping down behind the Parthenon from here was spectacular. She sat between Klaus and Nikita, with Hector on the other side of Klaus, all dangling their legs over the cliff edge. It was peaceful and beautiful up here, as the tiled rooftops sparkled in the evening sun and the lights of the city slowly began to twinkle as dusk settled.

The city below was not quite sleepy, however. Gertie could see cars, people, smoke from chimney tops, and lots of other signs of human activity. She looked at her phone for the time.

"I thought this place closed at eight-thirty," she said.

"We can climb down from here," Klaus said, showing his dimples, apparently happy for the adventure.

"Too bad Dionysus can't come out and bring us some of his wine," Gertie said with a laugh. "Thanks a lot for giving me ideas, Nikita. I'm thirsty now."

The other three didn't laugh, so Gertie added, "Just joking." She thought Europeans were more open-minded about the drinking age; maybe she was wrong.

They were quiet then as the wind lifted their hair in its breeze and cooled them down.

That's when Gertie noticed two people climbing up from the hillside toward them.

Hector stood up. "Don't say anything to them when they come by."

Gertie bent her brows. They'd been surrounded by people all day. What made these two any different?

"And don't make eye contact with them." Klaus stood up too.

Gertie gave Nikita a quizzical look.

"They're tramps," she whispered. "They just want to take advantage of you."

"How can you tell?" Gertie asked.

The boy and girl making their way up toward them didn't look much different from anyone else. They wore summer tanks and blue jeans and had dark, wavy hair. They looked like brother and sister but were thicker and taller in stature than the Angelis kids.

As the two hikers climbed closer, Gertie's brows shot up even higher. She recognized one of them. He was the boy from the bus.

The boy noticed her, too, and smiled.

"The girl from the bus," he said. "The vampire lover."

"Vampire lover?" the girl beside him asked.

Hector helped Gertie and Nikita to their feet. Then he positioned himself between them and the newcomers. Klaus stood beside him.

"This is my sister, Calandra," the boy said, ignoring Hector. "Calandra, this is...sorry, I didn't get your name."

"Don't answer," Hector muttered. "Xasoy apo ta matia moy."

"It's okay," Gertie said. "I've talked with him before."

"But you don't understand, Gertie," Klaus said.

Hector turned to Klaus. "Way to go."

"Gertie? Nice to meet you. I'm Jeno."

He gave her his brilliant smile, and she was suddenly reminded of the dream she'd had on the bus, of him looming over her with his mouth full of fangs and blood. She shuddered, but, out of habit, said, "It's nice to meet you."

"We were just leaving," Hector said, pulling the girls down the hill in the opposite direction.

Klaus followed closely behind.

"I hope we meet again!" Jeno called after them.

Gertie couldn't understand how the friendliest people on the planet could be so rude, but she waited until they were at the bottom of the hillside, on the street, walking back toward the car, to bring it up.

"They seemed nice," she said. "I don't understand why we had to leave."

"We need to get to the ferry anyway," Nikita said.

Hector stopped abruptly and turned, looking down at her with his face fierce and close to hers. "Never talk to them again, okay?"

"But why?" she asked.

"Trust me," Hector said, his breath washing against her face.

"But I've just met you." She narrowed her eyes. "In fact, I met Jeno before I met you. That means I've known him longer. Give me a reason why I shouldn't talk to him."

"Because he's dangerous," Klaus said.

The muscles of Hector's jaw tightened. "Dangerous and selfish. He'll try to hurt you."

EVA POHLER

Eva Pohler is a *USA Today* bestselling author of over thirty novels in multiple genres, including mysteries, thrillers, and young adult paranormal romance based on Greek mythology. Her books have been described as "addictive" and "sure to thrill"—*Kirkus Reviews*.

To learn more about Eva and her books, and to sign up to hear about new releases, and sales, please visit her website at www.evapohler.com.

www.ingramcontent.com/pod-product-compliance
Lightning Source LLC
Chambersburg PA
CBHW061237210726
48293CB00003B/798